Clay

Clay

A NOVEL

FRANK MEOLA

GREEN WRITERS PRESS *Brattleboro, Vermont*

Printed in the United States

10 9 8 7 6 5 4 3 2 1

Green Writers Press is a Vermont-based publisher whose
mission is to spread a message of hope and renewal through
the words and images we publish. Throughout we will adhere
to our commitment to preserving and protecting the natural
resources of the earth. To that end, a percentage of our
proceeds will be donated to environmental activist groups.
Green Writers Press gratefully acknowledges support from
individual donors, friends, and readers to help support the
environment and our publishing initiative.

Giving Voice to Writers & Artists Who Will Make the World a Better Place
Green Writers Press | Brattleboro, Vermont • www.greenwriterspress.com

ISBN: 978-1-9505840-0-0

COVER PHOTO BY GLENN LUNDEN
Fresh Kills Panorama

The paper used in this publication is produced by mills committed
to responsible and sustainable forestry practices.

PART ONE

ONE

It was an unquiet time, that spring to fall, alive with clashing and threat. Other summers blur, but that one stands distinct, sharp as a wounding edge. The world doesn't change in a summer, of course, but so much happened, so much opened up. You could say we were all awaiting that violent opening, that deep gash in the normal fabric of things.

Our town was clustered at the remotest end of the farthest island in New York, city of islands. When I say farthest, I mean of course from Manhattan. That island was The City; ours was not. We could sample its splendors but we felt safe from its depravities and dangers. Like most communities on the city's fringes, we believed we were different, separate. But that spring, it seemed the larger world was creeping nearer. Crime had erupted: a burglar broke in on the Agamos down the block and threatened Mrs. A with a gun. She identified him vaguely as "one of those lowlifes from the North Shore"—the brown and black neighborhoods closer to the inner city. A girl was raped in Huguenot Pond Park, and people blamed those Brooklyn punks who sullied its pristine lawns with their beer-bottle detritus and who knew what else. It was all the city's fault, as it moved closer and closer in people's perceptions like some miasmic cloud. Locks clicked shut on doors day and night now as many wondered what was next.

This was the summer of Nixon's resignation. Conspiracy and confusion were in the air. Nothing makes sense anymore, my mother kept saying, as if once everything had.

By the end of June, my parents were bickering daily; my sister was cutting classes and losing or finding herself in Eastern religions. My grandfather started imagining things and talking crazy. I would be turning thirteen in September and felt like I wasn't one thing or the other, vacillating in some middle, muddled state, a moody mix of innocent and precocious.

For me, though, all the strangeness came to center on one person: a guy named Jimmy Gerthoff, who twice that summer nearly died. And twice came back to life. Or so it appeared to me. It seemed, for a while, that he could transcend all limitations. He was a sort of human bridge from where I was to where I could be—an older in-between, almost out there in the world but still tied to home. For some adults, insular ones especially, he was a flagrant example of a local kid who'd been corrupted by the wider world, with its dangerous attractions, its disruptive mysteries, its restless diversity. Lots of people felt that way about him. And so Jimmy became a focus, a lightning rod in the social storms that summer—even more so once he got involved with Claytown, an old African-American settlement a few miles from town.

He was a deep-rooted Wardville boy, from a bigshot old family. At eighteen, he seemed a lot older, and wiser—or hipper anyway, with his denim jackets patched with peace signs, religious symbols, and rock group logos, a cool jumble. His long, lank, sandy hair suggested a slightly hippie boy-next-door, but with a certain privilege and freedom denied us younger boys from less affluent families. He wore exotically round glasses like John Lennon's that I couldn't find at our mall opticians; Jimmy had bought them in some hip Manhattan store. He could do that, go wherever he wanted, buy whatever he wanted. We didn't know each other well, which only added to his glamour in my life-hungry eyes. I'd always seen him around, and he'd dated my sister in his last months of high school and for a while after he'd begun college. He would talk and joke with me sometimes before disappearing with Diane into her bedroom, from which I heard laughter as well as stranger sounds—creepy, exciting.

It seemed Jimmy had a kind of confidence my sister and I lacked, a sense of who he was, so he could move in and out of the little worlds of school as if playing a game. I wanted to be part of the social in-groups while still detesting them; Jimmy had been part of them while seeming free and indifferent. He'd give me advice sharper than Diane's, or he'd comment on my clothes or a book I was reading, his pithy judgments tossed with an easy authority that could seem both concerned-brotherly and smug. And underneath ran a nasty current, at times erupting wildly: one day he'd rubbed his boot sole into my brand new sneakers, smudging the spotless white canvas, hurting my foot, ragging me to get them dirtier and implying that I ran a risk of sissyhood. Even the nastiness, though, seemed worldly and enviable, wise guy and wise at once.

That spring, months after he'd abruptly stopped dating Diane and pretty much vanished from our lives, he'd begun to wave at me from his gleaming car when he saw me walking on the street or riding my bicycle. Once he'd even stopped to ask how I was doing. That felt weird and heady, since I'd always wanted to know him better, along with the things I imagined he knew—so that I could speed away into all those possibilities that were open to guys like him.

Of course, summer always seemed full of possibilities, like gifts with endless time to enjoy them. And for outer-borough New Yorkers like us, in our peninsula community jutting into Raritan Bay, summer meant an opening to vaster places, even if that only meant New Jersey. When we were younger, we took trips to blue Garden State lakes or the better beaches of the Shore, the ones without rabble and honky-tonk. We rode in the ample back seats of big cars. I sat with my sister as she listened to her leather-encased transistor radio through an earpiece and I read Encyclopedia Brown or attempted Poe, Jules Verne, or some daunting book of history. From the dashboard floated the radio voices of singers from the forties and fifties, whose string-backed crooning made me think of our doctor's waiting room, a feeling reinforced by slight nausea from reading in the sunny car.

In my mind, Jimmy never had to endure such family rituals. In the driver's seat, he went anywhere he wanted. Early on, he'd driven his parents' Lincoln Continental, a huge silver machine. Later, it was a Chevy Camaro. He could tune the radio to whatever station he liked, his blaring speakers painting loud streaks of rock across our town's pale canvas as he shot by, most times with a girl.

Nevertheless, he still lived at home in Wardville and commuted to Emerson Hill College on the north side of the island. "Well, sure," my mother once said. "He's got it good at home. Meals, laundry, all the comforts. Why should he leave?"

No, Jimmy wasn't leaving. In fact, we were seeing more and more of him. He seemed to be deliberately driving past our house, on a side street he didn't need to use. I asked my mother about that, and she told me to ignore him if he signaled or spoke to me. Naturally this puzzling command only fueled my eagerness to talk to him.

I got my chance in an unexpected way on a Saturday morning in June. I was playing Stevie Wonder's *Innervisions* at top volume in my bedroom with the door open wide: I thought this was radical black music that would disturb my parents in a way that the Jackson Five never could. Blasting songs about urban racism, squalor, and violence into the living room where Mom and Dad were trying to relax was like a declaration of fantasized independence for wild, nameless things clamoring for release. (This was unusual behavior. I was the good boy; Diane was the rebel, five years older and a belated counterculturalist.)

Since the living room and bedrooms were all on the upstairs floor of our "high ranch," the music carried directly.

Dad's voice carried too. "Luke! Turn down the noise, will you?"

I slammed my bedroom door, inviting another reaction, which wasn't long in coming: my father screamed that if I slammed the door again he'd slam my face—an angry threat as uncharacteristic of him as the door slam was of me.

I sat down on my bed, above which a crucifix hung alongside a plaque depicting a guardian angel with his arm around a small blond boy. It was a First Communion gift from my grandmother, and though I no longer believed that it was *my* guardian, I still wanted the picture there.

I couldn't sit still. I got up and paced back and forth between the angel/Jesus wall and the opposite one, with the *Outer Limits* poster: an image of oscillating light waves obscuring a blurred, oblong alien face. I kept looking around the room as if some exit other than the door might

7

open up—some instant transporter that could take me into the future or into history, anywhere but the here-and-now.

I thought about where I could go. I wouldn't "run away" (impossible and stupid), but I *wanted* to run away. So I decided to take a bus hardly anyone ever rode, one that ran past deep woods on the outskirts of town, interspersed with abandoned buildings like ruins slowly being absorbed into the enveloping green. You could get on in Wardville and in a few minutes find yourself beyond the last few houses in town as you rode along the Kill (Dutch for creek or river, as I'd learned in school), which narrowly separated Staten Island from New Jersey. This less-taken route seemed adventurous, even rebellious, with the frightening blissful feel of the unknown, largely because of two places along that meandering way. One was the big hilltop house where Riveredge Road took a sharp turn north, a mile or so after it ran under the approach ramp of the bridge to Jersey. People said the house was haunted, cursed.

The other place along the way, riskier and vaguer, was Claytown, several miles beyond the big old house and farther than I'd ever traveled on that bus route before. Claytown was a small and isolated community dating back to the nineteenth century. I'd been more and more attracted to the place, partly for its history but also for a stronger reason: we weren't supposed to go there. "We" meaning the white people of Wardville, and back then that included pretty much everybody, even my family and those like us, "new people" of dubious immigrant origins. There wasn't a lot of outright hatred (actually, many old Wardville families had abolitionists perched on the family tree), but Claytown barely existed in Wardville's fenced-in consciousness, even though Claytown people came to "our" schools, shops, and offices. We never went over there, and in fact we hardly thought about them at all. The two communities were separate. I knew that even then and wondered about it.

But as whites fleeing from inner-city neighborhoods began to settle near Claytown and encountered black people where they'd expected none (and in the woods, in dilapidated clapboard houses!), contact and conflict intensified.

I left without being noticed and caught the big green 113 bus. Soon we were making our way through the backwoods outside town, along the lonely river that wasn't really a river, I knew, but a sort of estuary, a long narrow extension of the bay and the sea. There were only three other people on the bus: a couple of teenage girls giggling in the back seats, probably on their way to the mall, and an elderly woman holding a Bible close to her half-moon eyeglasses and moving her lips as she read.

Out here stood formerly grand old homes that once looked across the Kill to a bucolic New Jersey, greening into distant hills. Now they could gaze only at storage tanks and refineries on the opposite bank. Between the neglected houses, dense woods obscured the river view.

We passed the majestic turreted house peering down from its solitary hill. I'd learned from a book that it was a Queen Anne Victorian, and that it once belonged to a rich family who had owned a nearby brick factory. They had all died off, retribution (the story went) for evil deeds in the past. I watched the house disappear behind trees. A few minutes later, I pulled the cord to signal what I thought would be the stop closest to Claytown. The fat, sweaty driver turned to me as I stood waiting to get out. His brow formed two tight mounds of disapproval.

"Son," he said. "You want to get off *here*?"

"Yes," I said.

He pressed the door lever, his eyes still narrowed and fixed on me, and the door folded open with a thwack.

"Okay, kid, but watch yourself. Pretty deserted around here. Only them colored off in the woods."

I didn't answer as I stepped off the bus. It growled away, leaving me alone with the wind wafting the summerleaf scent of trees and the sealike aroma of river water once the bus exhaust had dissipated. There was no traffic on the road. I turned off Riveredge and started walking up the much narrower, barely paved surface of Clay Road, named, like Claytown itself, for the old clay pits that sliced the area and had supplied the long-gone brick factory. In the distance rose the three huge hills, brown and bare, of the Kills landfill, once flat marshland but now much higher than Claytown, towering over it, I imagined, and encroaching on it. I hadn't realized before how close the dump was to the town. You could smell the garbage. You could hear the cawing scavenger birds that swirled above it.

Those birds and my sneakers crunching gravel were the only sounds until I heard a low hum behind me—a lawnmower, I figured, or a motorboat on the river. But it got louder, along with heavy rock music like waves bumping me forward. I turned and saw Jimmy Gerthoff's sky-blue Camaro approaching. I stopped as it got closer. It was a cool car: long hood thrusting forward from the interior, smooth fastback sloping down.

I wasn't surprised to see Jimmy—like I said, he could go anywhere—but I was startled by his passenger. It wasn't one of Jimmy's girls. It wasn't a girl at all. It was Bentley Riley. Bentley Peter Riley, as his mother liked to call him. Bentley was my age and a schoolmate, but I knew him mainly from religious instruction classes on Wednesday afternoons and Sunday mornings, after Mass, at Our Lady Stella Maris. His mother came from one of the old English families in town. She'd converted to Catholicism when she married Pete Riley, a policeman, now a detective in the department. He was another of Dad's acquaintances; they'd gotten to know one another when Bentley and I were teammates in Little League. Bentley had always been tougher and stronger than I was, with a self-sufficiency and assurance that could ratchet up to arrogance, which meant that I sometimes wanted to be his buddy and sometimes wanted to shut him up. We were both loners, though, and that had led to an odd sort of hot-and-cold friendship. Hotter on my side, since I liked being around him and didn't always hide it. And I was impressed that his dad was a detective, which had a shadowy coolness about it.

Jimmy slowed down and looked over at me, leaning across Bentley, whose blue eyes flashed surprise and suspicion.

"Hey, kid, what're you doing out here?" Jimmy asked, with a friendly grin hinting at amused superiority. He continued looking at me as the car kept moving.

I had no answer that wouldn't sound dumb and dorky. My face throbbed and burned, as if I'd been walking in an August heat wave.

"Exploring," I finally said.

This got a laugh out of Bentley, hard yet giggly, somewhere between Jimmy's hip-guy dismissal and a kid's nervousness. I laughed with him, at myself, all the while fuming.

"Where are *you* guys going?"

"Got some errands over in Claytown," Jimmy said. "Saw Bentley sitting on his front steps looking bored as hell so I asked him along. There's someone there I'd like him to meet'"" He looked at Bentley, then back at me, as if considering.

"So," he said. "Wanna join us? You should meet this guy, too."

I stared at them without answering, as I took in the dizzying facts: Jimmy knew people in Claytown, Bentley was going there with him, and Bentley's parents must have allowed him to ride with Jimmy. I wondered if Jimmy had known I was headed there, through some eerie connection between us. Or had he somehow followed me? Was he ambling around town offering rides to boys? Why bring us to Claytown? It seemed to be an ordinary destination for him.

"Well, do you wanna come or don't you?" Jimmy's grin had turned smart-ass, but all I could think was: *He's asking me to ride in his car.* This was overwhelming, a fine new thing, but I kept that to myself.

"Sure," I deadpanned.

I got into the car's backseat and felt the engine throb and rumble as Jimmy revved it. We turned onto a narrow pockmarked road, and houses appeared between stretches of forest—old two-story wooden houses, some of them freshly painted and sturdy, others with sagging roofs and junk-strewn yards. They looked like they'd been there forever, like part of the woods around them. So high and narrow, so steep-roofed, with so many rough and patterned surfaces. The newer screen doors or windows stood out like modern pictures in ancient frames. I imagined some sect with antique customs living there, swooping down from the cracked front porches in long dark skirts and vested suits. I had an inkling of circumstances I couldn't fully understand back then—that this oldness was a form of invisibility, that these people would be cast aside, squeezed between the growing landfill and the efficiently spreading suburbs.

Farther along, the houses clustered closer and shops appeared: a grocery, a tiny barbershop, a five-and-ten, each sagging and splintered like the houses. And then a larger building, the only brick one, with gaps in the brickwork like wounds. The two front windows held patched stained glass, and the frosted-glass side windows were riddled with spidery cracks. A sign above the arched front doors read

"Claytown AME Zion Church." The sign was semi-cryptic: Zion a vague locale from religion class, the initials a puzzle.

Jimmy cut the engine, then turned toward Bentley and me. "You guys wait here a minute, okay? Got some business with the minister here."

I was baffled and let down—Jimmy had business with a minister? Was he the one Jimmy wanted us to meet? I had my fill of church on Wednesday and Sunday.

As soon as Jimmy got out, I leaned forward toward Bentley. A trickle of sweat ran down behind his ear into his shirt. "What's he doing?" I whispered.

Bentley shrugged and wiped away the sweat. We watched Jimmy shaking hands with a tall, thin black man in a clergy collar on the steps of the church. The minister went back inside and quickly came out again along with a boy I recognized—he was one of the few black kids in our school, a grade ahead of me. But I didn't know him. The minister said something sharply to Jimmy while pointing toward the car where we sat staring at him. The boy followed Jimmy down the short front steps. Everything seemed unclear—definition blurring into mystery.

The door across from me opened, and the boy got in, with his head down, and sat as far away as possible. His head was close-shaved, with dark stubbles in his otherwise smooth caramel skin. His khaki shorts exposed long, muscled legs.

"This is Solomon, guys," Jimmy said as he settled himself into the driver's seat. "Solomon, this is Bentley, and back there next to you is Luke."

"Hi," I said. Bentley was silent.

Solomon glanced at me and gave a nod. His brown eyes flicked nervously.

Bentley turned, wrinkling his brow and cocking his head in the other boy's direction, as if Solomon couldn't see him. Was he asking me something? Making some sly comment? I wasn't sure. I shrugged, feeling privileged and uneasy, as if Jimmy was drawing me into some vaguely criminal activity that promised subversive freedom. As we sped away, I let myself go with the strange fun of it, thinking about Diane riding in Jimmy's car, crossing bridges, speeding to the Shore. The smell of trees and grass and swampy landfill swept through the open windows as the radio blared bass-thick Led Zeppelin. Solomon sat gazing out the window now as dappled light passed over him.

We were driving away from the river, south toward the bay. Jimmy said nothing about where we were going; he drummed on the steering wheel with the radio beat and gunned the engine when the rhythm kicked harder.

We swung abruptly onto Ward Road, and I was thrown sideways into Solomon, who pushed me away. I turned to push back, but he looked at me as if I'd lunged at him, as if he'd defended himself by reflex. I mumbled "sorry," feeling disoriented, jittery-excited at this sudden close contact.

Bentley was watching us, smirking. He seemed stuck-up, as though the two of us in the back were just cargo. As if the blond boys up front were in charge.

We drove up the road past well-kept old homes with wraparound porches whose furniture and swings had emerged from winter covers to meet the ocean air. The houses yielded to woods and past them the bay and the marina with its sailboat masts and outboard motors in bobbing rows. To the left were the seaside grounds of South Island Hospital. On the right appeared the low walls of the Ward estate, and beyond it through thick-trunked elder trees the huge house itself overlooking the bay. We had a side view: the evenly spaced windows with small, square panes, the dormered roofs front and back above the long colonnaded porches.

So there it was, so familiar yet fantasy-like: the ancestral home of the clan for whom Wardville was named.

The family lived there still, in the person of Sebastian Ward, descended from Wards going back to the eighteenth century—farmers and ship owners and (their prime distinction) oystering royalty. I'd researched it all for an article in the junior high newspaper. Back when the island's now-grubby waters were thick with oyster beds, the Wards farmed the tides as well as the land; they harvested sea and shore. Ward oysters traveled from humble Raritan Bay to the great restaurants of New York and London. And Ward trading ships brought the big world to Wardville. Of all the grand waterfront houses along the bay, the grandest was the Wards' pillared mansion, looking like it had been plucked from a Georgia plantation and dropped amid marshy creek mouths up the coast from Wardville proper. Sebastian Ward lived in the house alone—the final Ward, my father would joke. Sebastian Ward, town legend even to us: portly leisured gentleman, real estate baron, antiques connoisseur, charity benefactor, with a gentleman's bad habits like drinking and, the whispers went, worse.

The gates to the long graveled driveway stood open, and Jimmy turned in with swift ease, as if he'd done this many times. I wasn't surprised that he'd obviously been around here before, probably to park with girlfriends, since you couldn't beat Ward's view of the marina, the bay, and the nighttime lights of the Atlantic Highlands suspended like low stars above the Jersey shoreline. And of course Jimmy was local aristocracy, too. But I didn't expect him to enter the grounds.

Even I, carless and girlfriendless, felt the tug of the place. I always had. When I was younger my parents had concocted grim, Grimm-like stories of disobedient children who ventured near the house (forbidden!) and were snatched up and imprisoned there with other wicked kids. These tales scared and sparked me about equally. Later they hinted about drugs and "the bad element" that hung out nearby. Ward, it was implied, encouraged these reprobates.

We pulled up to the back of the house, which faced the bay across a lawn sloping to a low brick wall, beyond which a short gravel road ran along the water to the woods. The wind brought a salt smell. The massive trees stood alongside the house like guardian creatures from a green mythic world.

Jimmy cut the engine but left the radio on. He got out and pulled his seat forward for Solomon, who hesitated a few seconds before getting out, too.

Jimmy leaned in and flashed his smile, the charmer now. "You guys wait here, okay? I'll be right back." He closed the door.

On the radio, Deep Purple gave way to the news, the usual stuff: Nixon and his cronies, secret tapes, conspiracies.

Solomon and Jimmy made their way toward the back door of the house. Halfway there, Solomon stopped and shook his head, but Jimmy leaned down, put an arm around him, said something close to his ear. Solomon looked up at him and shrugged. They continued walking, more rapidly, and Jimmy patted Solomon's back. The door opened before they got up onto the long porch, and a man (not Ward) dressed in shorts and a polo shirt waved them inside.

Bentley and I were both breathing hard now in the warm car, and I felt a tense anticipation. He looked at me as if he wanted to tell me or ask me something, but neither of us spoke. At the sound of a door closing, we both looked back at the house. Jimmy stood there alone, staring down at his black sneakers, hands in his jeans pockets, hair falling over his glasses. He stood awhile like that, then he looked up as if responding to a sudden command and walked quickly back to the car. He got in, slammed the door shut, started the engine, pumped up the radio.

"Good kid, that Solomon," said Jimmy on the way back to town. "Had some problems but, hey, haven't we all?"

He turned down the music and told us how much he'd like it if we got to be friends with Solomon. Bentley laughed but Jimmy was completely serious, even intense, and said he'd like to arrange something we could all do together, that it was a shame how no one paid attention to those people in Claytown.

"Solomon hardly ever gets out of that place," he told us. "Always alone or with his grandparents. It's like he lives in an internment camp and they just let him out for school."

This sounded crazy and exaggerated, and Bentley was smirking again. To me it wasn't funny—hard to understand, maybe, but that was something else. (Why only grandparents? Why was Solomon so moody?) And it all seemed personal and imperative to Jimmy. Claytown and the Ward house were connected somehow, I knew that much, and Jimmy played some part in that connection. But he wasn't telling, only hinting as usual, revealing just enough to impress us with all the things he could tell—if and when he wanted to.

We drove down Jimmy's block when we got back to Wardville, and he stopped the car in front of his house. The Gerthoffs lived in a large, multi-winged brick ranch framed by a brick wall and wrought-iron gates. It sat on family property, overlooking the river, next to the house that Jimmy's father had grown up in, where Jimmy's grandmother still lived. Her German parents had built the older house, whose gabled gingerbread bulk accentuated the ranch's spare modernity.

I figured maybe Jimmy was checking on his mother, who rarely left home; rumors were she'd undergone a terrible trauma that no one knew the truth about and spent much of her time cleaning the house in anticipation of some transformative event that wouldn't happen, of visitors who wouldn't arrive. I had never seen her drive the car. Sometimes I would catch her scurrying along the sidewalk, looking around as if fearing she'd be noticed. Spotting Anna Gerthoff was something like glimpsing a rare planet in the night sky or a seldom-seen animal on a hike. "Look," kids would say, "it's *her.*"

Mr. Gerthoff was more "normal"—confident, certain in his opinions and eager to express them, devoted to his construction business. He and Dad were casual friends; he was far wealthier and more of a local insider than Dad. I can see them standing together, Dad squat and dark-haired with his thick, black-framed eyeglasses, like some bookish Portuguese *paisan* in casual American clothes. And Gerthoff Senior, tall and ice-latitude blond, wearing a pressed shirt with neatly folded-up sleeves and a discreet logo from a fancy old-line store. He looks comfortable in his clothes and in his skin, contrasting with Dad's nervous stoop. Gerthoff was a big man in that little world, which was still big to me. He introduced my parents to the Swim Club and the Country Club, where they attended swank events. I often wondered why Dad liked him. Maybe he was just flattered by the attention, which always seemed condescending. He called my father "Portugal," as if our ethnicity summed us up, a cute little joke. "Hey, Portugal, I bet you could get a bundle for that house," he'd say. His exchanges with my father mostly involved stocks or real estate or taxes, on all of which Gerthoff expounded while Dad mostly listened. They saw less of each other after Jimmy and Diane broke up.

We waited in the car only a few minutes before Jimmy emerged from his house. He got back in the driver's seat looking preoccupied, distressed. He drove me the few blocks to my house in silence, and as soon as I got out he gunned the engine and pulled away.

Two

Those first rides in Jimmy's car, those visits to Claytown and the Ward house, gave me a closer look at things that had always seemed half-real, like countries you know exist but have only read about or seen in pictures or maps. They suggested entire lives lived in ways I could only imagine, full of things off-limits, things whispered and unspoken.

I knew more about Ward than about Claytown. Everybody knew Ward, if only from seeing him around town. In summer he strolled in white suits, grasping a walking stick; in winter he sported fur coats and berets. He would emerge Sundays from gleaming gothic St. Anselm's Episcopal Church and greet people along with the priest, like small-town gentry (he was among the leaders of the dwindling congregation). He presided over his restaurant in one of the many old houses he'd saved and restored. Ward's antique piles stood like eccentric matrons dressed up for a fair, looking down their noses at the casual young ranch houses crowding them. Mr. Ward himself looked like an old matron, or so the jokes went, at least among those of us with no ancestral respect for his family. My parents thought he was weird; to me he seemed both weird and romantic, like some wondrous old book given life.

Of course, Ward wasn't really the oddity in Wardville: people like my family were—Portuguese-American, Roman Catholic transplants in the venerable Anglo-Saxon garden. We were very late arrivals by Wardville's reckoning. Even as more and more "ethnic" people moved in, we remained anomalies, most of the newcomers being Italian or Jewish. As I saw it, my parents and I had different attitudes about the small circles of Wardville: they aimed for the centers, and I was drifting toward the edges.

The night following the car ride I dreamed that Ward was leading Jimmy through the old mansion while Jimmy grasped Solomon, pulling him along. I was walking behind them as if invisible. Shadows and cobwebs clung in darkness. We climbed stair after stair until we reached a small remote room, and Ward told Jimmy to put Solomon inside the room. Jimmy pushed him in and they closed the door, which Ward locked with a huge key. They walked down the miles of stairs and out a back door, and suddenly we were all in Claytown. Jimmy and Ward were loading children into a van parked behind the AME Zion church. The children weren't struggling, but they didn't look happy. And I woke up. Or I thought I did. On the wall above my head, my ex-guardian angel was speaking garbled words in a weird metallic voice. His usually bland kind face looked intense, as if trying to communicate some vital, urgent message. The blond boy recoiled from the fierce angel.

All seemed ordinary in the warm morning light. My angel in his long bodiless robe and silver wings hovered silently again on the wall, wearing his usual expression: untroubled, creepily sweet, in contrast to the pained face of the crucified Jesus beside him. And yet I was still in the dream, and the dreamlike events of the day before—especially Solomon transported, reluctantly it seemed, from a church in Claytown to that big old house where we'd left him. What was he doing there? What were they doing to him?

From the kitchen came my sister's voice, rising in another tense discussion with my parents. There'd been a lot of those recently. That spring, she'd read the *Bhagavad Gita* and decided she was working off some past-life karma by promoting social justice in our oppressive home and community. Her Hindu interests had developed out of sitar lessons she took from a guy named Rolf who claimed to be half Indian but looked entirely Nordic.

I loved my sister and even liked her when she wasn't condescending and bossy. She taught me a lot, even if it was mostly through teasing; her jokes (like Dad's) were comments on things I didn't yet fully understand. She was a magnet for flecks of information from books and magazines and music and the wider world they mediated. She had access before I did to some of the young adult books at the library, moving freely through the checkout, which was also a checkpoint guarded by Mrs. Foy, our no-nonsense librarian. Diane would pass along forbidden works to me or sometimes just read me passages hinting of sex, teenage trauma, social and family conflicts. I eventually caught up with her book knowledge (I loved looking things up), but she had already raced beyond, into more tangible forms of knowing, into more radical questioning.

She'd been my pal on family outings, and there were lots of them back then. Like those summer Shore trips, with my parents under beach umbrellas laughing—they were always laughing then it seemed, enjoying one another's talk and company—while we played in the sand and my sister dared me to go a little farther out into the water, even as she was there to grab me as our parents looked on, relaxed but sharp-eyed. In winter we'd all skate on Huguenot Park Pond, where Diane was tutor, skating smoothly while Mom and Dad, who'd only learned after they moved to Wardville, sometimes had to lean on one another. Often she let me slip, laughing as she watched me learn by falling.

Now, the next morning after the dream, Mom and Dad were busy preparing for the Fourth of July luau at the Wardville Swim Club. When I came in to breakfast, the parents were still arguing with Diane and didn't seem to notice me.

"Luaus," Diane was saying. "What phony crap." She was slumped at the table in cutoff blue jeans, artfully patched and torn, and a tank top without bra. I had recently become more aware of my sister's breasts, maybe because more was on display.

"You don't have to use that kind of language," my mother responded. "A luau is a Hawaiian tradition we adapt for parties. We raise money for charities. And it's *fun*."

Diane snorted. "Bullshit, ma. Hawaiians don't do this silly stuff except for tourists. They have their own traditions, or they used to until the almighty white people got there and wiped everything out. And now all these squares play at being Hawaiian in their backyards. It's disgusting."

"Look," my father said, glancing up from his legal pad. He seemed to be making up a list with a column of figures next to it. "You don't have to come to the luau if you don't want to. Who needs your gloomy mug around there anyway?"

"Don't worry, I wouldn't be caught dead there."

Diane roused herself. She pushed her empty cereal bowl away, knocking over the box of granola, which only she ate, and got up. As she walked by me, she paused. "Hey, bro, what's wrong? You look freaked out."

I shrugged, still dazy from dreams and confused by the luau argument. Diane ruffled my hair, but I pulled away. She laughed and continued down the hall.

My mother now noticed me in the doorway. "Well, look who's here. Our little wanderer."

Her tone clashed with her bright, cheery outfit—white shorts and a button-front blouse with a bird-of-paradise pattern. The clothing brought out the dark strands in her hair. She bleached it blonde, but her natural shade was so coal-black that the resurgent roots overpowered the bleaching. Diane and I had both inherited that black, curly hair—Diane's was profuse or, as Mom called it, "wild."

My father looked up as my mother spoke, and the combination of his look and her words signaled trouble.

"Mrs. Lindeburg said she saw you get out of Jimmy Gerthoff's car yesterday in front of the house. Did he give you a ride?"

"Why should Mrs. Lindeburg care?" I answered.

They stared, waiting, as if I hadn't said anything.

"Yeah," I continued. "He gave me a lift from the library."

To my surprise, they seemed satisfied with this lame but safe explanation. My mother went on examining recipes in *Better Homes and Gardens*. My father returned to his list making. But I didn't calm down. Something roared inside me like a motor stuck on high. I wanted a stronger response from my parents, and I almost blurted the full truth, like a threat. I wanted the truth to invade the kitchen. I kept thinking about the things I'd seen during the night: Jimmy shoving kids into that van, the angel's looming face. Somehow it was all part of that truth, lurking, ready to spring. I had to remind myself that it was only my night brain's reinvention, not what I'd actually seen.

But instead I spat out something else I knew might bug them. "How's Avo?"

This was my grandfather, my mother's father. "Avo," we called him—"grandfather"—one of the crumbs of Portuguese that had been allowed to fall for Diane and me to pick up. Avo lived alone in a colony of beachside bungalows on the wooded southern edge of town. Most of Wardville—especially newcomers—did their best to ignore the place. We'd passed it on the way to Ward's house, so I'd been thinking about Avo.

My father looked up again, as if I'd said something nasty. He and Avo maintained a friendly distance, clashing if they got too close. Dad's reading glasses enlarged his light brown eyes, magnifying their keen look but also revealing a sort of weariness. His face had tensed into creases around his nose and eyes. Or were they permanent, new lines I hadn't seen before, like the gray I'd recently noticed speckling his hair?

"What brought this on?" my mother said.

"I had a dream about him," I said, almost convinced that Avo had appeared among all those shifting figures.

"A dream?" She looked briefly alarmed before her face locked up. "Well, he's fine. I talked to him on the phone yesterday, as a matter of fact."

I nodded, and then I ate breakfast in silence broken by the sound of my Cocoa Puffs crunching, my mother turning the pages of her magazine, and my father the banker scratching figures on his pad.

We were considering the question of Purgatory and its relationship to Heaven, but my mind kept wandering. All of us in religious instruction class wanted to be outside on that warm afternoon a few days later. Through the windows came scents of trees and flowers, and sounds of balls bouncing and kids shouting from the park across the street. Public schools (mine included) were done for the day, but there I was, still stuck in a classroom.

Sister Michael Mary was telling us about Heaven, a wonderful place without hatred or violence or one group of people dominating others. People's better selves came together, as in Communion, a spiritual sharing. The Church was an earthly version of that sharing, or it should be.

I felt like she was telling us a story that might or might not be real.

We were preparing for eventual Confirmation, still a year away. I was much less enthused about this sacrament than I'd been about First Communion, back when I was still trying to figure out who Stella Maris was and why they'd named a church and a school after her. My Confirmation would be later than normal because of the general ambivalence about religion in my family. It was left up to me. The sacrament is all about reasoned choice, after all, and responsibility. But it is also about accepting one truth: the Holy Spirit would descend upon us like some swooping bird and we would be sealed as Christians, different—better, really—than those who weren't. It seemed thrilling, yet bizarre.

The Stella Maris school was a much quieter, cleaner, and more intimidating place than our own school. Yes, it fit the stereotype, with both "nice" and "nasty" nuns gliding through its polished hallways. Sister Michael Mary, our catechism teacher that year, was one of the nice nuns. She smiled, spoke gently, told jokes. She had asked us to call her "Sister M," which became "Sister M&M" (or worse) for the wise guys outside class. Diane said that "Sister M" sounded like something from *The Wizard of Oz.* Sister Michael Mary strayed from the strict catechism. We read the Bible, with Sister M giving dramatic emphasis to the stories of visionaries and dreamers and outcast souls transformed. She gave us passages from St. Francis and St. Teresa and told us they were true revolutionaries. She strummed guitar in the folk

mass, prompting Dad to joke that maybe we'd see her singing on TV like that Belgian nun ("or like Julie Andrews,"
Mom added, more earnestly). Through Sister M, religion
had mysterious power—raising big questions and avoiding
stark, dry answers. These were the best mysteries, the ones
without easy solutions, the kind that made you dizzy like
heights. Sister herself was mysterious, with her habit covering all but her hands, lower legs, and face—and the fact,
revealed to me by a classmate in an awed whisper, that she
was married not to a man but to Christ.

Sister was now explaining that Jesus, whose body we
joined through Communion, had suffered in that body to
redeem us. We were at an age when we would begin to
understand that pain is part of being in a human body that
suffers and dies. This was the basis of compassion, especially toward the poor and the afflicted. I listened, half comprehending. Suffering was elsewhere—in other people, on
television, in books, in the failing bodies of grandparents,
but not yet in my own body, confused and awkward and
alien as it often felt.

I was suddenly more aware of the bodies around me:
that body of Jesus slumped nearly naked on the cross—
God's body but also a mortal body like ours, and the covered body of Sister M, of whom I was sometimes in awe, as
well as the bodies of all the kids at their desks. They were
pink-skinned and wheat-haired mostly, Irish or German or
Polish, with a few darker Italians and one Puerto Rican girl,
darker still, like me.

One seat in front of me sat Bentley Riley, who was also
being confirmed at a later age than most. Bentley's hair was
freshly clipped in a crew cut, a style required by his father.
(My father let me grow my hair longer, but not so long that
it would look girlish or suggest hippie squalor.) The back
of Bentley's neck was bare and smooth. His fresh scent
mingled with the floral-soap fragrance of Sister M herself

as she swooshed by us in the aisles, gesturing to emphasize her points.

"You see, we don't live in Heaven," she continued, lifting an arm. "We are not in paradise. We live in the world, and we have to work and experience pain and sadness. And conflict. That is what Purgatory really means: those experiences in life we must endure. But we can work to ease that pain and sadness in others who suffer far more than most of us do. We can work to reduce hatred among people. Such work will make us more worthy of God's grace and bring Heaven closer."

She had paused in her progress and stood at the head of our aisle. Her blue eyes surveyed the class, her mouth open slightly as if she'd been interrupted, revealing her perfectly shaped white teeth, like Chiclets. The word *Purgatory*, she explained, was related to words like *purge* or *purging*. She asked for definitions, and Bentley raised his hand—a rare occurrence.

"Throwing up," he said, straight-faced. "Or pooping."

Laughter melted the classroom's silence, and Sister smiled before quickly retracting the smile and ordering quiet. She gave Bentley a steady, on-to-you stare.

"Thank you, Mr. Riley," she said, and went on to explain that Bentley was actually correct, since purging had to do with letting bad things pass through you so you would feel better. More laughs followed—strangled, quickly dying out. Bentley reddened but otherwise didn't let on that Sister M had doused the little fire he'd set.

Sister continued the lesson, and by its end we were all reminded of what a long and treacherous road we had ahead of us. Growing up would be a journey through more and more difficulty: hard work, disappointments, complicated choices, and the ever-present possibility of falling into bad behavior and maybe never finding our way out again. Good and bad were not always easy to tell apart. But we were guided by love, God's love, through these difficulties, these experiences of Purgatory, toward a good life.

Bentley was smirking now. Most likely, a lot of this was dull and goody-goody to him, and some of it was to me, too. I often craved Bentley's approval and his hard-shell invulnerability, but right then I wanted to say something that would knock the smile off his face. I wanted to believe in that good life. But I just stared at him.

I thought about Jimmy Gerthoff drawing both of us into new places, into his frenetic, near-adult world. Maybe it was all part of God's guidance. Or maybe not.

I barely looked up from my book and the back of Bentley's head through the rest of that class. After we read stories about Old and New Testament Josephs and their dreams, Sister M spoke about our upcoming summer vacation—what should we do with it? She made a distinction between time put to good use and time wasted.

"Now," she said. "We throw things away that we don't need, right? They can be things that serve no further purpose, but also things we could use if we knew how. Why do we get rid of things that *might* serve a purpose? Luke?"

My head shot up and I met her eyes. "We don't think they're worth anything," I said. It was the first thing that came to mind.

"Yes," Sister M said. "It has to do with what we value and what we do not."

Time is a gift, she continued, God's gift, and we can either value that gift or we can take it for granted. People's lives can be seen as precious or they can be seen as waste. Our society, she said, tends to use people and throw them away, just as it throws away things. Sometimes it never finds a use for people at all. But people aren't things. They should be valued far more than things. Perhaps we—she opened her arms, as if gathering all of us in—should use part of our free summer time to pay more attention to people and less to things.

"I want each of you to think about this over the next week," she concluded. "And write 500 words on how you might spend some time this summer doing some good for other people, helping to value each and every life. This could be what St. Paul calls 'redeeming the time.'"

She swept her gaze across our confused, reluctant faces.

After class ended, Sister asked me to stay a few minutes, so I sat unmoving as all the other students left as rapidly as the rules would allow. Bentley leaned over and whispered, "What's up?" I told him I didn't know. He shrugged and left with the others, maybe surprised and happy he wasn't the one kept behind.

"Luke Montalegre," Sister said, gently, as she sat at her desk facing me. "Is something wrong? I noticed you spent most of the class with your head down."

"No," I said. I glanced up at the crucifix above the perfect handwritten alphabet letters, in upper and lower case, running along the top of the blackboard. (Sister M also taught first grade at the school.) I looked back. Obviously that wasn't enough of an answer. She looked at me as if expecting a better one. As though she knew what I'd been thinking about: Bentley, Jimmy, the boy from Claytown, Sebastian Ward. They'd all mixed in my head with the words of her lesson that day, it seemed, and her questions, her closeness, her calm contrast to my inner turmoil and jumble—all of that tied my tongue.

"Do you know anything about Claytown?" The question spilled out of me.

"Claytown?" she said. "Why?"

I told her that Bentley and I had been there together. With Jimmy Gerthoff, I added, feeling it was a daring secret that I immediately wanted to unsay. She watched me in silence, and I could almost see her thinking.

"The people in Claytown," she finally said, "have been living in that place, their ancestors have, for well over a hundred years. They're good people, but they've been through a lot of hardship. They keep to themselves, and I suppose they don't really trust outsiders. They were always very isolated there, kept apart. Living in another time, really. I taught some students from there, got to know their families. A little."

She told me briskly that I should go to the library and ask for a book on the history of Wardville, that it would be good for me to learn about Claytown. *Good*—that small huge word, raising doubts and hopes and questions. I was eager to follow her suggestion, even if it sounded like another assignment. I had never read about Claytown, and its history wasn't taught to us in school. I already sensed that Claytown was a place you couldn't really know just by getting on a bus and walking around there for a few hours. Or even if you stayed a long time. There was something bigger you had to know.

"Is there anything else?" Sister asked.

"No, Sister." I hurried out into the warm air, feeling there was plenty else, like the questions brought up in class, the things going on all around me. But it would be like trying to describe a puzzle picture from its scattered pieces. I could see it only imperfectly, with wonder and dread, as the pieces slowly came together.

THREE

My mother was having problems with her muu-muu. It was much too big on her, and would have to be taken in. As I sat in the living room reading about Claytown, Mom stood looking down at the vast peach-colored tent surrounding her body. Diane sat on the floor beside her, gathering folds of fabric and letting them drop.

"That doesn't seem to be helping," my mother said.

"It'll take some doing because you're thin for this kind of dress," Diane replied, pinning a fold. "Just stay calm, be in the moment, center yourself."

"I'm trying to center myself in this dress," Mom said. "And I don't think you know what you're doing. Didn't they teach you anything in that home economics class?"

"Domestic arts. No, as a matter of fact they didn't," Diane said, in a tone of determined patience.

The Fourth of July was fast approaching, and my mother was panicking. Not only did she have her dress to deal with but menus and decorations as well, and she hadn't begun seriously rehearsing the *South Pacific* medley she planned to sing during the festivities.

Diane had agreed to help with the muumuu, probably because this was one aspect of the luau preparations she could relate to. Muumuus were cool: Mama Cass, for instance, had worn them. They were part of some California dream of Polynesia that Diane seemed to want to believe in. So she was willing to practice some domestic arts despite her usual attitude that Mom had wasted her life after giving up her secretarial job to become a housewife.

It was a week or so after Sister Michael Mary had kept me after class, and all this muumuu stuff was background interference as I sat reading. I was learning a lot about Claytown and trying to figure out its link to Sebastian Ward. I loved the feel of the book as I turned its thick pages, which smelled slightly musty, like wood in an old house.

Fed up with the bickering, I took my reading outside and sat on our front steps. My ordinary ranch-house block receded as I learned about nineteenth-century black strawberry farmers who marketed their prize produce alongside throngs of fellow hawkers on the grubby-fancy Manhattan sidewalks. About black oystermen who'd owned their boats and houses. About clay quarry and brick factory workers. And about how most of that had vanished. I felt like I'd been let in on a long-hidden secret, with stranger secrets beneath it that weren't clear. Yet.

"What're you reading?"

I looked up. My friend Doris Patera stood under the canopy of a plane tree, watching me. She pushed her dark brown hair away from her face, below which another face looked at me from her chest: Uhura on a *Star Trek* T-shirt. Doris talked a lot lately about becoming an astronaut, a goal her father joked about, calling her his "astronette." She and I had become friends late in elementary school, when I started finding girls easier to talk to than the loud, rough boys around me. But that was ending: I was pulling away from Doris, maybe from our similarities. From all that assuredness in her chatter that no longer seemed prematurely wise but know-it-all, insecure.

Now I showed her my book, and she performed a yawn. History wasn't her thing. I told her a little about Claytown, and she gave me a baffled look.

"Jeez, my dad'd have a fit," she said. "He told us never to go near that place. Kids have like disappeared from there, no one ever saw them again. Probably got chopped up and thrown in the garbage dump, he says." She smiled. "Of course, my dad likes to exaggerate."

The Pateras lived up the street, having moved from Brooklyn a few years earlier. Mr. Patera was an engineer at Garden Petrochemical over in Jersey, and Mrs. Patera owned a small clothing store in Wardville. There were a lot of lame scientific jokes in their household: Mrs. Patera had also been a science major in college, where they'd met, so Mr. Patera would say it was "chemistry." Doris already knew all the elements in the periodic table. She and I shared a liking for science fact and fiction, even if we diverged on history.

She started talking about Brooklyn. Despite her outer-space dreams, Doris lived in a narrow world. She would express intense curiosity about things while dismissing them. She was afraid of places outside Wardville. She had no interest in terrestrial geography; she'd been surprised when I'd informed her that, like me, she had always lived on an island, that Brooklyn was the western end of Long Island, the head of a huge fish.

The stuff she was now saying was a variation on things she'd told me before. She and her parents had escaped great dangers. Brooklyn had gotten "unsafe." Crime in the "bad" neighborhoods north of theirs had begun to spill over. When they'd occasionally driven through these neighborhoods (they never walked there), Doris had been told to lock her door and roll up her window. She would gaze through glass at rundown buildings and trash-strewn sidewalks. Most of the people walking around were black. She got the fearful message, even as she was warned against prejudice. She was happy when they'd moved out here, far from cramped old buildings into a bright and roomy new house.

Yet I knew the Pateras weren't exactly at home in Wardville: they'd been tagged as "different" when they'd first moved in, themselves now the feared Other. Mr. Patera was Italian, Mrs. Patera Jewish, and Doris was being raised Jewish. Like us, it took a while for them to be accepted. Like us too, Doris and her parents occupied a strange middle ground: socially involved yet insular, happily settled yet uneasy.

Before Doris had finished her litany of Brooklyn horrors, a car sped down our block, and we turned to look. Jimmy sat with one hand on the steering wheel, the other arm tightly holding a girl—a black girl I didn't recognize. Music crescendoed and faded as they swept by.

Doris and I looked at each other, and she let out a little laugh that seemed embarrassed, surprised. I felt a pulsing tightness low down in my belly as I imagined riding in Jimmy's car, with Doris in her Uhura shirt or—better yet—without Doris, riding with Jimmy alone. I told Doris I'd talk to her later and retreated quickly into the house, just in time to see Diane tearing the muumuu from my mother's body.

"How can I do work as spiritual discipline under these conditions?" Diane was saying. "You're never satisfied with anything."

I stood staring: my mother in a pair of shorts and her brassiere, my sister kicking at the fallen muumuu.

•

As it turned out, a few days later the luau was seriously threatened. The head of the organizing committee at the Swim Club had suffered, in my mother's words, "a sort of nervous breakdown" after his son ran off to Canada, denouncing his parents as government lackeys. There were other factors: Mr. Slade, descended from one of Wardville's "old families," was under a lot of pressure to produce a grand celebration. We were building toward the Bicentennial, two years away. The older club members in particular wanted a very big party, a showpiece of old-fashioned American optimism represented by the wonders of our newest state, our farthest frontier (they weren't counting the moon, I figured). Maybe they wanted to celebrate away the lingering fog of Vietnam and Watergate. There hadn't been a lot of donations, though, and it was hard to get the event going. Maybe luaus themselves seemed to some like relics of an earlier, more innocent time. And then there were rumors that Slade had gotten a large chunk of the money from a waste-hauling firm, Randono and Velman, that might have "mob connections." We knew both the Randonos and the Velmans—my mother and Mrs. Velman were friends.

My father was also on the committee, bringing his accounting skills. But he too had doubts about the luau. I discovered this late one night, when I woke up shaky and dry-mouthed after watching *Invasion of the Body Snatchers* on *Creature Features*. I crept into the kitchen for some water and stopped at the end of the hallway. The dining room light cast angled shadows down the hall, and my father sat at the table with sheets of paper spread out before him next to a bottle of whiskey and a glass. He was mumbling to himself, and foul words emerged out of the general dissatisfied murmur. I got closer. "Damn Hawaiian crap," he growled. "What the hell is all this shit for anyway? I work my ass off so I can dress like some tropical fruit? Fucking bullshit."

I had never heard my father talk this way; I choked back a giddy-shivery laugh. He seemed like a different person, some substitute dad. The walls looked dark and strange, as if they concealed unfamiliar doorways into rooms I did not know, engulfing depths into which I might vanish. I couldn't let my father discover me there, looking, over-hearing. I went back to bed without the water, keeping my eyes focused forward on the door of my actual lamplit room, as if those phantom doorways might pull me in if I looked toward them.

After a long while, I fell asleep and dreamed of pod people replacing all the residents of Wardville. But the morphing angel emerged from my wall, like a great swift bird with a pale silver alien's face, and grasped me in his talon-hands, pulling me off into the warm night. We flew away from Wardville, over woods, and Claytown appeared below: those ancient-looking wooden structures clustered around the weathered church. And the town was on fire; people were running from the tinderbox houses. I was holding a glass of water and I began to pour it down over the fire, and the water continued to flow from some endless source through the small glass. But the fire burned on. I woke up as the angel swept me from the flames. We flew high above and away.

Dad was grouchy at breakfast and flinched at every loud noise. He didn't look at me, and I wondered if he'd known I was there the night before, watching him, hearing his drunken grumbling. I wanted him to look up and say something to me, maybe crack a joke.

The radio was on at low volume: *Rambling with John Gambling* on WOR, my mother's favorite show. (In the afternoon I'd tune in to the same station for Bob and Ray.)

Mom stood at the stove scrambling eggs as I sat down at the table. She turned to put the eggs on our plates. Her eyelids were reddish and swollen, and she spoke cheerful words as if from underwater. Something felt wrong. Something had crept into the house overnight. My eggs looked like unnatural-yellow blobs.

I forced breakfast down, though, and told Mom I was going over to the beach to see Avo. I was trying to rework my uneasiness into further defiance. I got the expected look: sharp disapproval modulating into resigned impatience.

"I hope you won't hang around there, bugging your grandfather," she said.

She was doing it again—discouraging me from seeing Avo. Sometimes it seemed like he was an embarrassment to her. If her friends visited while my grandfather happened to be there, Mom would speak for Avo, as if she was afraid of his roughness, his accent, his left-wing politics ("left-over," my father had joked). She would correct his use of her real name, Libertade, insisting on the Libby everyone knew her by. I hated all that.

"I don't think Avo minds having me around," I said now.

"Well, be careful going over there. Lots of construction activity. And I'm sure your friends will be around looking for you, so don't spend the whole day there."

I nodded, while resolving to stay there as long as I wanted. Contrary to my mother's words and wishes, there wouldn't be a gang of friends searching me out.

I felt, in an uncomprehending way, my mother's fear that I'd be friendless, abnormal, a misfit. I often felt like I really was all those things, and sometimes I didn't care.

I headed toward the woods and beach, away from town.

Of course, I sensed even then how much my parents wanted us all to belong, not to be isolated, like Avo. Despite their efforts, they didn't really have close friends in town.

Mom had Mrs. Velman and Mrs. Patera (fellow usurpers of Wardville's old turf) and acquaintances from clubs and neighborhood groups, but it didn't seem that she confided in these women or that there was much affection between them. In their presence, she maintained a guardedness, a sort of mask.

Besides James Gerthoff and Pete Riley, my father had a few other friends in Wardville, the result of shared father–son rituals, the athletic and boy-club and church-sponsored activities that occupied Saturday mornings (back when I still participated in them). But Dad's only close friends were from the old neighborhood in Newark, people he'd bonded with early and who remained the models for any later bonds—models never equaled. Even though Dad rarely saw these old friends, he kept in touch, and they featured in stories spun into near-legend. (My mother, on the other hand, kept silent about her frayed old ties.) His tales were full of joking and horseplay and, I think, genuine camaraderie—you could see it all in his lively face as he told these stories. The newer friendships didn't seem so real.

There wasn't much close family, either—only Avo on my mother's side, since she had no siblings (an infant brother had succumbed to polio). Dad's parents were dead and he hardly saw his three brothers, nearly dead to him, too, out in their separate seaside towns on Long Island and in Jersey. All the brothers had left Newark, moving nearer to the ocean, as if back toward the transatlantic ancestry they had aspired to escape. They centered their lives on their own nuclear families, their green water-edge suburbs.

I had decided to try writing about Claytown for the paper as well as my journal, and I figured Avo could tell me some things about the old town. He lived in a similar sort of place, a community apart from Wardville that, like Claytown, was an object of aloof indifference and sometimes suspicion.

Avo's house sat a hundred feet or so from Wardville Beach, in a cluster of cottages named Spanish Settlement—former summer residences whose original inhabitants had been a group of nature-loving socialist Spaniards who thought they could find there a safe retreat from the city and the larger society. They had faith in self-sufficiency, communal resources, and vegetarianism. They had tried to keep their lives as simple as possible. My grandparents were among the first nonmembers to move in—they too were fleeing urban life to find a seaside haven, and they shared many of the colony's beliefs. But now the value of the land outweighed other kinds of values, and a development of large homes was encroaching on the few remaining cottages. It was called Capri West. The builder, none other than James Gerthoff Senior, was buying up small houses to demolish them and erect in their places boxy faux-palazzos—stucco and red tile grafted onto ranches, with pretty views across Raritan Bay. My grandfather's house was one of those unsightly little bungalows, obstructive anachronisms stubbornly resisting the flow of modern development. No one was sure how much longer Avo would be able to stay in the house.

All this had intensified Avo's already robust feelings about American injustice. He had always been passionate about politics; the mention of any Republican might provoke him into expounding an extensive social history of the twentieth century, with Franklin Roosevelt as its unquestioned hero. Unlike my parents and most of their friends, Avo was an unreconstructed lefty Democrat—no post-Kennedy shift in *his* allegiance (except to oppose LBJ on Vietnam). True, he had moved with my parents from Newark's Portuguese enclave, called Ironbound for the railroads around it and now hemmed in by rough neighborhoods. But Avo never developed my parents' detachment from the poor people still packed in urban slums that, after all, weren't very far away. He'd volunteered in soup kitchens and shelters. He'd marched for civil rights with others from the Settlement.

I rode to Avo's house on my bike with the banana seat and high handlebars and new electric turn signals—arrows in a small box above the rear wheel. This short ride always made me feel like I was leaving Wardville far behind, as if the woods were wilderness. Out there it felt easier to say or think what I wanted to, and I could ask questions I couldn't ask at home. The colony nurtured my grandfather's off-center, nonconformist views, which I linked to all the books (mainly history) stacked and scattered in his house, to his advanced-seeming age, to the inflections and accent of his speech. His English, although fluent, had the flavor of a distant, alien place—far beyond the wide bay that widened further into ocean that appeared to have no end. (Sometimes it seemed as though that other land was his true home and mine too, and as if America was the alien place, and his accent the trace of our true language that I did not know.)

He'd never been a demonstrative man—leaving that sort of thing to my grandmother—but he'd always shown a keen interest in Diane's and my welfare, a concern that often took the form of stories and secular sermons, as if he had a duty to make us aware of the world we were growing into, aware in ways that our parents couldn't or wouldn't make us. So we both became very close to him, reliant on him even, while he remained, at some level, enigmatic and unapproachable. These days I was seeing him much more often than Diane was.

So I guess it was more than information about Claytown I wanted from Avo—it was something like support for my near-fixation on the place and the people there.

Avo's house stood at the waterfront end of a row of the one-story cottages, all very much alike, with simple

A-shaped roofs not much higher than their front doors. The houses, mostly uninhabited now, lined one side of the street. On the other side, the woods stretched nearly unbroken to the bluffs at the island's end. A grassy area separated Avo's property from the narrow rust-colored beach. The house behind his was boarded up and empty; it had belonged to a couple named Alvarez (Juan, Ella), garment workers and labor organizers who had died years before. The place was abandoned. Next door lived a widow we knew only as Señora Cruz (Avo never used her first name), a ramrod-thin woman with gray-blue eyes that scrutinized and judged. Like most of her remaining neighbors, she grew vegetables and fruit in her small, thickly planted backyard, which my grandmother had called "the farm." Señora Cruz had formed a friendship of sorts with my sister based on radical politics and alternative foods, but Diane hadn't been to the Settlement in months.

I carefully kick-standed my bike on Avo's uneven front walk, buckled by the roots of a huge oak tree. I walked up the brick path bisecting the small front garden to the screen door and called into the dark interior. There was a sound of shuffling feet before Avo's face appeared, floating for a moment in the dimness, and then his stooped body. He seemed, for a weird moment, not to know who I was, but the hazel eyes in his creased brown face seemed to drop their guard as he recognized me. They kept their sharpness, though.

"Ah," he said.

Inside, the house looked much as it had when my grandmother died, of cancer, five years earlier. Two bulky armchairs, one a half-decade more worn, dominated the tiny living room, where my grandparents would sit together reading or watching TV. Their old black-and-white set retained its place atop an antique cabinet on the opposite wall. It was tuned to the Yankees game. Beyond was the small dining room, made smaller by the huge old dark furniture they'd brought down from their Newark apartment. A round doily rested on the table's center, beneath a bowl of dusty carved-wood fruit—my grandmother's decorations, untouched. Avo ate in the kitchen, the brightest part of the house.

"You want something to drink?" Avo said. My grandmother had always fed us as soon as we arrived, and he had taken over that role in his own rougher way.

Shakily (I didn't dare offer help), he poured out cranberry juice for us ("good for the bladder," he said), and we sat at the small Formica-topped kitchen table. Crusty scotch tape on the plastic-cushioned chair scratched against my thighs. Avo settled himself slowly, with a wince, wordlessly enduring his arthritis while still letting you know it hurt. We could hear the ballgame from the living room; Phil Rizzuto's commentary and the background crowd noise floated through the kitchen as if carried directly from the Bronx on the grass-scented breeze wafting through doorways and windows.

Avo leaned toward me. I could smell his bath powder, faintly medicinal. "Something wrong? You worn out from just a bike ride, *menino?*"

Until recently he'd never used that term of affection (or any other); it was my grandmother's word, and because I never heard it anywhere else—you heard Spanish sometimes, yes, but not Portuguese—it belonged only to her. I looked down the dim hallway toward their small bedroom and remembered my final visit: she lay there skeletal and silent, on morphine, recognizing no one, and I wondered what she was seeing behind her closed eyes or when she briefly, blankly opened them.

I told Avo about the dream that had broken into my sleep and swept me away. He didn't react well.

"Angels? What is this *merde?*" he said. "Too much of that church school, I think. You know, that church talk will make you crazy." He tapped a finger against his head. "Oh, what I could tell you about the Church!"

Of course, he *had* told me, many times, even before I was remotely able to understand. There were vaguely Marxist rants against Church authorities, but what stuck were the stories, which carried me to a place much older than Claytown or Newark, to a country whose stony, damp green fields yielded pitiful crops only grudgingly, after long slavelike labor. The church was the largest building, and the priest would hobnob with big landowners while feeding piety to the poor. Sometimes he'd come to talk with Avo's mother while avoiding Avo's priest-hating father.

Now Avo launched into one of those recurring stories: the winter day his mother asked him to deliver a pot of stew to the priest. Soft-footing to the rectory through the darkened church that smelled of old wood and incense, Avo saw the priest scoop money from an offering box near the altar and press it quickly into his pocket. Avo halted, but a stepped-on floorboard creaked, and the priest looked up. His startled eyes met Avo's, and he grasped his arm, nearly overturning the stewpot. "Little spy," he said, threatening God's punishment if Avo said a word. Avo fled and told no one, unsure what he'd witnessed but feeling sick and shaken, as if he'd done something evil. He told his mother that the priest wasn't home.

As with every retelling, Avo's reawakened fear and confusion ran through me as if we were both suddenly boys in that dark sanctuary, space and time dissolving.

Before he could start on further tales and tirades, I told him I'd gone to Claytown. I'd meant to sound proud, but it came out wavering, doubtful.

"Did you?" He laughed again. "Did your parents know? They wouldn't want you over there with those poor dark people, would they? They forget when *we* were poor dark people."

I stared at him without answering, and he shook his head. "I know that place a little," he said. "We used to swap with them sometimes, fruits and vegetables, back when they still had farms. Nice people, most of them. A little suspicious, always holding back some—who could blame them? But they didn't care about our accents or where we came from."

Claytown started as a farming and fishing town, he told me, where free blacks lived, from the Chesapeake some of them, and later freed slaves from the South. It was a stop on the Underground Railroad—did I know what that was? I nodded. Most of what he told me about Claytown I'd gleaned from my book, but his speaking it made all the history seem like news. The past was urgent present for Avo, recurrent cycles of oppression and justice.

He paused to take off his glasses and fiddled with the tape holding the frames together. He looked at me awhile.

"They weren't always treated good, you know," he said.

He watched me again, the baseball sounds still drifting in. I figured he was considering how much to tell me, how much I could handle, coddled and sheltered as I was in that fancy new house (he'd lectured Mom and Dad openly, in front of me).

"At least not by some people," he continued. "They hired the blacks and like garbage they treated them. This was way back. Nineteen hundreds. Terrible, cruel things they did to those people."

But it wasn't finished, he told me. Power and greed hadn't gone away; they were after Spanish Settlement now, and their next goal was Claytown. I could almost see them, Power and Greed, snaky creatures gobbling up these neighborly places whose time was passing.

Biking back home, I thought about Claytown—what might have happened there and what might be happening now. I had only half-formed ideas, distressing feelings more than ideas. I kept hearing Avo's words again, about past and present threats, or one big threat, recurring, that he always felt.

As I waited at the light to cross the wide road separating the main town from the seaside cottages, I looked around at the thick trees. I knew their names from walks with my grandparents: the tall dusky-barked oaks with their twisting armlike branches, the mottled sycamores, the reddish maples. The woods were an old Indian hunting ground—some said a burial ground, too—and I would dig up arrowheads, abundant as pebbles there, while remembering things I'd read about the Leni Lenapes. One late afternoon, sitting at a grassy pond edge listening to birdcalls and rustles, I saw a dark outline on the other side of the water, deep in the leafy shadows. It was an Indian brave, watching me. I was amazed but not frightened. I glanced toward the pond, and when I looked back the figure had vanished.

Now, waiting to cross, I could hear them, the Indians, rushing through the forest, free and powerful ghosts. If I turned back, I might disappear amid the trees with those ghosts and never return to town.

But I slammed my pedals as soon as the light changed and raced across the intersection. As I rode toward my street, an engine vroomed behind me and I felt a tickle along the back of my neck. The engine got louder, and now the radio blared too as the car caught up. It was Jimmy. He had his arm around the front-seat passenger: the same girl as that afternoon on my block. Two boys about my own age sat in back. Not Bentley, not Solomon, no one I knew. The car shot by, and if Jimmy noticed me, he gave no sign. I wondered where he was going with those kids. I felt a rush of anger and desire and curiosity and envy and fear.

The subject of Claytown came up again the next day. I'd been shooting baskets in the driveway—missing most of my shots, since I didn't practice much—and came inside for a cold drink. My mother was sitting in the kitchen with Grace Velman, she whose husband, Stan, was a partner in Randono and Velman Waste Management. Mrs. Velman had attained a prominent place for herself in town, having broken down the barriers keeping anyone not "old" Wardville out of lofty institutions like the Swim Club and the Bridge Society. She had joined with a vengeance, becoming important on committees and governing boards, and so naturally she was now up to her lei in luau. But they weren't discussing the luau.

"It's just empty lots," Mrs. Velman was saying as I climbed the stairs to the kitchen. "And now the black people there, well, they claim it's their property. But I happen to know—"

This was where Mrs. Velman saw me, and she never finished her sentence, so I didn't learn what she happened to know. But I figured it had something to do with Claytown and probably with Stan. I felt as if I'd been cut off from learning something important—and unsavory enough that I was deemed too young to hear it.

"Hi there, Luke," she said, smoothly shifting gears. She examined me through her pointy-cornered eyeglasses. "You're quite sweaty. Running around?"

I nodded. "Have some iced tea," said my mother, pointing to a pitcher on the table between the two women. They were a contrast: Mom wavy-blonde and thin-faced, Mrs. Velman with dark straight hair and cheeks that looked like she was storing food in them.

Mrs. Velman looked at me now, her lips pressed tight, as if she'd exhausted her supply of small talk and amiability and was waiting for me to leave. It was familiar to me, this combination of friendliness, self-doubt, and arrogance. Like the Randonos, headed by Dom ("Dump-King") Randono, the Velmans were unsure of themselves, judging from the talk about them inside and outside my family. They were, as my father put it, as loaded as their trash trucks, but they were also different from most of their affluent neighbors. The trash business, however lucrative, didn't quite measure up in old Wardville's eyes. (The new money didn't care so much.) And then there were the Mafia rumors. So Mrs. Velman was, no doubt, doubly eager to scale the spindly Wardville social ladder. I didn't know all the nuances, but I felt the attitude—snobby, gossipy, suspicious.

I directed a revoltingly sweet smile at Mrs. Velman, but it had no effect. I gulped the tea and excused myself.

So now I knew there were more connections: Randono and Velman had some interest in Claytown property. But why all this focus on Claytown? My imagination swiftly conjured hidden gold and buried treasure, but I knew that was a kid's view; I already sensed the grimmer reality. Bursting with half-formed, creepy questions, I hurried outside. I walked rapidly down my block and then began to run, heading toward the ocean but with no specific destination, propelled by a fierce need to get somewhere or to get away from something that was quickly overtaking me. After a few blocks, I noticed Doris up ahead walking toward me, and I slowed down. At first I wanted to turn back, run the other way, but I kept going. I wanted to tell her all I was thinking; I wanted, for some reason, to disturb her.

She was already looking alarmed when we both stopped. "Where are you going?" she asked. "What's wrong?"

"Nothing," I gasped, still trying to catch my breath. "Well, something, but I'm not sure. Just felt like getting away from my house."

She gave me a concerned look as if from some height of sense and maturity, which made me want to bug her all the more. She was silent as I told her about Jimmy's car and Claytown and the rest. But when I mentioned that I'd like to get inside the Ward house, she asked me sharply why I'd want to do that. There was something going on around Claytown, I told her, and Jimmy was involved in it somehow, and maybe it all had to do with Sebastian Ward. Doris shook her head with a sort of shudder and replied that Ward was just strange, an old degenerate—that's what her father said. I didn't exactly know what a degenerate was, but I knew it wasn't good. I wasn't sure that Doris herself knew what it meant. I had a sudden prickly feeling along my arms and legs. I told her I'd talk to her later and hurried off, continuing the way I'd been going.

I walked quickly down to the wide road, which was quiet—no cars racing anywhere. I crossed over to the woods and entered the cool, green silence. I sat by the pond, whose still surface reflected the tall trees and the sky, making the water's depths seem infinite. I felt calmer, less afraid of the questions filling my head. I sat a long time, half-waiting for those spirits that still might appear there amid the trees, benign and terrifying, to lure me away.

Later, back home, I looked up *degenerate* in my Webster's Dictionary. The definitions were as murky as the word itself. None of it seemed to have much to do with Ward, and I wondered why people would call him that. I figured maybe it was linked to Ward's involvement with Claytown. So it further stoked my curiosity about Ward, Claytown, and—of course—Jimmy's connection to both. Yes, it was all strange, as Doris said, and it scared me, but that only made me want to get closer to it.

FOUR

Jimmy had been free from school for a month already by the time my vacation began. He had just completed his freshman year at Emerson Hill College, named for Ralph Waldo's commonsense brother William, a judge whose house once stood there among the bay-view hillside homes of fellow abolitionists. The campus looked toward Manhattan across the bay, and most students made the twenty-minute crossing every weekend, ferried from leafy calm to urban frenzy, from secluded corner to the center of the world. Jimmy looked out from that campus, too, of course, part of him yearning to get to that other island and out of his father's business for good.

But it was clear that one foot was deeply sunk in home soil. He had that cozy arrangement—no rent to pay and lots of money to be made filling the island's remaining open space with efficient suburban cubes for Wall Street workers and city employees fleeing the urban core. And there was also his mother, mysteriously housebound and needy, wanting him there partly to help stave off the demons from which her house was inadequate protection.

What spawned those demons I wasn't sure; some said a childhood tragedy had left her orphaned and craving security. Others pointed to abusive boyfriends in a long pattern extending into her marriage to James Gerthoff, who had been witnessed shouting nasty putdowns at her in public places. Jimmy had hinted at bullying, too, and might have told my parents things I never heard. There was also the formidable mother-in-law, a stern and judgmental next-door presence.

Whatever the reasons, Anna Gerthoff had withdrawn from the world. She would close the curtains in daytime, and no doubt Jimmy sat there with her in the darkened house, reassuring her, consoling her for losses he wasn't even clear about except for the loss of her domineering husband to long hours of work. And Jimmy would grow restless, unable to sit still, unwilling to look into her reproachful eyes awash in sadness and confusion, until finally he couldn't take any more and so would assert his need and power to get away, running out of the house to his car.

This getaway need seemed to be growing; it had pushed him toward a college major in architecture and planning and away from the family business. He was learning more and more, from books and from people who saw things differently from most on the island, and he was moving outward in a larger and larger radius. Since entering college and breaking up with Diane, he was meeting girls he hadn't known through high school; they were wild by his mother's definition, but he likely thought of them as liberated, adventurous. At first they were wealthier girls, attending the Hill College or home on breaks from more-distant campuses, and later they were working class, from denser, multiracial neighborhoods. Probably he liked their attitudes, especially the North Shore girls, the way they moved with grace and self-possession, their sassy talk that fired back at bullshit, their total lack of fawning toward him. Later in life, maybe, he recognized that they'd been the antithesis of home and his mother, but for now they were like a brisk sea breeze through a newly opened window.

This was the college Jimmy—restless, torn, experience-hungry—emerging out of the Jimmy I'd encountered through Diane.

And our encounters continued, as if following some unseen pattern guiding me into a wider, freer, weightier world. One late-June morning I was mowing our front lawn while Diane, in another rare burst of helpfulness, watered the impatiens bordering the walk. With a roar that sank to a restrained growl, Jimmy's car came up the street, slowing as he passed by. He glanced at us but kept moving, and I wondered again why he was driving down our block. He was shirtless, and his backseat was piled with beach gear: towels, a cooler, a large radio.

Diane tracked his slow movement tight-lipped, fiddling with a bracelet on her wrist. "He'll probably spend a few nights down the Shore," she said, as if I'd asked about it. There was a resentful edge in her voice. "Parents have a place they never use."

I had come up close to my sister. We watched Jimmy drive off, the roar resuming once he got farther up the block. He seemed to trail some of the Shore's rock-&-roll, carnival romance.

"I'd like to ask him if he'd take me someplace," I said.

Diane gave me such an alarmed, censorious look that I backed away. "What do you mean?" she said.

"Well, like Sebastian Ward's house. Inside."

"With Jimmy?"

"Yeah, I think he'd drive me there."

"Did he suggest that?"

"No," I said. "Not really."

She told me there wasn't any need for Jimmy to take me anywhere, that if I wanted for some strange reason to see the Ward place inside, she would take me herself on one of Ward's open-house days.

"But I don't want you to take me," I said.

She threw down the hose she'd been grasping. "Fine," she said. "Do what you want. Why you'd want to go anywhere with him is beyond me, though."

She strode back through the garage into the house. I stood there bewildered and shaken. She'd seemed sad after the breakup with Jimmy, very sad sometimes, and she wouldn't talk about him or answer questions about their relationship. But if she'd felt this kind of blazing, pained hostility, I never saw it before this.

I didn't need to ask Jimmy, as it turned out. He asked me— or rather, Bentley and me—on behalf of Sebastian Ward. I wondered why he would invite us there, but my eagerness blew away my doubts. It was irresistible, getting inside that old mansion, with all its strange, risky possibilities, and its secrets that seemed obscurely linked to Claytown. Jimmy must have known that my parents wouldn't want me riding in his car to Ward's house, but he didn't seem to care whether I told them about it or not.

In any case, I didn't tell them. When he picked me up, I rode in back again and kept looking at the empty seat next to me and seeing Solomon. I wondered if he'd be at the house. I was worried about him without knowing why.

This time, after Jimmy parked in the driveway, we walked around to the front door. Everything looked quiet and dark inside. A note in elegant calligraphy taped to the brass knocker read: "Greetings, young visitors. Please knock."

Jimmy laughed at the note and said, "I think he means you. Go ahead." The knocker was an old man's face; you lifted his beard to knock. "Neptune," Jimmy said. "God of the sea."

I pulled up the beard and hit Neptune's chin a few times, but nothing happened. I tried again. After footsteps and creaking floorboards, the door opened, and there stood Ward himself, in a pale blue jacket, white pants, and a straw hat with a multicolored band, worn at a rakish angle. His round, gold glasses glinted in a shaft of sun. He looked startled for a few seconds at the sight of us—as if we'd surprised him—but he quickly regained himself and beckoned us in.

Up close, he seemed almost exotic. He was so different from most of the men I knew in Wardville, with their hearty speech and sharp, forceful motions. They kidded you, gave you quick punches in the shoulder, asked *How ya doing*, pausing for a *just fine* or *okay* so they could return the ritual *attaboy*. I felt weak, strange, awkward around them. Models of masculine energy and strength and optimism, these men. They'd gone through wars and into ambitious, difficult postwar work that gave us the modern, foursquare homes we lived in.

Oh yeah, Ward was different. He had all the time in the world, like a boy at play. As we walked into his house, he bowed to us, a peculiar and funny gesture, especially with his stocky build. "Welcome, young gentlemen," he said. He looked at me and smiled, but his eyes didn't seem to be kidding. It was like he was joking and earnest at once.

We followed him to the left off the entry, into the "parlor." Heavy curtains were drawn back from long windows, but not much air or sun was getting in. The room was full of antique objects. Polished wood surfaces gleamed in amber light: glass-fronted desks and bookcases, highboys and butler's tables (Ward told us the names), chairs that seemed the shape of the plump women who once sat in them. Carpets whose intricate patterns might be deciphered to tell stories of their distant Asian homelands. Painted jars and figures on finely crafted wooden stands. A marble-and-wood mantle. Tarnished mirrors, smoky dim as if they contained these rooms in an earlier time, so if I walked into one I'd fall right through into the startled company of a nineteenth-century family on a similar sleepy afternoon. They'd take me in like an orphan left on their doorstep, and I'd be a different boy altogether, transformed, no longer dark and odd-ethnic and awkward but a confident master of the house, a fair American prince.

I was staring into one of the tall mirrors when a figure appeared there, distorted and spectral. It took me a few dizzying seconds to recognize the current, living Ward. I whirled around to face him.

"James just conveyed this mirror here for me from a very nice shop in the Village," he said.

He was looking at Jimmy like a proud parent, but his look changed, and he put a hand to his head, as if he suddenly had a headache. "That reminds me, James, I need to you to pick up that armoire out in Bucks County for the blue bedroom."

Jimmy's mouth tightened and he looked away. "Yes, when I get a chance, Sebastian," he said. "I'll have to borrow a truck again."

"I'm sure they can spare one," Ward said. "Unless they need it to haul away the wreckage of some cottage."

"Can we talk about this later?" Jimmy said.

"Of course."

"I'd like to show them the house." Jimmy's voice had calmed, as if to placate Ward.

"Fine," Ward said. He looked at us. "Feel free to wander through the open rooms, but watch what you touch. I'll be taking a walk around the grounds until the others come. My regular young guests. One is already here. You can stay to meet them if you like. I was hoping you would."

We made a circuit of the first floor, pausing awhile in a room filled with books, more than I had ever seen outside the town library. Most looked very old. I ran my hand across a row of leather-bound Dickens and pulled out *Great Expectations*. Jimmy slid the book from my hands, muttering, "Careful," then returned it to its place. We walked back to the entrance hall, from which a wide staircase branched left and right from a middle landing. A chandelier high up scattered rainbow light fragments into the otherwise shadowy second story. We walked up. No one else was touring the house. At the landing, Jimmy told us to continue on upstairs, that he wasn't our babysitter and we'd be fine on our own. We could meet him outside in back. His mood had taken another sudden swing toward impatient, self-questioning haughtiness, like he was wasting precious time on us.

There was a hallway at the top of each staircase; we chose the left one, which had five doors, three closed. Bentley and I walked into a very large bedroom, with a four-poster bed and huge, ornate dressers. Through the long windows you could see far out across the bay, with sails and masts white against the gray-blue. Above one dresser hung an oil painting of the Ward house (in the nineteenth century, I figured) surrounded by fields and forests, like a plantation manor in some unspoiled dream of a landscape. There were no people in the scene, no well-dressed Wards on the wide porches, no workers laboring in the fields.

We walked past all the open doors, peeked into rooms similarly antique, and I felt like our time, Bentley's and mine, was racing by while the house's time was longer, slower, as if the place existed in a kind of eternity. I would sometimes ponder these mind-bogglers of time and eternity, prompted by science fiction and by questions my catechism suggested but did not ask nor answer: Would we exist in time after death and, if not, how *would* we exist? Was eternity time's extension? How could it go on forever?

After looking in all the open rooms, we returned to the middle door, which was closed but unlocked. We ventured inside. It was a completely different kind of room, the most amazing rec room I'd ever seen. The walls had murals of trees, all sorts of trees close together, as if we were in a forest; the ceiling dazzled with white stars on blue, some in constellation patterns. Shelves overflowed with games. There were easels and chalkboards. A ping-pong table and a trampoline. Tops and jump ropes. Lionel trains running around the periphery. Toy cars and trucks. Building kits, gadgets, spyglasses and microscopes, a rocking horse, a fortune-telling witch in a glass cabinet: it was all too much to take in at once. Bentley and I looked at each other, and I could see that his cool was shaken. I felt a sort of awe at all that stuff, but the room also creeped me out; it seemed so enclosed, so separate from the outside world. There were no windows. And all the objects looked out of date, like relics of an earlier generation's childhood. Bentley pointed down. Underfoot was soft blue carpeting inset with a white map of an unidentified, unfamiliar-looking island, floating by itself in a wide sea.

"Boys!"

The voice came from behind us. We turned. Sebastian Ward stood rigid, hands at his sides, face flushed.

"Sometimes doors are closed for a reason," he said. "James should have locked it. He really shouldn't have let you wander alone. Come along, come on out."

I said, "We didn't know."

"A lot you don't know." He made way for us to pass and, as I did, I could smell his body, a weird amalgam like damp dough and cologne.

Ward followed us as we walked downstairs, and he told us to head straight back through the long main hallway.

We entered an enormous kitchen of gleaming chrome. A center worktable was piled with sweets: cakes, chocolates, cookies, tubs of ice cream. Ward paused, looked at us. His face was calmer. "These are for our guests later on. But you're welcome to some. Not too much. I'll be outside."

This implied, of course, that the true guests, the real objects of Ward's generosity (most likely Claytown kids) had a deeper need for, a greater right to, this mountain of treats—a month's worth of permitted dessert at my house, probably a year's worth at Bentley's. There was something indecent and entrapping about this abundance, like the upstairs rec room. It seemed unreal, a conjurer's trick. Yet it also promised some huge fulfillment beyond the sating of appetite. Some greater hunger might be banished by such patronage. And I see now that maybe it was an expression of Ward's need and desire to provide.

Warily, I took a cookie while Bentley grabbed two handfuls of stuff.

Out in back was a garden: roses climbing white trellises, perfectly trimmed low green hedges, pink-gravel pathways. At the back of the garden stood an old-fashioned wooden swing with facing benches, on one of which sat Jimmy, with Solomon next to him. On the opposite bench sat the girl who'd been in Jimmy's car. Behind the still swing stood Ward, with one hand on Jimmy's shoulder and the other on Solomon's. Jimmy was clasping Ward's right wrist with one hand, just holding it, while they laughed and talked, showing no signs of their earlier gruffness. The woman and Solomon were neither laughing nor talking. Solomon looked uncomfortable.

I was glad to see Solomon (I hadn't run into him at school), but something about the way he and Ward and Jimmy were interacting, and the way the girl was looking away from them, put me off. I hesitated, sensing trouble but then asking myself what trouble there could be in this garden. Bentley strode forward, and I hurried to catch up, apprehensive and eager, like I was moving from a safe but confining place into the open.

As we approached the swing, Ward noticed us, and his laughing shrank away. He removed his hands from Jimmy and Solomon and pulled himself back into formality. The conversation stopped. The only sounds were the swing's slow rhythmic creaking, the hum of insects, and the distant whine of boat motors from the marina.

Jimmy had stayed relaxed and now clasped his hands behind his head. "Well, hello again, boys," he said. "You remember Solomon here. And that's Theona." This welcome had the usual joking edge, piercing the sudden tension. Theona gave us a reserved nod and turned away again. Strands of her long straight hair fell across her face.

"Hi," said Solomon, glancing at us.

Ward coughed and said he had to get back inside to greet guests. He looked at us with a sort of appraising suspicion as he passed. Bentley was hurriedly chewing the last of his sweets.

"Glad you guys are here," Jimmy said once Ward had left. "Did you enjoy the tour? Great place here. Solomon and I have a great time here."

Jimmy put an arm around Solomon, who smiled but still looked squirmy.

"You guys wanna try out the swing?" Jimmy asked, getting up and nimbly hopping off. "They'd be glad to share, I think."

"Sure," Theona said. But there was hesitation in her voice and in her light brown eyes. She slid over to let Solomon sit next to her, but they didn't look at one another. Bentley and I sat side by side and pushed the swing into motion, faster and faster, in wider and wider arcs. Solomon started laughing but Theona still held back. I relaxed into the rhythm, the breezy bliss.

Jimmy stood watching us with a smile on his face like some combination of kid and parent at the playground. His look spurred us on as we pushed the swing higher, and then he started talking to us, in a riveting, hyperactive flow, a meandering but intense riff. He liked it here so much, he said, away from town, it was like a whole different world, and Ward had created his own little family, yes, they were all a sort of family here and Ward was almost a father, and sometimes you could really sympathize with those kids from Claytown, especially the ones whose fathers had left them, not that he blamed them since there was hardly any work there anymore and they sure weren't growing strawberries or digging up clay or harvesting oysters, but he was glad he could be a brother to them like Ward was a sort of dad and yet not the kind of dad who tells you what to do all the time, not a boss, nope, there was plenty of freedom here to do what you like, have fun, be happy for a change instead of worrying about the goddamn future or people trying to trap you, yes, you could breathe out here, really breathe, feel independent, you guys, Luke and Bentley, you should come out here whenever you like, get to know Solomon better, it's good that we all get to know each other better, and it would get you away from all those small-minded people.

Through all of this, Bentley pressed the swing into faster pendulum arcs, thrilling swoops, until the old wood creaked and the swing began to wobble like it was about to tip. Trees, house, garden, Jimmy—all of it had come loose, it seemed, and I felt thrill veering into terror, not of falling but of never stopping, with nothing fixed in place and me just one more thing in motion, endlessly.

Theona gripped Solomon through Jimmy's rambling speech as the swing flew up and back and up again. Solomon tried to push her away, telling her to calm down, and maybe telling himself too.

"Stop," she said. "Stop it now."

Nothing stopped, not Jimmy's fluent pep talk nor the swing's momentum.

"Stop it! You're crazy, stop it right now!"

Jimmy quit talking, and Bentley relaxed his pressure on the swing, letting it slow.

We all looked at Theona as she stared at Jimmy, her eyes teary, confused, livid. The breeze off the water felt suddenly cold on my arms and legs. I wasn't sure if Theona had screamed at Bentley for pushing the swing or at Jimmy's manic talking or at all of us. But her outburst shook me more than the swing ride, and it felt like something hurtful and dangerous was happening. Not someplace else, but here, invading the garden. And Jimmy was in the middle of it all.

FIVE

The day after our visit to Ward's house, I sat on a lawn chair in our backyard watching my father put together stage sets for the upcoming luau. I was listening to the weekly Top 40 countdown on my radio with a notebook open in my lap and a Bic pen poised to list each song as Casey Kasem announced and played it, leading up, of course, to the all-important Number One. On the facing page, I had begun my already-late composition for religious instruction class: "Summer gives us plenty of free time not only to enjoy ourselves but also to fulfill our responsibility to help make the world a better place." That was it, before the Top 40 siphoned most of my attention. But it wasn't only the radio that kept me from my description of intended good works (and from helping my father). Part of my mind was still wandering through Ward's house, taking delirious flight on his swing to the sound of Jimmy's voice.

After shouting at us, Theona had run off toward the driveway, leaving Jimmy in stunned silence. But then he'd laughed and plopped himself again, legs spread wide, on the swing bench next to Solomon. Don't worry about

Theona, Jimmy had said, she was probably off sulking in the car. He'd then started telling us more about Ward and Claytown: he was such a good guy, Ward was, bringing kids up here and giving them the run of the place—they could go to the beach, take rides on Ward's boat, enjoy all the fun stuff up in the "game room," go on day trips to the park or the zoo. And he didn't take a dime for any of this, it was a gift to the community. Jimmy was proud to lend a hand with that kind of giving-back. Some people do good with their money, he'd said.

He'd then stopped talking, looked off toward the house, pensive. Neither of us had asked him what the big deal was about the game room, why we weren't supposed to be in there, but I got the feeling that, like the mountain of treats, it was something carefully hoarded and ritualized, like an offering, only for Ward's regular guests. We hadn't stayed to meet them, except for Solomon.

Now, in my backyard, I pictured Ward's hand on Jimmy's shoulder as I watched Dad sticking green cellophane branches onto a cutout plywood palm tree. Our orange cat, Rusty, swiped at the cellophane and Dad whooshed him away. I recalled something else that Jimmy had said—he'd abruptly asked us, Bentley and Solomon and me, if we'd like to go for a ride in his car, one day during the week when there'd be less traffic, would we like to drive to the Shore? Bentley and I had looked at each other—surprised, eager, a little unbelieving. But I knew I wouldn't be allowed to go. Bentley had quickly agreed, leaving me to mumble some excuse.

After that, I tried not to think about Jimmy's invitation, but now it seemed to be all I could think about. I had to ask my parents—Dad first, since my mother would definitely say no.

•

They discussed it when they thought I wasn't listening, but I'd left my door open. At first they seemed to agree: I couldn't be allowed in Jimmy's car outside of town; my mother didn't much like the idea of my being in his car at all. But Dad began to change his tack: maybe the kid needed to learn something, get it out of his system, see what this idol of his is really like, firsthand, up close, see his clay feet. But is it *safe*, my mother objected. Life isn't safe, Dad said, he's gotta learn that. Dad began to argue that I should go with Jimmy, while Mom repeated her doubts, saying she'd had enough of Jimmy, and the more she objected, the more Dad dismissed her. He nearly shouted, and she stopped arguing back. I almost shut the door to stop hearing. It didn't really seem like Dad had had a change of heart toward Jimmy—it was more like he suddenly wanted me to know more about Jimmy because I somehow needed to, and because Dad himself, for some reason, was getting more and more focused on him.

In the evenings I could hear the cars out on the divided four-lane road between town and beach. The big guys racing, or just exercising the engines of the cars their parents had bought them. One night I'd gone on my bike to watch them, and that's how I learned for sure that Jimmy was among them. They growled, screeched, roared—shaking the pavement like earth tremors as they raced past, unbelievably loud and fast in the otherwise still night. I knew it was dangerous. I knew it was irresponsible. I knew they were a little crazy and far more daring than I could be or wanted to be. I knew. Yet the sound and sight raised the flesh on my arms and made me want to race after them, with them, shaking the town awake.

•

The day before Jimmy's drive to the Jersey Shore, my parents still hadn't made up their minds about it. The issue got pushed aside that day by a crisis. Señora Cruz phoned my parents to alert them that Avo was sitting on the roof of his house. He'd told her he was angry about the development threatening Spanish Settlement and wanted to protest in a way that would get noticed.

I'd known that Avo wasn't just going to wait to be thrown out, because he'd said so. But I hadn't imagined he would do anything like this. For one thing, I didn't think he had the strength.

He'd climbed up a ladder to sit at his roof's apex—not very high up but high enough to be visible to prospective buyers of houses and tracts in Capri West. He taped a large sign that read "Save Our Homes" to his small chimney. He brought his lunch, a thermos of water, a pillow, and a book, and sat leaning against the chimney. He had on a Yankees cap, khaki slacks, and a rarely worn white linen shirt that my parents had brought him from their honeymoon trip to Honolulu, a trip they had described to us many times with enthusiasm and nostalgia—as well they might, since it was the last trip of any distance they'd taken unless you counted the journey we all took by car for a wedding in Terre Haute, Indiana, where somehow a small colony of Portuguese—all related to my father—had settled.

My mother refused to confront her protesting parent while he occupied his roof. She walked through our house manically tidying, upset about the humiliation of it all and the aggravation in the middle of her preparations and how could he behave in such a ridiculous and dangerous way? It was my father who insisted that *somebody* had to go talk to the old man, after all, because the situation couldn't just be ignored. Dad spent an hour on the roof with my grandfather while I stood at the base of the wooden ladder they'd used to climb up; they drank cold water together and talked about the state of the world. Avo quoted Thoreau and Gandhi and Martin Luther King. He refused to leave his perch except to use the bathroom, after which he climbed right back up. A small crowd gathered. My grandfather became the focus of excitement and rumor. A reporter from our local paper, the *Island Vantage*, came to interview the eccentric rebel, and my father came down from the roof to face the press. He was animated, almost giddy, as he discussed the situation, and I got caught up, too. It was like all those protests on TV, and I was awed by the pro journalist. But soon I noticed Avo had turned his back on the crowd below, and on my father, who was making a joke out of something Avo didn't consider funny at all. I wanted to tell them all to leave us alone.

Of Avo's neighbors, only Señora Cruz came out of her house. There weren't many neighbors left, of course, and most of them were much older than Avo and therefore ancient to me. Now I fully grasped how easy it would be to get rid of the whole colony. A lot of it was gone already. Avo's protest was solitary.

"Antonio," shouted the Señora from her abundant yard. She stood waist-deep in tomato plants, wearing a long housedress and a kerchief around her head. "You trying to kill yourself? You think the *jefes* care you're up there on your roof?"

Avo didn't answer. My father walked over to the shouting woman and I followed him. She shook her head and explained how Avo wouldn't listen and wasn't facing reality. She herself would be moving in with a daughter in New Jersey.

"It's all finished here," she said. "How can this be a community when there's nobody here?"

Eventually the *Vantage* reporter departed with his notebook and camera, and the crowd began to sense that this was no longer the place to be, that the excitement was ending. So they gradually dispersed back into the dull calm of a Wardville summer day. It was then left to me to talk with my grandfather, since he and I had, in Dad's words, "a special relationship."

As I walked back to Avo's house, I heard an engine grumble and a blast of loud music. I turned to see a green pickup truck hard-braking to a dusty halt. The side of the truck read "Gerthoff and Son." (The "son" was Gerthoff Senior but the name also implied a future partnership.)

The truck door opened and Jimmy got out. He wiped his hands on his white T-shirt, already streaked with reddish soil. His sneakers were caked.

"Hey, I heard you're having a problem here," he said.

Dad's face stiffened. "Yes, but we're dealing with it," he replied in the voice he used with telephone salesmen.

He was looking from me to Jimmy and back with an expression somewhere between worry and hostility, and I thought this surely meant there'd be no riding with Jimmy the next day.

"Okay, just thought I might help. I was real close by, working with my father."

"Oh? What's going on there?" Dad said.

"We're hauling stuff out. Junk mostly. The Randono people are helping us. You wouldn't believe the crap people threw in there while it was empty lots. While it was woods, probably. All kinds of trash, even big stuff like refrigerators, stoves. Cars even."

"Waste," I said. But neither of them heard me, since they were intent on one another.

"You! You down there!"

The shout came from the roof. My grandfather was leaning forward to look at us.

"Pop, sit down," Dad said. "You're gonna fall."

"Is that James Gerthoff down there? Tell your father and his Mafia pals they won't scare me away. I don't care what gang of goons you bring around here. You got that?"

Jimmy looked stunned. He had shifted from his usual slouch to full height, combative and agitated. Without a word, he turned and strode back toward the truck.

"Fine," came Avo's voice again. "Get off my property, punk."

My father stared at Jimmy's retreating figure.

"Dad," I said. I felt abandoned, like Jimmy would now cut off my sudden access to his larger, cooler, more adventurous life, while at the same time I hated the idea he was working with the construction people. My father gave me a look that didn't seem like him at all—a kind of giddy intensity.

"Go after him," he said. "You wanna go with him tomorrow, you go ahead."

I stood there bewildered, trying to read my father's face. There were no clear signs there, though, only a strange, unsettling confusion.

"Go ahead." Now I knew Dad meant it. I ran after Jimmy and caught up as he yanked open the truck door.

"Hey, I'm sorry. My grandfather, well—"

"It's okay, man, I understand."

I nodded, relieved—and buoyed that he'd said "man" rather than the usual "kid." He got in and slammed the door.

"We still going on that ride?" I asked.

"Sure," he said. "You bet. I think you need to get away from these people. I sure as hell need to get out of here for a while. Pick you up tomorrow? Ten or so?"

He gave me a look full of jumpy insistence along with a more welcoming grin. I nodded. He gunned it, and the truck screeched forward, raising another sand cloud.

Get away from these people: the words replayed themselves in my head and I wasn't sure if they pleased or miffed me. Jimmy seemed to have voiced some daring need in me that I'd never say aloud. But did he have something against my family? And they against him? I was involved in it, somehow. He was trying to cut through tangled things, and I could feel the sharp blades.

I did succeed in persuading my grandfather to leave the roof late that afternoon. We talked for over an hour, or rather he talked and I listened, watching the light shimmer on the bay and fade. I think the speaking out was what he needed, as if no one had been listening for a long time. All the while he spoke, an American flag fluttered at half-mast on his flagpole, stirred by the early summer wind that smelled of sea and trees. From up there, you could look past the bungalow backyards into a large, weedy field mounded with bulldozed soil. Beyond that foundations sprouted and, past them, new homes in neat rows.

My grandfather talked and talked, about things he'd never told me in such detail or with such force: How much he and my grandmother had loved that small house from the first time they'd seen it. How it felt like a reward for all the hard times, all the work and saving, all the not-having in Depression-era Newark, when their neighbors couldn't afford the food their small market sold, and how those people, in low, humiliated voices, asked for credit, as if for charity. How he and my grandmother would end up giving things away, knowing that most of the customers wouldn't be able to pay what they owed, despite their sincere, pride-saving pledges. They weren't just customers, he said, they were neighbors and friends. People cared about each other—why did it take hardship and tragedy to make people care? Why, he asked me, as if expecting an answer, and then he was quiet awhile, looking toward the bay. Then he continued, addressing some audience out there on the water. People used to be generous, he said, as long as a person was willing to work. But now—the selfishness, the greed. If they don't like people or people can't afford a fancy house or high rent, they throw them in the street. They want them out of sight, that's the truth. Used to be you could live the way you wanted out here in the woods as long as you didn't bother anyone. But no more—he turned his head toward the construction site—now they're all in it together, and all they care about is money. They'd kill for money.

I couldn't get a word in as my grandfather spoke, but I had nothing to tell him anyway. What could I say or do about the vague enemy? I felt outrage and fear without fully comprehending it, a passive, daunting urgency. He let out a long breath. He kept shifting and grimacing. When I asked him for the third or fourth time to come down off the roof, he gave me a weary look and let me help him down the rickety ladder.

"You think your grandfather is a nut, don't you?" he said, after we'd stepped onto solid ground.

"Stop," I said.

"Maybe I am. But I know when to quit. I know who's got the real power. You have to fight, though, show them you won't give up easy."

"Sure, I know."

I walked him to the back door, and he told me he'd be fine alone. He looked at me as if I were somehow one of those others, part of that uncomprehending world that was defeating him. He seemed very distant, and I wanted to reach in and pull him closer, so we could be like we used to be. But I stood silent and turned to leave. His look stayed with me as I biked home, and it lingered for days afterward.

•

The car itself, of course, was a big part of the thrill. Although it was only a Camaro, Jimmy pampered it like a Corvette, and compared to my parents' practical Buicks and Oldsmobiles it was a racecar. You could get far away very fast. It was lean and quick, like an extension of Jimmy's own body. He pulled up in front of our house, and I was waiting on the steps. It would be cooler than the first two rides (brief, random); this time Jimmy had made a special trip to retrieve me—nearly as fantastic as if the Batmobile had stopped at my door.

My parents had no outward reaction to Jimmy's arrival or my waiting for him. But my sister did. She was sitting in the living room reading Hermann Hesse when I said I was going outside to wait.

"The goddamn nerve," Diane said, looking up from her book. "Coming around here. No friends his own age?"

I stared at her, then hurried out.

When the car pulled up, Jimmy was alone in the front seat while Bentley and Solomon sat in back. A further thrill: I was getting the copilot's spot, next to the driver. I climbed in, buckled myself in, and Jimmy clasped my shoulder, giving it an affirming shake. He wore cutoffs and a T-shirt with a picture of large globe-like thing. I asked what it was.

"Buckminster Fuller," he said. "His geodesic dome. I'll tell you about that sometime." He smiled, and I felt hooked and frustrated. I was beginning to see that it was the usual thing with Jimmy: offering a tidbit of hipness or sophistication but no more, making him enigmatic and grander in our eyes.

"Hey, guys," I said, turning toward the back seat.

"Hey," Bentley said. Solomon waved.

" Pick a tape," said Jimmy. A bunch of 8-tracks were scattered at my feet. I surveyed them, and slid an Aretha Franklin tape into the player that hung below the radio.

As I watched Jimmy bopping his head to "Respect," I thought again about how odd it all was. This guy who a few months ago seemed to exist in another world, who went to college, dated girls from the hilly neighborhoods, and stood to inherit a lucrative business had now chosen to take up with a North Shore girl and befriend three boys just turning teenagers—two from the town he hoped to escape and the other from a black area nobody paid much attention to. He treated us all like we needed his help and guidance, as if he were on some kind of mission, as if we all lacked something he could provide or that he lacked, too. And it seemed he was still taking a particular interest in me, almost as if he had some duty toward me. It made me feel important, as though I'd been admitted to a cool and coveted club, and I enjoyed his attention, but it also felt like I was some swept-up object in Jimmy's perpetual whirlwind. Diane's angry outbursts kept coming back to me.

Before I knew it, we were on the bridge to Jersey. Far below us ran the gray river, polluted from refineries upstream, from oil tankers, from the landfill along its eastern banks. My father had joked that the Kill was an apt name for it. Off to the left were the steeples and small brick apartment buildings of Perth Amboy, the closest city to Wardville but one we never visited because it was "almost as bad as Newark," in my parents' estimation.

The Garden State Parkway, the shore route, was hectic with beachbound traffic. Jimmy had the windows down, so motors hummed, radios blared, fumes hit my face.

Once we arced over the Raritan River, with New Brunswick in the distance to the west, the buildings thinned and a landscape of woods, marshes, and fields spread out on both sides. Cattails swayed along the edge of the highway, which seemed to go on and on into a boundless distance, unlike the short highways of islanded New York City. We were now part of a rolling rush, like another river. I felt grand and free, in a car that didn't belong to my parents or their friends—those cars felt like mobile versions of our living room, secure and dull.

Jimmy shot well over the speed limit and turned up the music. I grasped the side of my seat while some voice that wasn't getting into the fun told me this was not a good thing.

Jimmy gripped the wheel and focused forward as if aiming for a finish line or outrunning something. I glanced in the rearview mirror, imagining pursuers (the state police, my parents, his parents, Bentley's cop dad), but there was only a purple VW Beetle several car lengths back, the distance my father always kept behind other cars, for safety.

Jimmy reached out now and turned down the volume. "Solomon," he said. "Tell Luke here where we're going."

I wondered if he'd read my mind or just noticed my uneasiness. I looked back at Solomon, who was staring out the window.

"We're going to look at a view," he said. "Up in the hills. He says it'll give us a new purpose or something."

"Perspective," Jimmy said. "A new perspective. And I mean that literally and figuratively."

I wasn't about to ask him what that meant. "You're taking us to Atlantic Highlands? I've been there tons of times with my parents," I said. Jimmy was sounding like my sister in her wiser-than-thou mode.

"I know," Jimmy said. "But I bet you never really looked at the view. Anyway, there's a place up there we can get lunch, rap together, and you guys can get to know one another better."

It sounded good to me, but I wondered why he should care if we got to know one another, or why he felt like he had to be the catalyst for it.

Jimmy laughed now and turned up the music again as we headed off the parkway and skirted the decaying shore towns along Route 36, the underside of Raritan Bay, ignored by those continuing the highway trek south toward better summer places. We drove past sorry rusting gas stations, convenience stores topped with aging replicas of cows and milk bottles, pawn shops, bait-and-tackle huts, dingy bars, holdover drive-in burger joints, discount carpet and furniture stores, as well as small houses in varying degrees of shabbiness. This continued through the entire 8-track tape and into another, until Jimmy turned left and we began to climb a wooded hillside road that I didn't recognize. No surprise that Jimmy wouldn't follow the usual route up to the Highlands.

Solomon had chosen the second tape, Dylan, one I might've picked, too (Diane played it), but I was surprised at Solomon liking it. We talked about Dylan, and we both loosened up, eagerly naming favorite singers, bands, records. Solomon knew more than I did about R&B and jazz—from his grandfather, he told us. (My parents rarely listened anymore to the standards and swing music of their day.) Solomon thought Motown was okay, but "real R&B" was a lot better. Bentley said nothing, but Jimmy kept chiming in, as if to keep us talking, connecting. He was like some rebellious shepherd, coaxing his flock along while leading them beyond bounds.

At the hillcrest, the woods opened out to a sudden sky-high view, a panorama from Raritan Bay east to the Rockaways, with Lower New York Bay and the thin arm of Sandy Hook at the center and the vast Atlantic stretching to the horizon. Nearly the whole city was spread out below us. Jimmy turned into a lookout point and parked; the hill appeared to drop away just beyond the car's hood, as if we were dangling over it. Jimmy opened the glove compartment and pulled out a pair of binoculars. "We'll need these," he said.

As we walked toward the low-walled overlook, Solomon and I kept on talking. Solomon couldn't take his eyes off the expansive view. He'd never seen the city from that height. Jimmy led us to the edge and we all looked out, with the wind cooling our faces. Solomon stared, silent now, absorbed in the light and space.

"Take a deep breath," Jimmy said, and he did so himself, spreading his arms out so that his T-shirt rode up, exposing his flat, tanned stomach. We all breathed the ocean air. Jimmy's hair blew back, and he squinted into the breeze as if trying to make something out. Then he put the binoculars to his eyes.

"You can see way uptown," he said. He handed me the binoculars. I focused, and there it all was, suddenly close yet far below, as if I was swooping above it all. I looked past the new shiny World Trade Center towers, up the skinny island to the Empire State Building and the spaceship-sleek Chrysler Building gleaming in the sun. Beacons from a different world—impossibly crowded and chaotic and scary and thrilling. Jimmy knew that world, directly. "Imagine all that's going on there," he said. "Imagine what it took to build all that. But so many people on top of one another, all running after the big things, without thinking much about how it all works together."

"And look at our island," he continued. "Small. Smaller and smaller. People can't see what's important. Can't even see that they're all together in a tiny place. Think they're all little kings on their little plots of land."

I looked out at the beaches, the spine of green hills, the flat stretches of forest between the town clusters and, spreading out from them, rows and rows of houses. From this viewpoint, with the vastness stretching into haze to the east and west, our town no longer looked isolated—it was one with the chaotic, chockablock metropolis.

I lowered the binoculars. Jimmy was gazing across the bay as he spoke, and once again, at that moment, he seemed almost heroic to me, like some pilgrim or explorer cresting a ridge and seeing new lands revealed below him. Or some visionary dreamer, seeing the possible in the familiar, maybe some freer place out there. I wanted to follow his look and see what he saw in that view.

I handed the binoculars to Solomon.

"Find where you live?" I said.

You could make it out down there, Claytown, because there was a much larger reference point: the brown hills of the landfill rising above the little wooded cluster, looking from this distance as if they could easily tumble down and bury it. The town seemed lonely there, like some lost village, separated from Jersey by foul water and from the rest of the island by swamps and woods. Yet it too was part of something larger. The main flow of life was all around it: the highways, the prolific suburbs.

Solomon peered, squinting. "Well," he said. "I can sort of see it. It kind of blends in. Like it's inside the landfill."

"Yeah," Jimmy said. "Almost is. I've heard you can see those garbage hills from outer space. They'll just keep getting bigger if nobody stops them. More and more people, more and more waste and destruction."

We all stood awhile longer, looking at where we'd started from. Bentley still hadn't said much; he seemed reluctant to get to know Solomon and took his turn with the binoculars at the opposite end of the parapet while Solomon told me about growing up in Claytown, playing in the woods, running from his grandmother's "whuppins."

"You can get in those woods and feel alone, like they were your own little country," he said. "Like nobody can bother you." He kept glancing over at the view, as if his mind was still on what he'd seen through the binoculars. He joked about the on-and-off stink in his neighborhood—how they'd try to guess if it came from the dump or Jersey on any given day, or both. It never seemed like a big deal, he said. As he loosened up, Solomon seemed a different kid from the somber, guarded one we'd first met at Claytown. We laughed a lot.

Jimmy led us carefully across the road to a German restaurant with an outdoor patio where you could have lunch with a view. Solomon and I did mock-German accents like the bad guys on *Hogan's Heroes*, and that finally broke through Bentley's sullen mood. We all riffed on tyrannical Germans, with Jimmy really getting into it, until he shushed us as we entered the restaurant.

We had more fun on the patio during lunch. Home, school, church, all the stuff that was so overwhelming and large in my little room seemed puny here. It felt as if you could laugh them away.

Over lunch Jimmy downed three large steins of beer, which he let us take big sips from despite disapproving looks from our waitress, sweating in her Bavarian outfit. Afterward, we followed him to the car; he wove a bit from the beer, and he got us all singing a fractured version of "Edelweiss." I sang loudest and laughed hardest, since I knew the song well: my mother watched *The Sound of Music* every time it was on TV.

We drove off with a screech, and Jimmy sped along the narrow hilltop road. We were all still laughing, but I felt the laughs tighten in my throat, almost like screams. "Moondance" blared from the speakers. "Van the Man," said Jimmy.

After a gut-shaking glide downhill, we headed for Sandy Hook and the beach. Striding past the sunning crowds, Jimmy led us to an emptier stretch shaded by trees. He stripped off his shirt and ran toward the rolling green-blue surf, howling, "Here we go, guys!" After dropping his shorts on the sand and placing his glasses on them, he dove toward the oncoming waves in his underpants, sunlit starkly white against his skin. We followed, up to the water's edge, the cold foam washing our ankles in the smooth wet sand. Unlike Jimmy, we'd all worn our swim trunks. Jimmy swam through the surf and beckoned us farther into the water. The waves pushed and pulled us, and we shoveled water onto one another. Bentley tried swimming but a wave knocked him over and drenched him. We all dove into each swell of sea as it crashed. At one point Jimmy disappeared and I thought the ocean had swallowed him, and I felt its powerful underpull, too. I yelled his name, and I swam along the waves, following the shoreline, then took long sinking strides and got myself back to the beach, fighting the tug of water and fear. Solomon and Bentley were pointing from where they stood in the surf, and Jimmy's head appeared, dark and slick like a seal's, above the waves, much farther out. He kept swimming, risking and mastering the ocean's relentless roll, its stealthy shifts.

Solomon and Bentley joined me on the sand, and we sat swapping stories about Wardville's beaches, about the horseshoe crabs in springtime, how we'd turn them over and watch them try to right themselves, their many spidery legs wriggling helplessly. Bentley described sticking firecrackers inside them, blowing up their innards, and we were grossed out and impressed. We all agreed we'd never go swimming at those beaches, and Bentley added that the pool at the Swim Club was much nicer. Solomon looked at him silently, and I realized that of course he'd never been to the Swim Club—no Claytown people went there. I said the pool was no big deal, as if to dismiss Bentley's comment, and Solomon turned his steady, inquiring look toward me but still said nothing.

We watched Jimmy walk confidently out of the surf like one of those Olympic swimmers with their lean muscles and sea-creature grace. The absence of his hip-intellectual eyeglasses added to this appearance of easy, natural athleticism. But he also looked kind of comic in his clinging wet underpants; I caught Bentley's eye and we laughed—a masked-embarrassment laughing, at least for me. I kept furtively glancing at Jimmy's outlined cock and balls.

Jimmy put on his pants and shirt over his wet body and we went back to the car, holding our sandy sneakers. The water had tempered his drunkenness, so he drove more carefully as we made our way south along the ocean, past cottages and condos and big summer houses, seafood restaurants, and beachside bars. Jimmy abruptly pulled in at one of these bars, a white-shingled shack in need of paint with a neon sign that read "The Hook." We all followed him inside, exchanging looks as if each of us was daring the others.

The bar was crowded, loud, smoky, rank with beer and sweat. I'd never seen so many guys with long hair, beards, tattoos. A few of them stared at us as we followed Jimmy up to the bar. The bartender gave us a scowly look but laughed. Jimmy got a beer and led us to a corner where some guys were shooting pool. The pool table wasn't like the ones in our neighbors' rec rooms; this one looked old and shabby, with a dusty glass light fixture overhead. Smoke drifted through the lightbulb's beam.

Jimmy asked us if we played. Solomon and I shook our heads no, but Bentley said, "Sure." We watched until the game ended, wrapped in sounds: pool balls colliding and rolling, laughs and curses and shouts, music blaring from a corner jukebox. The smoke gave everything a blue tint, like old movies. Then Jimmy and Bentley started playing while Solomon and I picked some songs on the jukebox. Bentley leaned over so far he was on tiptoe, and the pool cue looked too big for him. But he held it firmly and moved it easily and surely, his eyes focused on the ball like it was the only object in the room. Jimmy was less focused, but his work-muscled arms had more power and precision. He won, but it was close. Afterward, he got Bentley's head in an arm lock and rubbed his stubby hair, laughing. Bentley pulled away and glared at Jimmy with a sneery smile.

"You wait," he said.

Solomon and I tried playing, and I shot the cue itself across the table once, but we made some points, drawing cheers from the three or four guys who had gathered in the corner to watch us. Jimmy again let us sip his beers, of which he had two or three. I got so much into the game that I forgot about time—until Jimmy looked up at the clock behind the bar and said, "Shit, it's almost five." He told us we had to leave, Wardville's adult concerns in his voice. My mother would be frantic, I realized. I also knew that Jimmy was what Mom would call "tipsy" again and shouldn't be driving, but then we were all a little tipsy from the beer and the heat and the smoke, and it didn't seem to matter.

We got back in the car and screeched away south, taking the loop back past the green estates of Rumson, toward the parkway. Jimmy slowed down and the broad cool lawns glided by, fragrant green seas islanding kingly houses. It seemed the lives lived there must be very grand, even grander than Ward's. I gazed at these palaces with a vague desire for what they seemed to promise: amplitude, grace, happiness. A magical kind of strength and power, too, that I didn't feel in myself.

"Unreal," Jimmy said. "You know, a few miles from here people are living in poverty." He glanced left and right at the leafy serenity. "But it's beautiful. Who wouldn't want it?"

He laughed strangely and hit the gas; the car blasted forward, and he tried to beat every red light, almost rear-ending an electric company van. On the parkway we wove through traffic. I kept reaching for the dashboard as if to steady the car, while thrilled by its surge and growl. Somewhere before the Raritan River, Jimmy turned down the blaring music and started talking again, as if resuming the conversation with himself he'd begun amid the suburban splendor.

Yeah, he said, back to the island, back to his crazy life. Sure, there was the work for Ward, which was good experience for his Planning and Preservation classes at the college, and he loved helping out at Claytown moving the kids back and forth and working on the old buildings, but that took time from the construction business, and he really should be doing more since his dad wasn't getting any younger. Of course, some of the stuff they built was kind of shoddy and ugly and could be a little questionable in terms of the environment and good land use, but the money was good, the money was great. And you're building whole new communities, from ideas you have, changing people's lives. Lately, though, he was having more fights with his dad, who could get pretty angry and wouldn't let him in on the plans for some of the new developments. His dad was spending a lot of time near the landfill, late into the evenings, but wouldn't allow him out there at night, and the city was planning parkland for a large chunk of woods near where his dad's Arcadian Estates was going up, and there seemed to be some kind of conflict going on there. It had something to do with the Randono company and clearing land near Claytown, and he hated the idea of doing anything that would hurt the people there—especially if his father was part of it, somehow, but then how could his father be part of it?

As Jimmy talked, I began to feel woozy, then shaky and sweaty, as if a violent argument were happening in that car, but of course it was only Jimmy talking while the car sped forward with the force of his pinballing emotions, barely controlled.

SIX

She looked at herself in the full-length mirror, model-
ing her long, loose dress, imagining her appearance
singing Broadway melodies in the breezy summer
night with the torch flames reflected in the still, quiet
pool. She hadn't sung much since those dances back in the
fifties, after the war, the ones she and my father went to
every week when they were both attending Newark City
College. How they had loved dancing! On special nights
they'd venture across the river to Manhattan—to Roseland
or Webster Hall or another of the dance palaces, and it
was like living a movie. She would sing sometimes too,
with a Cuban band, even though her Spanish was even
worse than her Portuguese. When she stood up there her
shyness would vanish in the rush and vibration of horns,
maracas, pounding percussion. For a while Manhattan
became a glamorous tropical island. The Spanish words
no longer felt foreign. She could even dream, in the soaring aftermath of performances, of becoming a professional singer.

It was all part of the romance (and maybe naïveté) of her
first years with John, who was Joao then still. He seemed

almost movie-idol handsome to her, admittedly not tall but with that wavy dark hair and the thin Douglas Fairbanks mustache. And she thrilled at the press of his strong body through his loose-fitting suit when they danced close. They were caught up in their desires and dreams, on those nights when the dingy Newark apartment seemed unreal, like a remnant of the life they vowed to escape. And they *had* escaped, and made this freer, easier life for themselves and their children, who were blessings truly and blessed, thriving as she'd wanted. And she herself had felt freer here, more in control of her life, in this tidy new house surrounded by lawn, trees, and gardens, flanked by other tidy houses with neighborly yet private people centered too on their flourishing families. Dreams, of course, could be ridiculous, and sometimes now they seemed alive only in the way that ghosts or dimming photographs were alive. So this luau party might at least give her a chance to feel the sort of joy she used to feel.

Of course, it *was* only one night, one event—but she was afraid now that it wouldn't happen, and rituals like this were so important. They brought people together and gave them something to celebrate in common. Things to carry into the future and remember. Otherwise life could just be a series of losses, with people falling away from one another. She had grown distant from her own parents, and she had come to regret it, at least in these reflective moments. Sometimes she felt she had no close connection to anyone. It even seemed she was losing her daughter now, and her son too might be in danger. There was a balance you had to maintain between letting them spin away into their own lives and keeping them within bounds. It was getting more and more difficult to do that. But it was a duty (and pleasure) to create small moments, recurring events that would shape life into a circle, a ring. A safe enclosure against time.

Every day, in fact, could have these moments. So you always had to be planning something; time shouldn't be wasted. Life had to be organized and lived by schedules. This wasn't regimentation, it was part of the natural cycle of things, like the sun rising and setting. Dinner was at six o'clock, and the family would sit together at the table (in the kitchen on weekdays and Saturdays, in the dining room on Sundays) in assigned places. (Her daughter's increasing lapses from this routine had become infuriating, but there was little point in trying to get her to eat with the family again on a regular basis.)

Community events were no different, really. The town, too, should be ordered and attuned to regular rhythms, with no dark or chaotic corners. They had moved here for that rationality, that predictability. This is why holidays were so important, anchoring the years. At Christmas the town's stark winter grayness was transformed by color and light, and her home was a warm oasis of decoration and food. Beyond these circles created by work and ritual, unfortunate souls languished in a sad wasteland. Memorial Day and Labor Day were summer versions, bookending the happiest season, with the Fourth of July more or less at the center.

It was almost the Fourth, and I was watching my mother as she looked at herself in that long mirror. Now I can summon words to speculate about her thoughts and emotions, but even then I had some sense of what she might be feeling—from the almost crazily happy look on her face as she swung around, sweeping the muumuu in an arc like wings, and the way she suddenly stopped and stared at the reflections, her look sinking.

She turned abruptly and said to me, "How could you go off with that reckless boy? You know I didn't want you to."

Startled, I was about to say that Dad had let me go and she should lay off about it, but she was looking at me now with such distress and perplexity that I couldn't say anything.

"Between you with this joyriding with teenagers and your grandfather making a spectacle of himself for the entire town to see. The whole island, with that humiliating picture in the paper. Oh, I don't know. Nothing makes sense anymore."

I couldn't think of much to say to that—pointing out that I was almost a teenager myself wouldn't help. I tried to think of something to make her feel better, to stop this spiraling unease that threatened to suck me in too, but all I could come up with was the fact that I'd gotten Avo off the roof.

"And he's back up there today," she said. "Screaming at construction workers. They'll call the police if this keeps up, and who can blame them?"

She had moved to her bed and sat down, but I just stood there, seething. Why couldn't she understand why Avo felt so strongly about losing his home?

Now Mom looked at me awhile, wiping her face with a tissue. She took a deep breath, smoothed her dress. "Oh," she said, "I shouldn't be taking it all out on you. I know you tried to help your grandfather. I know you care about him." She sniffled, blew her nose. "We all do. Come here."

She held out her arms, the pastel fabric again hanging wing-like. I hesitated, not

wanting yet wanting her hug, her sudden forgiveness and reassurance.

"Jimmy was just trying to get away from his family," I said. "They're kind of crazy. I think he's afraid of his father."

Her arms dropped, her voice cooled. "Who told you that?"

"I just heard it, around."

"Well, you heard wrong. They've always been hardworking people, important in the community. They worked their way up from nothing, the way our families did, your father's and mine. Jimmy's grandfather was a carpenter, started a company that built half the buildings around here. His father made the business grow, he even studied architecture, you know, but he never got the chance to finish because the company took up all his time. That's why he's sort of hard on Jimmy, because he wants him to take over. You should be so lucky to have something like that to inherit. But that kid always had a contrary streak, always. Since he was a little boy. I remember. You don't really know him or his family. So be careful about judging people when you don't understand what people have been through."

I wanted to object that she herself was judging Jimmy, and that she hadn't mentioned Jimmy's trapped, scared mother, but I felt silenced by her severity, the scolding urgency of this long defense of Jimmy's father. It was like she felt some threat from what I'd said. She no longer looked like she wanted to hug me, and that was all right with me.

I just said, "Okay." Arguing back was useless, and it seemed she'd had enough of the subject of Jimmy. She got up and began to examine herself in the mirror again, and I left the room.

Back in my own room, I kept thinking about Avo. How he'd crossed an ocean to a country of strangers when he was only Jimmy's age and worked at all those tough jobs, how he'd fought against injustices—he was a pioneer! Had Mom forgotten that? She'd experienced a lot, too, growing up with all that grit and noise and edginess in her packed city neighborhood. She'd encountered all sorts of people there, and all kinds of behavior. I'd heard about some of them from Avo and Dad. Gangsters strutting around.

Strange solitary men stalking children. Old ladies dispensing folk charms and illicit cures, telling fortunes and interpreting dreams. People shouting greetings and threats from tenement windows. Neighbors close as family—with all the good and bad of that closeness, that absence of solitude, that insistence on group over self. And the street fairs filled with music and food, the parades and dances, games on rooftops and in the streets, sidewalk friendships and flirtations (even Mom had hinted about those). It seemed so lively to me, so adventurous and weird, like you could never be bored or lonely or an outcast. But she kept all that carefully, safely in the past. (Her actual past, of course, which I was only imagining.)

Hours later, still in my room, I sat working on my essay for Sister M, trying to decide whether persuading my grandfather to come down from his roof counted as a good work. I was grateful that school was over and I wouldn't have to face all those smirking, joking kids after Avo's picture had appeared in the *Vantage*. Bentley had made a few jokes but dropped it, and Doris hadn't mentioned it at all.

I'd just started describing the crazy event when I heard a booming voice from the kitchen: Dom Randono, co-monarch of the Randono-Velman garbage empire. I knew Mr. Randono mainly through his wife and his son Robbie, who was in my homeroom class—kids called him Round Donut, since he had inherited the paternal physique. He had an older brother, Eddie, who was a good friend of the Velmans' son Andy. They were both about Jimmy's age and used to hang out with him. Dom Randono rarely came to our house, but he had a voice you didn't forget: loud and raspy, with a pungent Brooklyn accent. He was funny and sometimes intimidating, but always kind of nervous-looking—talking rapidly, pacing, like he was never at ease.

I walked down the hall and stood in the kitchen doorway. Dom was talking with my parents about the Fourth of July and gave me a raised-hand hello. The Swim Club luau plans had collapsed, and that event was now postponed until Labor Day, the outer edge of summer. Quick and urgent replanning had been occurring for the Fourth. In fact, the holiday had become an obsession for much of Wardville, taking on even greater symbolic importance than usual, absorbing vast investments of energy and hope. Of course, it was a difficult time in that big, mysterious world outside our enclave. Swaths of New York seemed dangerous and dirty, split into defensive ethnic tribes warring against one another and against those who wanted the tribes to mix. The federal government appeared to be unraveling. There was talk of holes in the ozone layer. Every week it seemed a new cult appeared. Teenagers were questioning everything, but their rebellion seemed secondhand now. Some (including my parents) saw these rebels as phonies, adopting a style temporarily until they could discover the easiest way to make money and indulge themselves without having to work too hard.

Dom Randono had teenagers on his mind now, as he talked about the failed luau, which he was trying to replace with some kind of Vegas extravaganza. "The kids need things to occupy their time," he said. "No wonder they get in trouble, with squat to do all summer. Pretty soon they'll all be like those punks in the city, dealing drugs and God knows what else." He went into a brief rant about the graffiti popping up "everywhere." It puzzled him like modern-day hieroglyphics or a demonic alien language.

Dom's jowly face flushed as he pointed a chubby index finger at my father. He pulled a handkerchief out of his golf pants pocket and wiped his forehead, across which a few dark hairs were combed, a bridge between the thin tufts on either side of his otherwise bald head.

"How many teenagers are actually going to come to this thing, anyway?" my father asked, maybe thinking about Diane.

"There's my point," Dom said. "You give em a little flash, a little dazzle. How about a few rock numbers? My nephew's got a band, the Warlocks. Yeah, they look like girls with all that hair and makeup, but it's all clean material. Gets their attention, though, the way they jump around and wiggle their asses. You should see them play guitars with their teeth."

"Oh, dear God," said my mother, putting a hand to her head.

My father mentioned that Sebastian Ward wanted to invite some Claytown people to the event, and a stunned, distressed look came over Dom's face that made him seem oddly vulnerable. His bluster sounded forced and desperate.

"Those colored people?" he said. "They don't have a pot to piss in. They don't belong at the Club. Their whole town's an eyesore, a drain on property values. Always was. That place has been deteriorating for years, ever since the clay mining. Even then they were taking up valuable land. And that Ward guy—why would anyone listen to that fruitcake?"

Soon Dom was pressing his finger against Dad's chest and reminding him where a bunch of the Fourth of July money was coming from. Not from Sebastian Ward, Dom said. Dad stood still and looked down at the shorter, fatter man, who was breathing hard in his kinetic anger. But I could tell by Dad's grinding jaw and intense stare that he was mad, too. He pulled himself away from Dom's jabbing finger and said, "All right. We'll work something out."

Once Randono left, I heard my parents talking in the living room: my mother was worried about the funding and my father assured her there'd be money for both summer events. He sounded confident.

"So what's up?" Bentley said as he let me in the front door of his house an hour later. It was a lot like my house, the mirror image in fact—familiar rooms reversed. His father sat in the living room reading the paper. He turned his blond, close-cropped head toward us and said, "Hi, Luke—how's it going?"

"Okay," I responded, ignoring Bentley's question for the moment. Mr. Riley nodded at me and returned to his reading. Of Dad's two closest friends in Wardville, Pete Riley was the more "down to earth," as my mother put it. Big-voiced where James Gerthoff Senior was soft-spoken, straightforward where Gerthoff spiced nearly everything with sarcasm. Now I'd say Riley was insecure and eager to be upper middle class, but back then he came across as a tough guy with manners who sometimes thought he knew the right way everyone should behave. He acted like there wasn't much you could tell him, since he'd heard it all or learned it in the streets. Like a lot of cops, he thought civilians were pretty naïve.

Bentley and I went downstairs to the rec room and plopped into a couple of beanbag chairs. Some *MAD* magazines were sprawled on the floor. The TV was on: a *Gilligan's Island* rerun. "You know who was just at my house?" I said.

"Spiro Agnew."

I laughed. "Randono."

"Dump King?"

"Yep." I explained what Randono had said about Claytown and Ward. We were both silent awhile, listening to TV chatter and laugh tracks.

"Come on," Bentley said. "Let's talk to my Dad."

We walked back upstairs and Bentley asked his father, in a sort of buddy-to-buddy way, if he knew much about the Randono and Velman company. Riley put down his newspaper. He asked why we would want to know that, and Bentley shrugged and said he was just wondering. They haul waste, Riley said, for businesses mostly.

"Where do they dump it?" Bentley said.

"Where? Out at the landfill. At least that's where they're supposed to dump it. In the section for private waste-haulers."

"Near Claytown?" I asked.

He paused. "Yes. What's this all about?"

I told him I was doing a summer research project on the landfill. Riley gave me a look appropriate to this unlikely story, and he told us to stay away from the landfill and not to ask Randono or Velman any questions.

"Are they criminals, Dad?" Bentley said.

Riley laughed and asked Bentley where he'd heard that, and Bentley shrugged again. His father told us that Randono and Velman were good men who'd built up a business from nothing, but in that business you run into bad guys, and sometimes you're forced into playing the game with them. He looked at us as if trying to decide what else to say.

"There's no proof of that, though," he continued, "and it's none of your concern. Keep your noses out of it."

Bentley and I looked at each other, pinching our nostrils, laughing.

"Yeah, okay," Riley said. "But I mean it."

We laughed down the stairs and out the door. I had the feeling, though, that we had touched on something that Riley didn't want us to know, something that bothered even him. I had no real idea what "game" he was talking about. But it seemed our small questions could stir up larger and deeper ones.

From the woods behind Solomon's backyard, we watched the trucks arrive, one after another, in a line that never seemed to end, municipal trucks and trucks with company names—all transporting garbage, the huge city's waste. Gulls circled and hovered above the stinking hills from whose sides sprouted patches of grass and a few struggling, windblown young trees.

On a very hot early July afternoon, Bentley and I stood with Solomon atop a small dirt pile that gave us a clear view. Bentley had agreed to ride the bus with me to Claytown—out of curiosity? Defiance?

Solomon pointed toward the hills.

"See those stacks?"

Yes, I could see them now—white tubes protruding from the bases of the mounds like smokestacks on some buried ocean liner.

"They're letting out a whole lot of bad stuff. Chemicals and who knows what. And it all ends up over here. When the wind's coming this way, you can smell it, even over the garbage smell. And some days it's like a low cloud. That's when we all go inside. My grandpa's got lung problems, and he's really bad on those days."

The stacks looked scarily close. I remembered how the town had seemed to disappear in the landfill's shadow when we'd viewed it from the Highlands, and Solomon's awed, jittery reaction to seeing his community dwarfed by the dump. It must have confirmed what he already felt here every day. I imagined the toxic cloud groping through the trees toward us like some monster-movie version of the amoebas I'd examined through my bio class microscope.

We looked at the trucks awhile longer. Some had "RANDONO-VELMAN" written in bright red arches across their battleship-gray sides. When we got tired of looking, we raced each other down the dirt pile. Solomon won. We walked to his grandparents' house, where he lived, and crossed their deep yard that stretched back to the edge of the woods. The house was the only one on the road, which curved away from the main part of town toward the clay pits and the landfill. It was a two-story A-frame with faded blue clapboards. We came up to the small, screened back porch, where Solomon's grandmother stood behind the door. He'd told us she knew we'd be coming.

"Where you boys been?" she called out. "I hope you didn't go too far into those woods. God only knows what's back there. Dangerous. Come on in and have some lunch."

She held the door open and we followed Solomon into the kitchen. Everything was different from my own house, older and more worn yet at the same time sturdier-looking. White cabinets with glass fronts, a simple wood table with mismatched chairs, a linoleum floor with tiny starburst patterns. Long propped-open windows with thick, mullioned panes covered only by white rollup shades. There was a small Frigidaire rather than the huge Amanas I was used to, and on the very old stove blue flames—unknown in our all-electric house.

Large pots of food were cooking, as if in expectation of a crowd for dinner. Solomon's grandmother gave us a head-to-toe look with her brow knitted. She seemed to decide we were okay.

"Take a load off, boys," she said.

We sat down, the three of us, and she fed us all lunch as if we'd been invited.

"Gran keeps those pots on all day," Solomon told us.

"Not so much anymore. We do our quick meals and takeout."

"Except weekends," Solomon said.

"Well, it's a routine. And you never know who'll drop in."

"People used to come by."

"Still do," she replied. "Now and then."

It was all unfamiliar yet very familiar: I had queasy-hazy images of my grandparents' old apartment in Newark—the stained wallpaper and cracked linoleum, the dark furniture, the smell of gas. The food always cooking. Even some of the food itself—the green stuff Solomon's grandmother ladled onto my plate along with bits of ham looked like the greens in my own grandmother's Portuguese soup, which I'd gagged on after trying it once. But I couldn't really turn this down—both Solomon and Bentley were digging in, so I did too. The bitter tang brought back old aversions, but as I swallowed the stuff and kept eating, it got tastier.

Solomon's grandmother told us her name, Feen Peek, and said everybody called her Feen so we could, too; her real name was Josephine but she never liked being called Jo. Feen wasn't like TV images of black people, mostly on the news at the scene of some crime on a treeless city street, or being yelled at by angry white people, or showing a reporter the holes in their apartment ceilings that the landlord wouldn't fix. She seemed in control of this place she lived in, and centered here.

She poured us glasses of water, saying it was the best thing to drink with her soup. As she set a glass down for me, she said, "You know, it's not polite to look at people that way, boy, as if they've got two heads or something."

Startled, shamed, I couldn't answer. I wanted her to know I wasn't staring to be rude, that I felt like I had two heads myself, each full of questions. When I first started on the school paper, my father had told me I was a listener, like he was, not a talker, and I should try getting people to talk about themselves. I discovered that this worked pretty well: people liked to talk, and they would sometimes tell strange, surprising, possibly-true stories if you paid attention. Especially isolated people, or lonely ones.

"Sorry," I said. "I was just wondering about things."

"What kinds of things? If you're wondering, just ask."

"Well, like how long have you lived here?"

Her stern look eased back a notch. "Me, personally, all my life," she said. "My husband, too. Our families, though, have been here nearly two hundred years. When there was nothing much else here, we were here. Hadleys and Gibsons on my side, Morrises and of course Peeks on my husband's."

All this amazed me—it was history, not out of a book or from outsiders, but from someone who knew it like she knew the house she lived in. Two hundred years! An awesome stretch of time, it seemed. And to be in one family in one place through all that time—this seemed barely comprehensible, a little frightening, like some huge old building with rooms beyond rooms but no exits.

"There were farmers and fishermen here at first," she continued, as if carried by an ingrained story's momentum. "Then people worked at whatever we could find. We built a nice town here and had a good life. There were lots of things denied us, but we stuck together. Maybe we weren't as well off as some other places but, like I say, we had a good life."

I couldn't have given words to it, but I felt the sadness inside Feen's remembering, the sense of separateness and encroachment and loss, and the happier, dreamlike past. A rapt audience, I drifted into the dream as Feen described the area when she was a girl, how there was nothing around for miles except trees and grassland and open fields. So much wildlife, too, so many birds! Herons and egrets and all kinds of birds. You could look north and see all the marshes with the blue creek running up to the hills—the real hills way in the middle of the island, not the garbage hills. The garbage hills came later. They told everyone it was temporary, the dump, just taking up a few acres of farmland and swamp. At first, no one noticed a little city garbage. But the temporary was fifty years now.

She'd been standing with her back to the stove, watching us eat as she talked. Now she turned and stirred a pot awhile with a wooden spoon. "It's changing, though," she said. "It's like the world's gone crazy and Lord knows what. People moving in around here, acting like they own the whole place. And something's going on over near that dump, something not right. They want to build more houses here, but I think it's more than that. Had a man come by here and offer us a load of money for this place. I told him, mister, I've been here all my sixty-five years, how long you been here? He went away mad, called our house a 'shack,' said we'd all be gone soon anyway. Maybe that's true, but I didn't like the sound of it." She tapped the spoon on the pot's rim. "Can't say his offer wasn't tempting, though."

She had turned to look at us again. "It's the kids I really worry about. Off getting into all kinds of trouble. Guess it's understandable, in a way. Not much to occupy them. That's why we keep an eye on this one." She gave Solomon a not-so-gentle swat on the back of his head, and Solomon said, "Hey," rubbing himself where she'd swatted.

"Hay is for horses," Feen said, and I laughed.

"Isn't really something to laugh at," she said. "Day might not be far off there won't be any black folks around here."

I stopped laughing, confused; it was like some awful premonition. But it didn't make sense that anyone would bother people way over here in these houses that seemed as rooted as the old trees that sheltered them. But of course what was happening to Avo and his neighbors didn't make sense, either. Here, too, disappearing was on people's minds. It hadn't taken Feen long to start talking about it.

We stayed in Solomon's house a long while. As we were leaving, we heard coughing in another room, a man's thick hacking. Feen ignored it. Once outside, Solomon told us it was his grandfather. He said nothing about parents, and I wouldn't ask.

Solomon led us back into the woods. He and Bentley had stripped off their shirts by now, even though the air was getting cooler as the sun dropped through the trees. I kept mine on.

"Where we going?" I said.

"The pond."

A small one, it turned out, not much bigger than the Olympic-sized pool at the Swim Club, and without the pool's chlorine clarity. It looked muddy, and all kinds of plants and tree limbs reached up from its murkiness as if they'd been pulled in and trapped there. Beyond the water, trees thinned to reveal the edge of the landfill. The procession of trucks continued, close enough that you could hear their grunts and roars as they climbed up and over and down those great stark mounds. When I was younger, whenever we'd driven past the landfill—past Claytown, too, invisible behind woods—I had pictured myself driving one of those trucks, approaching the very top to add my haul to the gross stuff already piled there.

Solomon walked to the edge of the pond, stripped off his pants, and jumped into the water. Bentley did the same. Their shouts and laughs and splashing echoed in the woods. I pulled off my sneakers and socks and dipped one foot. The water was cold, and I still didn't like the look of it. But I wanted to be in there, too, swimming and horsing around. So I stripped to my underpants and joined them in the water. My feet sank in muck, and I raised my arms to steady myself. I was chill-stiff at first, but after a few minutes, I felt enveloped and held by the cool water—easy as Bentley and Solomon, swimming on their backs with the sun on their faces. It was as if we'd always swum together in this pond, this water mixed with Claytown's earth, and the three of us were part of that mixture.

We waded out and sat on the ground. Solomon and I pulled on our shorts again, with some shy yet curious glances at each other. Bentley stayed in his underpants, his dick outlined in the wet white fabric. We talked some more about music. About baseball. About school—mocking some teachers, praising others, mostly agreeing. Solomon didn't have a lot of friends in school, he said; there was his long ride home, and no one much liked coming to Claytown.

We sat in silence awhile. Solomon looked at the trees as if searching for something. The light was gold on the tree trunks.

"Usually I'm alone here," he said. "Feels like no one's around for miles. Like you've been here forever. Sometimes it's like I've been left here and everyone's gone."

I looked around, imagining the place without people. Only us. Was Solomon scared or happy, I wondered, at the thought of total solitude?

"So, wanna go to Ward's house again?" he suddenly asked.

Bentley and I looked at one another. I wasn't sure about it, and Bentley looked uncertain, too. But my curiosity about the place—and about Solomon—hadn't been satisfied, and Solomon seemed eager to go there, to keep on being friends.

"Okay," I said.

"Yeah," Bentley said, shrugging.

Solomon told us Jimmy was driving over there the next day and could pick us up. So it was Jimmy again, our transporter, moving among disparate, unequal places, as if trying—out of some need and belief?—to connect them.

SEVEN

We weren't the only ones Jimmy taxied to Ward's place the following day. Back and forth he shuttled all afternoon between rustic black town and opulent relic of white privilege. A boy and a girl shared our rapid ride, a brother and sister, born in Claytown but now living in a Brooklyn apartment with their mother. They'd returned to Claytown—like lots of others—to visit grandparents who'd stayed there, and so they were invited to Ward's house for the day. Ward had offered his place to help the youth program at the Claytown church, Solomon told us, which brought in a lot of kids who had moved away. Solomon knew the siblings, whom he introduced to us: Daryl, about my age but seeming older, with a seen-it-all city coolness, and Beth, maybe fourteen, tall, sort of aloof. Her full name was Bethel, she informed us, *not* Elizabeth. Daryl said hi to Solomon and gave a nod to Bentley and me. Beth spoke to us in a polite but distant way, like she had better things to do than make friends with younger boys.

On this visit we stayed outside, so I didn't get to explore the game room further, or the rest of the place. Instead we roamed the huge property, big as a dozen of our yards. We swung on the swing. We took turns on the tennis court. Solomon ran me all over it—he was sharp, focused, determined as he dashed in his tatty sneakers to finesse the ball where he wanted it or to counter my lobs and volleys. He'd been taking lessons from a coach Ward had hired—the polo-shirt guy we'd seen that first visit.

Out at the stables we inhaled straw and manure smells and saw three horses in varying shades of brown—large, powerful, mythically strange creatures up close. One was saddled for riding, a chestnut mare with a white diamond-shaped patch on her head like Indian royalty. Her name, Beth told us, was Miranda. None of us three knew how to ride, but we watched Beth gracefully mount the horse and take off toward the waterfront looking confident, happy, free. And mature, with a body almost like a woman's, her long legs fully straddling the horse's lean sides. Bentley stared. Solomon seemed less interested; he was shy around her, as I was. Beth spent the whole day riding her horse and tending it in the stable, alone.

Solomon seemed to be enjoying himself, in his quiet, self-sufficient way. Ward made everyone feel important and like they could do anything they set their minds to, which also meant that he would sometimes talk incessantly at you or hang around watching what you were doing. Solomon told us that Ward did this pretty often, and that after a while it wasn't much fun anymore and he would take the bus home. It sounded like he sometimes didn't know where he wanted to be. Now and then that look would come over him, that mixture of preoccupation and solitary inwardness, like he wanted you to stay away.

No one seemed afraid of Ward, though, and I began to think that my uneasiness about him was stupid. But I still got that tensed-gut, agitated feeling when I saw him touch a kid or when he got close enough that I could feel warmth waft from his body and catch his sweet-sour smell. At lunchtime, he brought out a tray full of food and snacks and set it on a glass-topped table. He put his hands together and drew them apart over the food, in a way that made me think of Father Drinnon saying mass. "Enjoy," he told us.

Jimmy left after dropping off his last riders. On the way out he stopped and, putting a hand on my shoulder, asked if I was having a good time. "Yeah," I said. He suggested taking me and Solomon for a ferry ride into Manhattan the next day, if that would be okay. He didn't mention Bentley. I hesitated, but he gave me a look I'd seen before, that combination of a dare and a brotherly sort of concern, and it somehow overrode my doubts and convinced me. I couldn't say no to him. He told me he'd pick me up at the top of my street around one, after his morning work. He smiled and asked if we were "mixing." "You know," he added, "joining in." I said we were.

Actually, Bentley and I hadn't really talked much with the others there, North Shore kids mostly; we were the only white kids. Everyone seemed to know one another, and there was a sort of barrier. Daryl looked like a tough guy, or like he was trying to be one. He tossed around slang that was like a foreign language to me (and to Solomon, it seemed). It was like they didn't want us too close to them, as if they were afraid or suspicious of us. Or maybe they just didn't know what to make of us, suddenly here with Solomon.

After we'd stood there awhile, Bentley walked up to Daryl and said, "Hey," meant as some half-assed greeting I think, but it came off like a taunt or challenge and Daryl paid no attention. Bentley said, "I'm talking to you," and Daryl stepped up and looked him in the face.

"Yeah?" Daryl said, returning the challenge.

I pulled Bentley back. "Let's go," I said. "Leave it alone."

He shook off my grasp but turned to go with us, mumbling some nasty stuff. We went and sat on the swing, since nobody else seemed much interested in it. With sudden force I felt something here that had always been like a dull, steady ache in Wardville, something that Solomon must have experienced all the time at school: not being what everyone else was, not sharing some bond that I might not ever share. And yet Solomon was hanging out with Bentley and me most of the day. My sense of who belonged where was spinning loose, which didn't seem so bad.

Toward the late afternoon, Bentley got bored and went home, and Solomon and I took a walk, circling Ward's house. We peered into the old windows that nearly reached the ground. Through their antique distorting panes the interior looked unreal, full of spectral objects. We joked about apparitions that were actually chairs, sofas, grandfather clocks, but I got that feeling again of floating in time, like some ghost myself. I backed away from the windows.

We continued around to the other side of the house. Up close, you could see peeling paint on the wood shingles.

"Like Claytown," I said.

"Not really," Solomon said.

"I guess not."

We dropped rocks into an old well near the swing, listened to the plunks in water so far down you couldn't see it. We joked some more, talked about records, TV, movies. And books, which most kids didn't talk about. He told me about his tennis playing—how he'd only started recently, here at Ward's place, and how great it felt to get the hang of it.

He sometimes hated going back to Claytown, he said, because it felt like the whole place was falling apart and soon there wouldn't be any people there. He would end up taking care of his grandparents and their house, and someday he'd be left alone in it. He was almost joking, but there was fear and worry underneath. It seemed strange, far-fetched—I might find Wardville confining and dream of running off, but it was only a matter of time before I'd actually leave. For Solomon, time seemed longer, heavier, as if getting out was only a sort of fantasy.

Here, he said, he felt different, like he was part of a rich family who could do whatever they wanted.

"But we're not part of it, and it's mostly gone," I said. "And we can't do whatever we want. Ward can't, either." I wasn't sure why I'd said all that, but it seemed true. I felt like I was damping my own wild dreams as well as Solomon's.

"I guess not," he said.

I felt a sudden loneliness, as if it surrounded us.

"Want to come back to town with me, to my house?" I asked.

The suggestion felt risky and lame as I spoke it, but it also sparked something, like a subtle charge up through my legs, groin, chest.

He stared at me, a sort of eager questioning in his eyes, along with some alarm, but then he shook his head as if answering himself. "Can only go there for school," he replied.

"Okay," I said, let down and relieved, acknowledging the rules that constrained us. Him more than me.

I didn't bother asking my parents about the next-day excursion with Jimmy. I told them I'd be bike riding, maybe to Avo's house. Jimmy met me at the corner; we sped to Claytown, picked up Solomon, and drove to the ferry terminal. Dad passed through the place every workday, but I hadn't been there in a very long time, since the rare family trip to the city in recent years had been by car. The terminal was a dim and grimy place, thick with pigeons and their shit.

But the boat ride! Starting with the view of the dark water from the upper deck and the shuddering blast of the horn as the engines rumbled and the squat orange vessel pulled away, leaving the island quickly behind. Then the opening-out into the wide bay and a feeling of expanding limits, multiplying possibilities.

We stood on the outside deck, cool sea-smelling wind in our faces, looking toward the Narrows and the bridge's huge suspended arch and the great ocean beyond it. Jimmy started talking about the amazing engineering of the bridge and how bridges like that linked the city together but also destroyed local neighborhoods, places where people felt they belonged. You gain mobility and freedom, he said, but you lose something, too.

He turned abruptly and we followed him across to the more crowded deck on the other side of the boat. Tourists lined the railing, snapping photos of the Statue of Liberty, which they knew from photos. As we passed it, Jimmy joked that she was looking and probably feeling pretty sad these days, but I was remembering Avo's stories about his first sight of the statue and how, to his surprise, it really had seemed the most wonderful and strange structure he'd ever seen, like some New World goddess. I tried to see it that way, but it was just the Statue of Liberty, a familiar object, a little more impressive up close. The really cool thing for me and Solomon was that you could climb up inside it—which I'd never done. Neither had Solomon. We bandied facts and speculations: how you couldn't go up to the torch because the whole arm might crack and fall off, and how deep the water probably was and how dirty it looked, and whether if you fell off the boat you'd get sucked under it before you could swim to Liberty Island.

We pulled into the South Ferry dock, massive boxy buildings rising behind it, getting bigger and bigger as we approached. The Trade towers rose above them all, so high you'd tip backwards trying to see their tops. Jimmy led the way, and we followed his bluejeaned, T-shirted figure into Battery Park. Amid the tourists and lunch-eating office workers, we saw several people lying on benches: dirty people with tattered clothes, one of whom, a gray-haired woman wrapped in an overcoat as if she was cold, opened her eyes and looked at me as we passed. Her eyes were clear light blue, like the only light in the darkness of her body, young eyes, and I paused as Solomon and Jimmy walked ahead. Sister M had once told us that we should think of every poor or suffering person as Jesus, and so I thought, Is this Jesus looking at me with that sharp expression, not asking anything, but somehow compelling me to pay attention? But if so, Jesus smelled pretty bad and I wasn't going to touch him, or her, and what was I supposed to do for this woman who seemed so completely alone? I wasn't sure what the eyes were saying to me, if anything, but I felt a shiver go through me in the hot park. I looked ahead, where my friends were beginning to get lost among the crowd, and glanced back a couple of times, but the second time the woman's eyes were closed.

We ate ice cream along the promenade, watching boats on the upper bay. Jimmy would point out lower Manhattan buildings and tell us when they were built and what their architectural features were, smiling the whole time and eager for us to find it all fun, too. The new buildings, he said, were mostly pretty ugly, didn't we think?

I'd never looked at the buildings the way Jimmy described them, as real objects in a real place where people lived and worked, a place you could actually enter into and be part of. But there was that recurrent ambivalence in Jimmy: the sense of wonder and opportunity soured by distaste. "All those glass monuments to power and money," he said.

After nearly an hour of walking around, I was getting tired of Jimmy's tour-guide thing, and I started interrupting his smooth comments with facts of my own, partly to show him I knew as much as he did (even if I mostly didn't). Solomon had been asking questions, and telling us about trips to the city with his mother, how loud and fast it had all seemed, and how he couldn't stop looking at everything and everyone, as if he'd never seen cars or people before. Now, for a while, he seemed to be re-experiencing those thrills, but he lost interest, lagging behind us, looking like he'd retreated into his own thoughts from the hectic surroundings. At one point, as we walked along the waterfront promenade, I glanced behind me and Solomon wasn't there. I tugged Jimmy's arm; he stopped talking, and we looked around, finally spotting Solomon on a park bench next to a woman holding a sun reflector under her face. He waved a hello but didn't get up.

Jimmy and I went up to the promenade railing and looked toward the Jersey buildings, squat and dull. He told me he thought Solomon was coming out of his shell and that I was helping him do that. I looked up at him, not really understanding. His hands were in his pockets and he was nodding his head as if agreeing with something. He turned to me and said I was a good kid and he hoped I'd be doing okay, and I wanted to laugh and tell him he wasn't my brother, but he wasn't joking at all, so it didn't seem right to say that. Looking back over the water, he continued talking, about how good a family I had, how important that was. It could all be a mess, he said, you think you're going one way but you're pulled in other ways, and you can start out loving things or people but it always turns into some kind of conflict. He looked at me again and, out of nowhere, laughed and told me he remembered how much fun it used to be to ride that ferry, how he would just enjoy things like that. He seemed like a little boy but also like some sad old man, reminiscing. He was opening up to me, or maybe to the broad bay and the land and sky, while I stood there overhearing.

"Freedom is the main thing," he said. "To be able to do what you want, go where you want. But it isn't so easy. People sometimes need you to take care of them, there are certain things they expect you to do, and you can't just abandon those responsibilities."

I figured he was talking about his parents, as if he needed my assent. I felt his guilty confusion like a heavy package he'd tossed to me that I didn't want. It seemed he might be afraid of leaving his parents alone with one another.

"Things can be so narrow," he continued. "Especially people's minds. Like circles." He made index-finger spirals above the lapping water. "They should always open wider, let more things in, more people, more ideas. But they mostly just close in."

I was still baffled, a little peeved. How could somebody like him have such discontent? And what did it have to do with me? At the same time, I felt enlarged, like I was moving further into vast, intricate concerns and mysteries. But I kept quiet. I could not be his confidant. I walked away and sat with Solomon.

Jimmy stood there awhile looking toward Jersey City, his energy gone it seemed, then abruptly shook his head as if he'd just emerged from the water. He clapped his hands together sharply. "Come on, guys," he said, upbeat, as though we suddenly had to be someplace on time.

Solomon was silently watching people go by as if looking for somebody he knew. "Gotta snap you out of that," said Jimmy. "Looks like you're carrying the weight of the world."

We walked farther up the promenade and over to the Bowling Green subway station, where Jimmy stopped. He stood a moment looking into the dirt-and-graffiti-streaked darkness of the station, then looked back at us. I was waiting for him to ask if we wanted to ride uptown, and I would have eagerly said yes. I'd only been on the subway a few times (never alone) and it seemed like a fun and daring prospect. Solomon didn't seem all that interested in the subway.

"We should be heading back," Jimmy said, as if he'd remembered something urgent and distressing that squelched his desire to take us farther away from home.

On the Fourth of July, I found out that Diane had been stealing things. She revealed this to me in a marijuana haze. We sat together on a bluff at the edge of the woods, a high-school hangout. Since neither of us wanted to endure the Swim Club picnic ("rah-rah bullshit," my sister called it), my mother had asked Diane to "take me" to Ward Point Park, a broad green slope where families frolicked on weekends and fireworks would be mirrored in the bay that night. We had wandered from the park into the nearby woods, where my sister led me to the bluff with its view of two or three Jersey Amboys, towns we'd blurred by on our Sandy Hook trip with Jimmy. We sat there awhile, and she pulled a large joint out of the canvas bag she'd brought along, containing the baloney sandwiches from Mom that I knew Diane wouldn't eat. She lit the joint and took a long drag. She held her breath in with her eyes closed and exhaled the sweet smoke. She pointed up at the tree next to us.

"A hackberry," she said. "Very rare tree this far north. Avo told me about it once when we walked here."

"Yes," I said. "He showed me too." Actually he hadn't. I got a familiar feeling of Diane's superior knowledge, her priority, but with strong undercurrents of jealousy and resentment. She took another puff.

I'd seen Diane smoke pot before, but never this openly—she'd always tried to hide it if I caught her and her friends passing a joint around, behind the school or (once, defiantly) behind our very own house. Of course she was afraid that her straight-arrow brother would inform the parents, though I never did. So I wondered at this sudden brazenness, this Jekyll-and-Hyde-like flip from her motherly warnings about Jimmy.

She offered me a hit, but I shook my head no. She smiled. "A waste," she said. "It's powerful. Can't smoke it all myself or I'd be jumping in the water. Naked." She

giggled. I laughed, too, but my face was burning.

That's when she told me about the thefts. Small things at first: cigarettes, candy, cheap clothes. One or two record albums.

"But the other day," she said. "I got this."

She reached into the canvas bag again and extracted a bright red transistor radio. She clicked it on. We heard the rapid, goofy-pal voice of Cousin Brucie on WABC.

"Diane, how could you just take that?" I said. "Where'd you steal it from?"

"Grant's." This was a big discount store. "And I don't feel bad. You know how much poverty there is in this country? You know how much people waste? I bet you saw plenty of shit in that Ward guy's house. The fat old snob lives there by himself, with all that stuff. Why? Cause he exploits other people. He's a crook. They're all crooks. It's a corrupt system. Why shouldn't people take what they need?"

"You don't need a radio," I said. "You *have* a radio. Just ask Mom and Dad if you want another one. Wait till Christmas or your birthday."

"'Mom and Dad.' Jeez, you can be so clueless for a smart kid. 'Christmas.' It's just this big commercial put-on to get you to buy stuff. And who knows how long Mom and Dad'll have money. Who knows how long they'll be living together, with all the shit that's going on."

I stood up and kicked my sister in the leg. She leaned forward, startled, briefly mad, and settled back laughing. "Oh, you do have lots to learn," she said.

"Shut up," I said, and my words seemed to echo through the woods.

I turned and ran away from her, toward what I thought was the open meadow of the park. I'd always been a little wary of these woods—unlike the woods near Avo's place, I'd never explored and mapped them. They seemed deep and mazy, although they couldn't have been more than a few acres. I soon realized that I didn't know where I was going. I was still hearing Diane's words in my head, about Ward, about our parents. I kept running and didn't stop until I saw the backyard of a house and knew I was reaching the woods' end. But I didn't feel relieved: this was the big ramshackle house with the half-collapsed mansard roof in whose attic rooms its owner, an old man named Van Todt, kept bats. Or so people said. I knew for sure he kept vicious dogs and that they might come after me if I went near his property.

I looked behind me at the woods. I didn't want to go back into that darkness and lostness, nor did I want to run into Diane. Ahead was a chain link fence, and I remembered that Van Todt's house was completely surrounded by it. The dogs couldn't get to me if I walked along the fence to the street. A narrow path led that way, at the edge of the woods. "Beware" signs on the rusty fence depicted gaping canine jaws with stiletto teeth. I hurried along the packed-dirt path. The house looked vacant. The yard was full of corroding junk, but there were no dogs to be seen. I heard them, though, from deep in the house—low, mean barks that nearly froze me. I forced myself to walk faster.

I did not go home immediately. I was gripped by the idea that somehow my parents would have been inwardly transformed, that they'd look the same but be strangers who wouldn't recognize me. (I'd had dreams like that often, but this felt real.) So I took the long way back, and I found myself near Jimmy's house overlooking the river in the oldest, quietest part of town, where Wardville's modest old money lingered in large Victorians and Colonials, some of them with cracking shingles and weedy yards. I came up to Jimmy's parents' property, with the two side-by-side houses: his grandmother's huge gabled structure, a freshly painted blue, with a large back porch looking out on the water and Jersey, and next door, farther back from the sidewalk, Jimmy's parents' house, its one level sprawling across two wings, with wide, high windows front and back, so you could look from the street directly through the house to the river. Graceful trees shaded the trimmed lawns. Parked in the ranch's driveway were Jimmy's father's truck and Lincoln Continental, and Jimmy's car. Behind them was another car, a Porsche.

On the front lawn near the cars sat Jimmy and two other guys: Eddie Randono and Andy Velman. They hadn't noticed me, and I stopped to look and listen.

"I don't think so," Jimmy was saying. "Got my own plans for today."

"Does this include some screwin' around with a colored girl?" Eddie said.

"That's none of your business."

"Oh, listen to Mister High and Mighty. Ain't there enough white girls around here for you? Or do the ghetto girls put out easier? I've heard they can be very fine." Eddie reached over and punched Jimmy in the shoulder, and Jimmy swatted his hand away.

"You're a pig," Jimmy said.

"You'll be missing the fireworks," Andy said.

"He'll be having some of his own," Eddie remarked.

They both laughed. Jimmy's face tightened up in a forced sort of smile, like he'd decided to play along. He'd grown up with these guys, but maybe now was moving past them, part of him still their old buddy, part wanting to hang out with his city friends instead. He told them he'd be with his girlfriend, watching the big fireworks over the East River, maybe checking out some clubs in the Village. That sounded cool to me, but the friends joked it away, further ragging Jimmy about Village fags and weirdos. Of course, that's why Jimmy went there, feeling strange himself. He could do what he wanted there, walk hand-in-hand with Theona along the indifferent sidewalks.

I was really scared now that they'd turn and see me, so I moved to where the front shrubs concealed me but I could still glimpse the three guys.

"My father's fireworks are fuckin' amazing," Eddie said.

"And illegal," Jimmy said.

"Like who's gonna care? Who's paying for the fuckin' Swim Club shit?"

"You know, Jim," Andy said. "You're worrying a lot about this legality stuff lately. Don't you understand how things work? You and your dad, always sweating the small stuff. There's so much more business we could do if you'd loosen up, be more friendly."

"'We'?" Jimmy said.

"Our company and your dad's. Trouble is, you're not very committed to working and I think it discourages your old man—he'd like to have someone to count on, I think."

"What the hell do you know about my father?"

"Plenty," Eddie said.

"Bullshit."

"Maybe we need to leave this guy alone to cool down and think," Andy said. "He'll eventually understand what's good for him."

"I know what's good for me," Jimmy said.

"Sure you do," Eddie said. "Sure."

Eddie and Andy stood up, a comedy-team contrast: Eddie round and squat, Andy a lanky tower. They brushed off their shorts with a sort of disgust and got into the Porsche. I ducked further as they pulled out of the drive. I looked back through the front gate to see Jimmy still sitting on the lawn, plucking blades of grass. He seemed to me like the odd boy abandoned by his rougher friends.

"Jimmy!" A faint but urgent voice, coming from the house. There, peering out from the inches-open front door, stood Jimmy's mother, wearing a robe and slippers. "Come in."

"Yeah," he said, but he didn't get up.

She glanced in my direction and, noticing me, pulled back and shut the door, but I saw her startled, sad eyes, as though the sight of me had triggered some deep, disturbing thing in her. Had she recognized me somehow from the few times we'd met while Jimmy and Diane were dating? Would she tell Jimmy that I was lurking there? I turned and hurried away, not slowing down until I got back home.

Bentley also didn't go to the Swim Club celebration. Solomon had invited him and me to Claytown for the community's annual picnic, and at first I'd said no, since I'd been assigned to my wayward sister for the day by my wishful-thinking mother. But now I wanted to be in Claytown.

Bentley didn't want to go to the picnic alone, it turned out. Solomon had told us there might be trouble; last year a bunch of white boys had disrupted the Fourth of July picnic at the Claytown church. This year Solomon's grandparents were hosting it in their backyard, and no one knew what might happen.

Solomon met us at his front gate, looking a little uneasy. We followed him around back, where folding tables and chairs were set up. Clusters of people stood holding plastic-cup drinks, some watching a man tending a large, smoking brazier. Most looked Feen's age. Talk, laughter, music, and barbecue aromas filled the yard. People looked our way; some stared, most went back to their conversations.

"Come in, welcome," said Feen as soon as she noticed us. She was sitting with two other women, all of them in loose summer dresses and wide-brimmed straw hats. Solomon's grandfather sat near the house, chin against chest, eyes closed. We could hear his wheezy breathing.

"How are you boys?" Feen said. "Excuse my husband George over there. Not too well today. He'll probably sleep for the afternoon. This is Thelma and Cassie, we do quilting together at the church." She introduced us by our names, adding that we were new friends of Solomon's.

Thelma and Cassie said "Nice to meet you" and asked Solomon if he'd brought any other friends to the picnic. Solomon said no.

"Well," Thelma said. "None of the young people in town want to come, the visiting kids especially. They're all off at the park or the beach. More fun there."

"And more mischief," Cassie said. "Lighting firecrackers and such."

I looked around; only a few kids were there, younger ones.

The three of us, though, had a great time that afternoon. After we ate, Solomon showed us a tree house he'd built himself a couple of years earlier, in an elm on the far side of the pond. As he extended a hand to help me up, he told us we were the first people he'd let in. I stopped, with our hands clasping; the clasp felt good, but I was reluctant, fearful, like I was crossing a limit. Solomon asked what was wrong. I had no real answer, none that wouldn't miff or hurt him, so I just shook my head and followed him onto the raft-like platform that rested on a thick branch over the pond. It was hardly a tree house at all. Sticks draped with canvas formed the walls, and he'd managed to suspend more canvas from some higher branches to form a sort of roof. It was like some hermit's retreat.

"They're all drop cloths," he said. "From my grandparents' cellar. They'll need em back when they get the house painted, if they ever do."

Inside, Solomon had worn-out rugs to sit on, a radio with a taped antenna, a stack of books, a Bible open next to them, an oil lamp, and a small cross made from two sticks, nailed to the tree trunk.

"It's my own place," he said. "I come here to think."

I looked at Bentley, who said, "Cool." But he smiled as if he thought it was silly and childish, this little hideaway. I thought almost the opposite: that it made Solomon seem older, like he'd been carving out a space for himself in the world, apart from his grandparents and yet near them. Bentley wouldn't understand that, since he saw himself striding confidently toward being a man—no need of retreats, no doubtful feelings.

Solomon switched on the radio. We listened to some songs, and he and I mostly agreed on which were great and which ones sucked. Bentley asked what we were going to do up there besides listen to songs. Solomon picked up a pack of cards that was resting on the top book, *The Last of the Mohicans*, and we played a few games: Go Fish, Casino. Solomon and I talked and joked, but he and Bentley mainly spoke through the cards: slapping them down, grasping them, holding them close, eyeing one another intensely, silently. The game got more like a battle, and Bentley seemed to be losing. His frustration spurted in grunts and mumbled curses until he accused Solomon of cheating, and Solomon froze, staring. He told Bentley to take it back, that he'd never cheated on anything. Bentley shoved him, and Solomon nearly fell backward but caught himself and stood up. Bentley stood, too, and they faced one another. Solomon didn't shove back, although he looked like he wanted to. Bentley was about to say something else, maybe something that would push things over a nasty line. A threat of physical danger had swept like sudden wind into the makeshift shelter. I could only say what seemed true, as if that would block the blast—Solomon hadn't cheated, I declared. Bentley looked at me and asked what the hell I knew, and I said I knew when someone was cheating. He gave me his smartass smirk and said "Oh," which I took to mean "Of course you're taking his side," and I almost shoved Bentley myself. We just stared at each other awhile, both of us pretty mad, until he finally mumbled that maybe he'd gotten carried away. But it wasn't an apology.

They sat back down and finished the game, while something lingered, something awful that had come from a place deeper than the friendliness.

After the game, Bentley and Solomon, as if at some signal I was unaware of, stood up again and jumped together down into the pond. I still felt jitters from the fighting, but they seemed to have gotten over it or channeled it into this sudden energetic leaping. I climbed down and waded in.

Later, on the warm bank, we lit some sparklers that Solomon pulled out of a box. We waved the smoky glitter in circles and zigzags, but Bentley tired of this quickly and told us he had firecrackers at home. Solomon and I both said we weren't allowed to play with firecrackers, and Bentley smiled.

"Neither am I," he said. You never knew with Bentley: he respected his dad and mostly hewed to the rules, but he also liked to smash them.

We talked about the Highlands trip with Jimmy. Solomon went into a long daydream riff about it, saying how much he'd like to have a car and get out of Claytown, take his grandparents with him, go somewhere and make money, somewhere with palm trees and open spaces and sunshine, and spanking new houses with only one floor so his grandparents wouldn't have to climb stairs. Arizona maybe, he said, where his grandfather could breathe.

We took another swim and walked dripping back to the picnic, where we sat with Feen and her friends. She'd removed her hat and was fanning herself. The women were talking about gardens. I asked Feen if she'd ever had a farm here, and she said, Well, her parents did, a long time back. She told us Claytown people used to grow a lot of the things we were eating today, and some still did. But farming got very hard. Her father started driving a truck and her mother worked as a maid for Wardville people. She herself had worked with her mother for a while, and that was trying—some of those people were slobs, and it was exhausting work. But she always did well in school, which is why she tried to get her grandson to apply himself. "I'd like him to be the first in the family to go to college," she said. "Maybe the college on the hill like that Gerthoff boy, though hopefully with more sense about what he wants."

Jimmy again. Everybody's point of reference that summer, it seemed. But Feen said nothing else about him. She went on to describe how hard it was to keep up the house after her parents died. They had both died young. She'd worked as a receptionist over at the hospital—a long, two-bus ride.

"Back then, though, people would help each other out," Thelma said. "You could rely on your neighbors."

"Oh, yes," Cassie added. "People shared food, and there were big community feasts—much bigger than this little thing."

"One time five men showed up to help paint our house," Feen said.

The women continued this interweaving of maybe rose-tinted memories until it formed a sort of story, overlapping, sometimes contradicting. And gradually sadder. How the town started getting smaller, with people moving away, houses going derelict, farms disappearing or shrunk to vegetable patches. Black people couldn't get many city government jobs yet, so either you got yourself educated and worked your way up in some business in the city or you got menial work.

"But most of us still here want to stay," Thelma said. "It's our home."

"Raised two kids here," Feen said. She turned to Bentley and me. "Solomon's mother and uncle. Out of state now, the both of them."

The women's voices seemed to grow steadier, more forceful yet calmer as they shared these stories about their lives, even when they talked about hard times. I was hooked. Bentley was restless.

Everything went smoothly until late afternoon, when only a few people remained; Solomon's grandfather had gone inside. There were Thelma and Cassie and Thelma's husband, Ray, a carpenter who'd brought some wooden birdhouses he'd made to sell at the picnic. The minister was there, the one we'd seen on our first visit. Reverend Wilson, his name was, and next to him sat a couple, Seth and Violet Woodrow, who ran the small grocery store in Claytown.

Off in a corner of the yard a younger guy was perched on a log bench; he'd been drinking beer after beer and shooting dirty looks at us.

"Hey you two," he shouted now. "What you doin' here where you don't belong? You spying on us?"

"What are you talking about, fool?" Solomon said. He'd stood up.

"I'm no fool. I know what's going on here. They're scopin' the place out so they can tell their friends where to vandalize. Why don't you both get the fuck outta here."

Feen, who'd been watching and listening, got up from her chair and walked toward the shouting man. All of us were standing now.

"Listen up here, Dalton, I won't have that kind of language on my property," Feen said. "We're trying to have a peaceful day. So you either keep your mouth shut or you leave."

Dalton was walking toward Feen now with a strange look on his face, distressed and bleary but attempting to focus.

"Very well, Miss Josephine, I will leave. But one of these days you'll wake up to what these people are doing to us. You hide away here in the woods and don't see what's happening in the rest of the world. You think people are your friends but they ain't."

He made his careful way toward the front of the house without even glancing at us. The gate slammed a few times. I had stepped back from everyone, as if I'd done something wrong but didn't know what it was.

"You boys stay where you are," Feen said. "Have some more lemonade. Don't you pay any mind to that drunk. I only put up with him because his mama and I used to be such friends in church and all. Drove her to an early grave."

We sat, sipping our drinks in the warm sun. I looked at Bentley, who seemed distant and amused, as if this was all too strange to take seriously.

"Let me tell you," Ray said. "That man's a little crazy, but he isn't altogether wrong. What about those punks riding by in their cars calling out filthy things to us. Spray-painting nasty words on the church wall. Never been trouble like that here." He looked at us. "That isn't your fault, boys."

I felt both accused and forgiven. I wondered who the punks were and if I knew them and why they would have done those things. It suddenly seemed like we didn't belong there, that we should get back to Wardville. Yet

I didn't move; right now I didn't feel like I'd belong back there, either.

"It's something we do need to be concerned about," Ray said. "There are people interested in this land, even though we still live here."

The reverend spoke up. "Yes, and you know we're working with some Wardville people on that. We've protested, gone to hearings."

"And it's all much ado about nothing, really," Seth Woodrow said.

Ray and Feen exchanged looks. Ray didn't acknowledge the other men's comments. "They'd love to build new houses here," he said. "Some of them would. But then there's others—"

"Raymond," the reverend said.

Ray waved him quiet. "Then there's others who seem more interested in the ground itself, or what they can put there. That's an old story, though. Goes back to the clay pits, people gettin' rich from that. White people, of course. We only had the little farms."

The reverend was shaking his head in dissent, and Seth looked at Ray as if offended into silence. It was like complex signals being exchanged, not easy to decode. I looked at Solomon, thinking he might explain things, but he was staring down at the grass as if he didn't want to meet our eyes.

"And what about the houses that burned down?" Ray said. "And the people who disappeared? Didn't that have to do with the quarries?"

Despite the warm sun, chilly bumps spread down my arms. Now Bentley's superior grin was gone, and he looked like he might be thinking the same awful things I was.

"Disappeared?" I said to Ray.

"So they say." He was calm. "Vanished. Of course, some people were bought out, others moved to find jobs. But there are still some unaccounted for to this day. Whole families. Killed for their land, some people say. And later, black workers died, the ones who did the crap work, pardon my language. A confrontation happened with the white workers, the Germans and Irish. Maybe it was an accident, maybe the quarry owners did it along with the white workers."

Ray paused, looking from Bentley to me and back, ignoring Solomon, who now had his hands pressed against his ears, his elbows resting on his knees. I thought he might be feeling sick.

"They say a whole lot of folks were buried in one big grave, in the marshes where the dump is now. Under tons and tons of garbage now, way down deep. And right in the quarries themselves."

"This is absurd." It was Seth, bursting from his quiet. "Why are you talking to children like that? Always repeating these old stories. They're mythology, not fact. Black folks had plenty here. Oyster boats, big farms, nice houses."

Ray spoke directly to Seth now. "I'm not sure any of us know all the facts. I'm just trying to explain why some people around here might be a little suspicious."

"Suspicious of what?" Seth said. He was leaning forward in his lawn chair as if he might lunge at Ray.

Solomon looked up now and shook his head—negating something, trying to rouse himself, I wasn't sure.

"Suspicious about people taking our property away again," Ray said. "About what they might be doing to the land around here."

"All this sentimentality about the land," Seth said. "The land's value today is what we can get for it. And we can get a lot. No one is stealing it."

"I wouldn't be so sure."

The reverend interrupted. "Do we have to talk about this now? Ruin a nice day?"

"Take it easy, everybody," Feen said. "Calm yourselves. No, we don't have to talk about it, and we won't anymore. Ray, there really isn't any point in bringing all this up again now, scaring these kids."

We sipped the remnants of our lemonades in strange silence as the wind whooshed through the tall trees and fluttered the tablecloths, knocking cups onto their sides with plastic plunks.

"I'd better start cleaning up," Feen said, and all of us, well-raised boys, got up to help.

When we'd finished, Solomon walked us to the gate; yellow-orange light filtering through the woods illuminated the landfill mounds in the near distance, almost making them beautiful. When we said our see ya laters, I grasped Solomon's arm below the shoulder, not really knowing why—some clumsy attempt at connection, cheering-up. He tensed, with a slight edgy smile, and I pulled back.

As Bentley and I started home along the road, we heard deep, grinding motor sounds above the rustling of trees; two trucks were moving in the landfill.

"Dumping stuff on the Fourth of July?" Bentley said.

We looked at one another, the question suspended, as the landfill grumbles grew louder.

On the bus ride back, thinking about the afternoon, I asked Bentley straight out why he'd gone with Jimmy to Claytown to begin with. He shrugged. "Something to do," he said. "Hanging around town is fuckin' boring." And his mom and dad told him not to, he added with a grin. So he, too, hadn't had permission, and his reasons maybe weren't so different from mine. Yet he didn't seem to care that much about it, whereas I, for some reason, did. I thought about Solomon, how he'd gotten so nervous and withdrawn when Ray was talking.

"What about that stuff Ray was saying?" I asked Bentley.

"What about it?"

"Do you think it was true?"

"Maybe. Do you?"

"Solomon seemed to think so. I mean the way he reacted."

"Hmm," Bentley responded, and we stopped speculating—out loud anyway.

Whatever was going on, it could divide us from Solomon, put us on the wrong side of some nasty things, and I didn't want that to happen. Neither, it seemed, did Solomon.

When we got to my house, my parents were still at the Swim Club. In my room, I took down my library book and opened it to some old maps of Claytown. Bentley and I sat with it on my bed. We turned pages over our bare legs, both of us smelling of sweat and pond.

The maps were chronological. Claytown began as a large area, buildings and houses marked with X's on winding roads bordering the woods and marshes and, along the river, the clay quarry. The quarry had belonged, I knew, to Albert Bultmann, whose factory had supplied bricks for many New York City structures. There was a small illustration of the eerie, rambling Bultmann house, isolated on its hilltop with acres of land around it, sloping down to Claytown.

As we followed the maps, they too told Claytown's story: the community shrank like a life form deprived of nourishment. Its boundaries retreated sharply between 1915 and 1925. Bentley ran a finger across the map and said, "They disappeared."

Looking again, I noticed two tiny mounds north of Claytown labeled "Kills Landfill."

Bentley didn't stay long; after he'd looked at some more maps, he got antsy and said he wanted to go shoot off some fireworks before his parents got home. After he left, I felt antsy, too, and kind of abandoned. I put the book on my desk, where I noticed another book that I hadn't left there. Atop the book was a note with my name on it.

"Bro," it said, "*Sorry I upset you. But you've got to grow up, or maybe be a little less grownup. Things are worse and better than you think. Mom and Dad are acting weird, haven't you noticed? And Jimmy, you think he's so strong and free, but let me tell you he's always running away. Yet he's under his father's thumb. And his mother's too, in a different way, the poor woman. He gets in over his head in a lot of things and doesn't know how to get out. OK, I'm probably upsetting you again. We've got to talk sometime soon. We never really talk anymore! Meanwhile, give this book a try—it might help you find your way through the woods. You'll dig it, I think, since it's sort of history, sort of fantasy. Kind of outside time, though, a different perspective. Love you, Diane.*"

The book was *The Fellowship of the Ring*. I'd seen Diane's tattered copy around the house before but I'd never opened it. Now I did, and I was quickly carried into its alternate yet parallel world, like the imaginary country I'd invented in grade school, an island off Britain. I was never sure if it was in the past or the future. I'd mapped it and given it a language. Sometimes in the woods I would imagine I was there. People were happy; they had everything they wanted—plenty of food, music, books, and games—and the ruling power was love. You could be as weird as you wanted. All the violent, greedy, hateful people had been banished and had turned into sea monsters always threatening to invade.

This world I was entering now was much darker, more menacing. More real. Yet not real: a sort of mirror reality. I kept reading late into the night. I left off with the pathetic, thieving Gollum and the rising power of evil Mordor.

•

In the morning, I dove back into the book and had reached Frodo's departure from the peaceful Shire when I heard voices from the kitchen. Diane and our mother in combat, loud on Diane's side. I opened my door to better make out their words: Mom lecturing Diane for taking me into the woods at the bluff's edge, troublemaker territory.

"So maybe he needs a little trouble," Diane said. "You might not understand it, but I'm trying to look out for the kid."

"Smart aleck," Mom said. "Here, I thought since you wouldn't go to the Swim Club you could have a nice afternoon with your brother, the way you used to, and get out in the fresh air, too. Maybe clear the garbage out of your brain a little."

"Well, we got some air, probably polluted," Diane said. "Took a little nature walk. Looking at the flora and the fauna, what's left of it."

"Everything is negative to you, isn't it?" My mother kept her voice low, but Diane was getting to her. "You should've grown up where there weren't any trees or gardens or open spaces to enjoy. It's like paradise here, but do you kids appreciate it? You're the ones who've ruined those woods. You think I don't know that's where the kids go to smoke their dope and do whatever else they get themselves into? And leave their garbage all over."

"Yeah, it's a shooting gallery up there. Needles everywhere. I'm turning my brother into a junkie. Jesus."

"Keep up the sarcasm, Miss Know-it-all." Mom was nearing a shout. "You're pretty smart for someone who's never in school. You don't even clean up your room—it's like the Collyers' mansion in there. Instead of helping, you make more problems. Like I don't have enough with the Fourth of July mess and now planning for the luau."

Diane replied that she certainly was too smart for the meaningless activities Mom wasted her time on, and I shut my door against their sniping. Later I learned the undercurrent cause of Mom's threadbare nerves: the Independence Day party itself. Very few people had shown up, the band was loud and awful, and the fireworks fizzled.

Before long, though, Mom had begun to transfer her hopes and efforts to the Labor Day luau, which was still two months away. It would salvage the summer, restore its tainted shine, a golden goal in the bright distance.

Later that day, I walked by my parents' bedroom door and saw my mother sitting on her bed with an open box of photographs and papers. I watched awhile. She would pick up one of these documents, stare at it, and return it to the box. It didn't seem that she was looking for any item in particular; she examined each scrap of paper, each photograph, as if trying to solve a mystery. It wasn't like her to be spending time with these old things. I had never been aware that she'd kept so much. To me, she had no real past; it remained unspoken, emerging in haphazard fragments I assembled much later. So that moment was like glimpsing some habit secretly indulged.

I stood there, trying not to breathe loudly although my chest felt like a too-tight shirt. I stood for several minutes, until I heard the side door creak open downstairs and slam shut, followed by my father's voice, urgently calling my mother's name. She jammed everything back into the box, except for one black-and-white photograph I figured she hadn't noticed behind her on the bed. She returned the box to the shelf of her closet, and I rushed back quietly to my room before she could see me. Once she'd gone, I went back and retrieved the photograph. In my room again, I looked at it: a young man in a suit and tie, with some sort of ribbon on his lapel, and a hat like detectives wore in old movies. He stood with his feet apart, firmly planted on a sidewalk in front of a brick building. He had a thin moustache and a direct, confident gaze. It was my grandfather. Staring down at the photo, lost in its silvery disappeared world, I again heard my father's agitated voice, shouting something about an accident. But it was only when I heard the name Jimmy that I dropped the photo onto my desk and ran out into the hallway.

"Big, big crash," Dad was saying. "Smashed the damn car right into a tree. Kid's in the hospital now, but they're not sure he's gonna make it."

The house was trembling.

"Was he drunk?" my mother asked.

"Or high. Who knows. But it was ten o'clock in the morning. Probably late to his job near the landfill, his father's project there. Probably took a curve too fast."

"Irresponsible boy. Always has been. Oh God, his poor parents."

Some part of me had feared this would happen, yet it didn't seem possible. Jimmy was too strong and sure and swift. How could powerful, heroic motion be stopped in this brutal way? He should be protected from such catastrophe. Through my panic and anger, I began to form an explanation, half-aware that it wasn't a heroic one: Jimmy had done this deliberately. He had aimed his car, his escape machine, at that tree. I remembered his outbursts in the car and at Ward's house—the manic urgency, the headlong argument with himself. The things he'd told me in Battery Park, the simmering confusion about what he did and did not want. His sad mother, slowly giving up on life. The conflicts with his father, who put him down and probably did worse.

I took deep breaths and wiped my eyes with my shirt. Now I wanted to see him, but I knew that was crazy. I wasn't family, I wasn't even a friend, I was nothing to him really. I wouldn't be allowed to see him, and I shouldn't want to so strongly.

I walked into the living room, and as soon as my mother noticed me, she said, "Come here." She was crying. I hesitated, and she repeated her anxious command. My legs moved me toward her, and she took my head between her hands.

"You heard?" my father said. I nodded in my mother's grasp.

"You see, you see," she said, her face a wet red. "You see what happens to these punks. You see now what could have happened to you."

"Stop squeezing the kid, for Chrissake," my father said. "He looks pretty upset as it is. I think he understands what happened. You do understand, don't you, Luke?"

I nodded again; my mother had loosened her grip but was still holding my head. I was almost crying, too. She drew me into a hug, but I could feel her shakiness, and I pulled away.

"I'm okay," I said. "Nothing happened to me."

"By the grace of God," she said.

"Is Jimmy going to die?"

My question seemed to calm her, maybe bringing her back to the bad-enough reality.

But it was my father who answered. "Well, he's pretty seriously hurt. He'll be okay, though."

Dad's voice had taken on a blustery confidence, as if to dilute his panicky announcement of the bad news. Maybe he had remembered that he'd persuaded my mother to let me go riding in Jimmy's car. His agitation and his control were disorienting, the way he swung between them. My parents' fear and concern about Jimmy seemed far deeper and more complicated than mine.

An hour later I was in Solomon's front yard, where things were getting even stranger. Solomon had something to tell us about Jimmy and the accident: he had witnessed the whole thing. He couldn't keep still now and paced the yard, repeatedly rubbing his forehead as if to scrape something away. Before he gave details, I blurted my notion that Jimmy had aimed for the tree.

"What?" Solomon said. "Why would he run his car into a tree on purpose?"

This shut me up, the fierce insistence of it. He told us he knew the facts; he had seen it all from right there in his yard. Jimmy had been going fast because someone was chasing him. Solomon described what had happened on the road next to us. First, Jimmy came speeding up with gravel in clouds around him (Solomon's hands made a sweeping motion and his face was all alarm), and then a dump truck appeared where no truck usually came and roared past on the tail of Jimmy's car, which (Solomon's head moved swiftly right to left, following the remembered vehicles) took the big curve in the road way too fast and with a loud screech and metal crunch and bang (Solomon slammed fist into palm) hit the big old oak there almost head-on. The truck's brakes squealed, and it halted before the bend and backed up all the way out of the road. It turned and headed out toward the landfill. Solomon saw this as he ran toward Jimmy's mangled car and then back to his house to call for help.

"So somebody was after him," Bentley said.

"Somebody driving a green truck with tape across the sides so you couldn't read the name," Solomon said.

"Green?" I said.

"Yeah, green, so?" he said.

"Nothing." If Solomon had been thinking what I had, he'd pushed away the thought, and I tried to push it away too.

Of course I wasn't allowed to visit the hospital and I'd come to understand that doing so wouldn't relieve my fear and dread or my restless wanting and curiosity, so the next few days were endless. I spent a lot of time alone in my room. I avoided my parents, and they seemed to be avoiding me, too. Even weirder, they seemed to be avoiding each other, and there was a lot of silence in the house. My father was staying up late at night again; I knew this because I was up late, too, unable to sleep. I was still having dreams of flying, now in spaceships piloted by those silvery alien-faced angels, swooping closer and closer to earth, nearer and nearer to fiery collisions. And now there were ogre-like space creatures pursuing us, too. I crept into the kitchen at midnight the day after Jimmy's accident and saw my father sitting alone in the dark living room with the TV on, grasping a glass of whiskey. He was pale with picture-tube light, like when we used to watch old movies together late on Friday or Saturday. Dad would explain who all the actors were (that's Cary Grant and Grace Kelly, kiddo, they had *class*; that's Johnny Garfield, every city boy wanted to be like him). But now there was no picture on the screen, only snow soundtracked by a faint electronic buzz, and Dad was staring at it anyway as if it were telling him something.

Avo examined the photograph I had handed to him, as if he was trying to recognize the person in it.

"Where did you get this?"

"Mom was looking at it."

He let out a laugh. "Your mother? She had this?"

"Yes."

He nodded. He continued staring at the photo awhile as I listened to the news from the radio next to us on his kitchen table. It was a couple of days after the accident, and I had come to my grandfather's house as if he might have answers, even if I wouldn't fully understand them. But he hadn't mentioned Jimmy, and I didn't want to bring up the subject yet; instead, I had shown him the photograph.

Even the latest news about the possible impeachment of Nixon didn't pull Avo's attention away from that fading image of himself. It prompted a story, one he'd never told me. The picture was taken at the time of the Spanish Civil War, he said, and he had dressed up for a labor rally. He had wanted to look respectable, since they were all tagged as communists. "Of course," he pointed out, "some of them *were* communists." But sometimes it was only the communists who put up any fight. The Russians were the only ones who helped the Spanish Republic, along with the volunteers from other countries, including communists. There was a march that day, probably May Day, to Union Square in the city. Along the route, the marchers were taunted by spectators—fascists, some of them, but a lot of them were ordinary Americans. They threw tomatoes, called Avo a spic, and told him to get out of the country. And there were workers who didn't like my grandparents because they were small-business people, even though they were having a hard time in Newark then. Some Newark white people looked down on the Portuguese, a tiny minority then, before the bigger migration. Some whites called them Africans, as if it was another slur word.

Avo paused in his telling. He briefly seemed to be listening to the radio. "She never liked Newark much, your grandmother," he continued. "No real gardens, no trees. Good people there, but too much conflict and getting worse. We wanted to get out. Promised your mother we would. Our princess, we called her, and not always in a nice way. Maybe we spoiled her. She was the only one after we lost our boy. We told her someday we'd live in one of those places we went to in the summer. And now we do, but she got here first, and we followed. Strange turns in life."

He slid the photograph toward me and nodded at the radio.

"So now they've taken over the government. Crooks. And it leads right down here to those land-grabbers. Too big to fight, maybe."

I looked down at the photo of the robust, well-dressed man who would one day become my grandfather. He looked like he could fight anything, with a clear sense of allies and enemies, persisting through detours and doubts. Stubborn but sure, knowing what he was, following some inner compass.

I couldn't talk to Avo about the accident now because I couldn't bring myself to speak Jimmy's name.

PART TWO

EIGHT

My grandfather's battle against the developers soon took another jolting turn. The closer the construction came to his house, it seemed, the more fantastic his resistance—and the more passive. He'd given up on direct confrontation and stayed indoors, trying to figure out the precise connections between the builders nearby and the larger powers controlling everything. He was doing his own constructing—of mental walls around himself. He arrived at a theory that he began to hold like a religion. Gradually, his speaking shrank toward one obsessive subject.

The construction at Capri West, my grandfather said, was linked to the work at the landfill, from which toxic substances were leaking into the ground and pouring into the air. Everyone for miles around was being slowly and secretly poisoned. He showed me the name of the invisible toxic substance, alongside a diagram of its chemical makeup, in a fat reference book. He had drawn an elaborate map with red dots indicating places the toxin had affected. It was largely invisible and odorless—all you could smell was the landfill itself. Some of this was true: I had read in the newspaper about toxins from the landfill, and Solomon had shown us the exhaust stacks. But that was mostly stuff you could both smell and see. Avo was talking about something far more insidious, and he connected it to larger patterns, amorphous and abstract. Our local poisoning was part of a nationwide plot by industrialists and the government. Once the facts were out, it would be far worse than Watergate, more scandalous than the FBI's surveillance of protestors. Invisible contaminants were everywhere, but especially in places where people had no influence, and where they'd lost the ability or desire to resist. They'd lost hope, too, and the toxic illness had increased their hopelessness.

Meanwhile, Jimmy was improving, according to my father's account. He'd learned this from Gerthoff Senior, whom Dad had called after the accident and even (weirdly, I thought) gone with to the hospital at least once. Jimmy hadn't in fact been at death's door, although he was on its front path, and he'd made a swift recovery from a serious head injury along with fractures and bruises. He now needed less sedation and was swimming back up to full consciousness. But not, as Dad put it, to playing with a full deck. He would have to be in the hospital awhile longer. For one thing, he had trouble recognizing some of the family and friends at his bedside. Not only that, but he was saying things no one could make sense of: he kept repeating the words *prodigal* and *sinner*, and asking to be forgiven. He talked about "atonement in blood."

I wrote these phrases down and read them to my grandfather one day as he listened on his ancient phonograph to a *fado* singer. This was music he'd always dismissed as morbid and medieval when my grandmother played it. But now it seemed to sadden him, and I felt a shaky sadness, too; it was like my grandmother was there in that room again, sitting invisibly in her chair. It felt doubly strange to be repeating Jimmy's delirious words above the music's wavering wail. The puzzling phrases only confirmed Avo in his belief: since Jimmy worked so close to the toxins, he might have been strongly affected. "But I'm sure his father protects him somehow," Avo said. "'Prodigal' my foot."

I asked what a prodigal was. Avo laughed. "A Bible tale," he said. "Anyhow, who knows if Jimmy said that? Maybe your father made it up."

"My father doesn't lie," I said.

"No, no. Not lying. Exaggerating. He's all caught up with those people."

I thought: *My grandfather really is crazy now. He's snapped.* I felt an awful mix of fear for him, alarm at what he was saying, and wanting him to shut up. Of course, Dad *was* saying all sorts of way-out things about Jimmy lately.

"You know, Jimmy was being chased by somebody," I said, and I explained what Solomon had seen, or thought he'd seen.

"Chased?" he said. "Or making trouble, along with the truck? Plowing through Claytown like he does everyplace else. He'll survive. Make his getaway. People with money and pull always do. Not the Claytown people—stuck there, caught in the middle. They'll be crushed. The way it always works. Already they're getting sick. Respiratory illness sky-high over there and nobody cares. Nobody ever cared. Put a power plant next to them, tore holes through their land, dumped the whole city's garbage on them."

"But Jimmy's helping out there," I objected. "And Sebastian Ward."

"Don't be so sure. I could tell you things. That Ward fella and Claytown. Jimmy too. Ward wants something, they all want something. Rich people. Dangerous if they don't get it."

Unspoken things lurked behind Avo's fragmentary words, things about Ward I'd been half-aware of for a long time. Maybe Ward wanted something Jimmy wouldn't give him, maybe he wanted to be around Jimmy the way girls did. I thought of Ward's hands resting on Jimmy and Solomon in that garden. But would Ward try to hurt Jimmy because of that? What really shook me was that I knew, deeply and directly, why girls liked to be with Jimmy.

I tried not to think these thoughts, but they persisted. Could Avo really be talking about these secret things? I examined his etched face as he leaned his head toward the phonograph. He had stopped talking, and I didn't know what else to say. For a moment, I saw him through my parents' eyes: out-of-touch, declining, filled with resentment and loneliness, and blaming a vague conspiracy for everything he saw going wrong. For a while it was the JFK assassination: I would listen to eerie, cryptic talk about a second gunman who was never caught and a lying Warren Commission. Now it was this. My grandfather had always had that cranky side. But that never seemed like the real Avo, who'd always made me feel it was okay (even a sign of distinction) not to want what everyone else wanted, even if you didn't yet know what you yourself wanted.

Looking at him now as he slowly shook his head, with his face drawn in as if tightened by pain, listening to the sorrowful music he never used to like, I thought: *There are things I can't tell him and things in his head I cannot understand.*

That night, the space angel piloted our speeding ship through wintry air into the window of a large old house, which was and was not Ward's. We stepped out onto soft carpet, and I looked at the angel's nonhuman face, with its narrow, catlike eyes and skin of an unearthly pallor. He was looking at something, and I turned to see Ward in front of a fireplace, dressed in strange, old-fashioned clothes, with a stiff high collar and a green waistcoat. I looked back, and the angel was now Jimmy. He was naked, and blood ran down his body and dripped from his semi-hard cock. I woke up and felt my own cock hard in my pajama bottoms, and a wetness under me where (still a new, amazing, and terrifying thing) I'd come.

I had to talk to someone about the things going on inside and outside me, if only to help tell them apart. I thought about Confession, a ritual I'd long ignored, despite the fact that Sister Michael Mary had told us we shouldn't take Communion without having listed our adolescent sins, the ones we could speak aloud (I lied to my mother, I answered my father back, I joined in taunting an ugly girl at school). Of course, she didn't make a big deal out of it, and I had in fact taken the body and blood without Confession many times. I dreaded the thought of that dark-wood booth with the screen-obscured outline of Father Drinnon like a shadow whispering, and his clean priestly scent making me feel I stank of guilt, especially since I wasn't telling everything and therefore the Hail Marys and Our Fathers I was assigned to speak probably wouldn't gain me true absolution.

And what could I confess? Weird dreams? Fears that my entire family was going nuts? My secret thoughts (sometimes while jerking off) about naked bodies, male and female? (Definitely not that.) I needed to talk to someone who might understand, and that wouldn't be Father Drinnon.

As it turned out, I confessed some of my fears—not all my thoughts, of course—to Sister M herself. I had handed in my composition, in which helping with chores became a service to humanity. But I also mentioned Claytown: the timeworn houses, the old people hanging on in them, coping. I didn't say anything about my grandfather or Jimmy. She had told me to pick up the composition the following Sunday after class. But when we met that day, she didn't give the essay back to me. She wanted me to go on writing and to meet with her through the summer to talk. I found this seriously weird, but I also felt special, chosen. And I liked being around her, abnormal as it might be, sort of the way I'd once liked spending time with Diane. Except, of course, Sister M had some silent, tranquil center from which she acted and spoke, something deep and strong and not easily shaken.

Or so it seemed. During our meeting she seemed rushed. Her face was tight with impatience, which didn't seem right for her. As I tried to tell her about Avo, at first I couldn't explain what I really meant, and she looked at me as if I were babbling. So I slowly described Avo's roof vigil, his fear of losing his house, and finally—hesitantly—his theory of poisoning and conspiracy. I realized I was shaking and very near crying. I squeezed my eyelids together a few seconds.

She said nothing for what seemed a very long time after I stopped talking. Her lips made a thin line as she stared down at me.

"My boy," she began, using a priest-phrase she hardly ever used. "You mustn't listen to that kind of talk. It is disordered. It is a confused mind speaking."

I was seated beside her desk. I looked up at the crucifix. Surely Jesus, with his broken body and agonized, sunken face, would understand the awful things that were happening. I was sorry I'd said anything, and I looked back at her, but she had followed my gaze to the cross. She shook her head as if dismissing some thought, and our eyes met again.

"I know a lot about your grandfather," she said. Her voice had relaxed some. "He didn't attend church, but your grandmother did—sometimes in secret, you know. She would talk to me about him. I think your grandfather sees injustice in the world, people doing evil things. Maybe he wants a simple explanation for that. But, of course, there isn't one. We have to work one step at a time to fix things that are wrong in the world. I think your grandfather understands that, but maybe he gets frustrated. We all do."

She told me that, yes, Claytown was in danger, and so was Spanish Settlement. They had always been vulnerable. And, yes, it was wrong for people to lose their homes. Sometimes protesting works, she said—in fact, she had done it herself, for civil rights, against the war. And sometimes you just have to be there for people, give what you can to them, even if it's only to listen. Problems can have many causes, so there have to be different solutions. If there *are* solutions, she added.

I thought about that awhile. I asked about Jimmy. People might be out to get him, too, I said. Yes, she said, she'd heard about the accident, that it was terrible, but she wasn't surprised. She knew Jimmy's mother, who had always had difficulties. She was raised Catholic and had become a Lutheran like her husband. He'd insisted on that, apparently, but the mother would come and talk to the nuns. The father, it seemed, could be a harsh man. And the mother was, well, troubled. Jimmy, of course, grew up with all that. She let out a long breath and continued to give me a questioning look.

I told her about Jimmy's hospital-bed mumblings, the phrases my father had reported that I didn't understand. She explained the prodigal story to me, and I felt inklings of something real and true in the parable of the wayward son. I wondered if Jimmy thought he needed to return to his father to be forgiven. Return from where, though, and forgiven for what?

"Tell me," she continued. "Are you seeing your friends? I don't mean James Gerthoff."

I picked up the hinted warning and said nothing else about Jimmy. I told her about Bentley and Solomon.

"Good, you should be making more friends," she said. "Kids your age. Maybe you can get to know this Solomon boy better. You know, he's probably reaching out to you, in his own way. It can get pretty lonely over there in that little town, I suppose, like any separate community."

She nodded as if confirming her own idea. She looked down at her desk, at the books and papers stacked there, and another long stretch went by before she spoke again. Her upper lip, I noticed, was beaded with sweat.

"Your grandfather is a good man," she went on. "But he spends a lot of time alone, thinking, and that's not always a good thing. The world can be overwhelming and frightening, but it's wonderful. Full of wonder, I mean. More wonderful than people's ideas about it." She laughed outright, and her laughter was loud against the classroom's silence. "Your grandfather will be okay. His heart is in the right place, as they say. But maybe sometimes his ideas get too big for him to handle. So he talks to you because he knows you'll listen, and you want to know about everything."

She sat back in her chair and looked at me awhile. Suddenly she laughed again as if she'd remembered a joke. It seemed a little nutty. This too wasn't like the person we saw in class.

"Now, get outside," she said, waving me away. "I've got work to do. Go ride your bike, have some fun. It's too nice a day to be stuck in here."

I didn't move, and she sighed. She said that maybe we shouldn't have regular meetings, maybe it wasn't a good idea. She suggested I keep writing things down when I felt I wanted to, and maybe show them to her from time to time. As I got up to leave, she added that I could come and see her anytime I liked. She was smiling, but it seemed the rest of her face was pulling against the smile. If I'd made a sort of confession to her, she'd given me a peculiar penance. I should enjoy the day but also reflect on it; make friends but find some of them in unlikely, neglected places. Combine pleasure in life with an awareness of the pained figure on the fringes.

The odd thing was, it could have been true that everyone was being gradually poisoned, driven crazy even, by some toxic substance, with Claytown on the front lines. Hints of strange and secret things continued.

One afternoon a couple of weeks after the Fourth of July, my mother and Mrs. Velman were sitting in lawn chairs on the patio, sipping fruit punch from Mom's new pastel plastic tumblers. Stirrers topped with palm trees stuck out from each glass. Above their heads swung paper lanterns in different colors, crisscrossed between a crab apple tree and a pine. From the intercom-system speaker on the back wall of the house came the voice of Nat King Cole, soft and smooth as the summer air itself.

I was nearby, sitting cross-legged on the grass. Diane had told me that you could meditate anywhere by focusing on a mantra and blocking out everything else. I'd tried it before, but I could never remain inside myself, since I was always too interested in what was going on around me. It wasn't working today, either. I was focusing on the two women talking.

"Who sees him?" Mrs. Velman was saying. "Day and night, working, working. You wouldn't think people had so much waste to get rid of. I guess it's all the new development. More businesses, more garbage. But I tell him, Stan, you're working yourself sick."

"What about Randono?"

"Eh, he's good at taking the money, not so good at working long hours. He and that fat wife, like two whales lying around the backyard. They love that little estate they live in. Have you seen it?"

"Yes. A little overdone."

"Oh, you're telling me. Versailles doesn't have so many statues and fountains. And inside—well, you feel like you're at a wake, with those curtains and that furniture."

My mother didn't respond immediately. Maybe she was thinking the same thing I was: that the Velmans' own house was more than a little overdone, too, with their huge wrought-iron gate flanked by brick pillars with stone lions sitting on them. It was a ranch house gussied up, and it contrasted sharply with our own house (plain shingle siding, fenceless lawn).

"Well, you know, they're running from where they came from. Trying to find the good life," my mother said.

"Yeah, well, aren't we all," said Mrs. Velman. "That's why Stanley works so hard. All that drive, drive, drive. I just don't want him to drive himself into the grave."

My mother leaned forward abruptly and put her hand to her chest. She set her glass down on the white plastic Parsons table.

"What's wrong, hon?" Mrs. Velman asked.

"Nothing. I don't know. A strange feeling. My mother would have said something happened to someone I know. She'd be expecting a bad-news phone call."

Mrs. Velman slapped her gently on the arm and laughed. My mother tried to smile away her feeling, but it didn't entirely work. It was odd, this mention of my grandmother and the half-endorsement of her Old World notions.

They both sat back, sipping their drinks. It was quiet, with only the pool's hum, a few cawing bluejays, and the intercom's soft music—now Doris Day singing about a secret love.

"Do you ever miss the old neighborhood?" my mother asked.

"Are you kidding, Libby? Miss what? The noise or the filth or the crime? And the people that were moving in— don't get me started."

Mrs. Velman's old neighborhood was not my mother's: the Velmans had migrated from Flatbush, Brooklyn. Mr. Velman had just launched the company back then, with Mr. Randono of Bensonhurst, and more and more of the business centered on our island's swamps (not yet called "wetlands"), happy dumping grounds aplenty. That, combined with the fact that their neighborhoods were "changing," prompted both the Randonos and the Velmans to leave Brooklyn (like the Pateras), all part of a refugee migration into the island and Jersey. I'd heard Randono call the Verrazano Bridge "the Guinea Gangplank," referring to all the Italian-Americans abandoning Brooklyn. Just as my parents and lots of other white people had fled Newark.

Now the two women were silent until my mother said, in a lower voice, "I remember happy times, though. People were closer. You felt connected to things."

"People were too damn close. I relish the space here." She spread out her arms, knocking over her drink.

My mother jumped up. "Oh, let me get you a towel, Grace."

"No, no, it's mostly on the patio. Sorry."

"Don't worry. We've got to hose down this thing anyway. You know those little apples that fall from the tree leave such stains on the concrete."

And they were back into the everyday concerns of a summer afternoon. Soon they were talking about the Labor Day luau, and my mother's mood brightened into enthusiasm.

But that look of apprehension on her face stayed with me, and a few days later I was confronted with it again, this time at the dinner table. It was one of those rare occasions when my grandfather ate with us, and my mother surprised everyone by cooking *bacalhau*, a dish she'd never made. She'd pulled out my grandmother's recipe from the oblivion-dark back of a drawer. We all watched Avo put the first forkful of the cod stew into his mouth.

"Not bad," he said. "You've got some of your mama in you after all, Libertade."

My mother's lips tightened briefly but eased into a shaky smile. "Well, yes, yes, of course I do," she said.

Fortunately, my grandfather said nothing at the dinner table about secret poisoning, and no one talked about his protest on the roof. But the conversation did turn to politics, a subject that only Avo or Diane normally raised at meals. In a subdued voice, as if rationing his words, Avo repeated a familiar lament: how the country would be a different place had Robert Kennedy not been killed. He had worshipped RFK; my parents had mixed feelings. In fact, I'd heard my father call him a "hypocrite rich boy" and make jokes about "the martyred widow Ethel and all those kids." He mumbled some such thing now but clearly didn't want to antagonize my grandfather, who had been quiet and reasonable so far. After his few broken, elegiac sentences about Bobby and all that had been lost, Avo drank down the last of his *vinho verde*.

It was Mom who got upset after my grandfather spoke. "Oh that poor, poor family," she said. "All that death and suffering. It's like they're cursed, just cursed. Remember how happy they all seemed when JFK was in the White House? That handsome, funny, energetic man. Those beautiful kids, like a little gentleman and lady. And Jackie so poised and glamorous, with all that nice clothing. Who could know that before long there'd be blood all over her clothes? That all the violence would take over and ruin our lives?"

She got up and hurried into the hallway with her napkin pressed to her nose and mouth. My father got up to go after her, telling us all to finish eating, it would be all right, Mom hadn't been feeling well.

My grandfather looked at me across the table, shaking his head slowly back and forth. Diane had a smirk on her face.

"All he did was get us into Vietnam," she said.

I couldn't help finding my mother's words weirdly funny, too, but her upset was not, and I hated Diane for smiling.

"Enough from you," my grandfather said quietly, fixing a stare on Diane. We finished eating in silence. I could hear my mother crying in her bedroom and my father's voice in that tone of reassuring reason, of practical sense, that had always kept things all right.

But Dad wasn't all right himself; that was becoming clearer and clearer. Instead of watching everything and keeping account in his quiet, composed way, he had lately become more volatile. His wry jokes, which had gently critiqued and corrected our behavior, got nastier. His outbursts of temper, effective because they'd been rare, came more frequently. Even publicly—one day he screamed at Diane from our front steps as she ran off after an argument, calling her a "slut," a word I looked up to get its full meaning and then tried to convince myself that Dad hadn't actually said. It was simple: that word had nothing to do with the Diane I knew, who'd had no boyfriends after Jimmy (at least none I'd met). There were more nights of Dad sitting awake in the living room staring at the TV, sometimes at old movies, sometimes at a blank screen, but always with the sound turned off. I'd stand there in the hallway, jolted from another dream of alien angel flight, listening to the tinkle of ice in his glass. He had stopped participating in the luau preparations. He denounced the "scum" dirtying up our parks and shopping centers. He complained that the liberals in city government didn't fix our streets because they didn't care about us nobodies in the boondocks. "Potholes like craters," he'd say.

And then there was his intensifying fixation on Jimmy since the accident. He was now reporting to my mother in greater detail about Jimmy's condition and his hospital-bed rambling, which seemed to interest Dad to a morbid degree. After visiting Jimmy early on and hearing some of that strange, meandering talk, he'd kept in regular touch with Gerthoff Senior. I picked up enough to be seriously freaked out by Jimmy's disorientation and self-blaming, and even more so by Dad's fascination with it.

One Saturday morning in mid-July, my father asked me to go for a ride with him. This was unusual, and potentially painful, since lately we didn't seem to have a lot to say to one another, and the intimate isolation of a car's front seat would only emphasize that silence. For one thing, there'd be memories riding with us of all those Saturday car trips to Little League and Cub Scouts, boy organizations I'd grown to dislike and had begged to drop out of, much to my father's quiet disappointment.

But a ride out of Wardville sounded good, even if Dad wouldn't say where we were going. Maybe it would even be fun, like driving to the park or the ice cream place or the toy store once was.

We got in the Plymouth Volare (it would be years before my parents would switch to Japanese cars), and I tuned the radio to WNEW-FM. A stomping T-Rex tune filled the car. Dad winced and grabbed the volume dial. "Jesus," he said, turning it down, tamping any notion of fun.

We headed north, out of town, along the wooded riverfront toward Claytown and the landfill. But we didn't get there. We stopped just south of the big mansion on the hill; Dad knew how much I felt drawn to the place. There it rose in front of us, all turrets and gables and lacey woodwork. I looked at its dark long windows, and I saw a thin, bony face looking back—the face of the old woman who'd long lived there, the last of the Bultmanns, although I knew she had recently died and the house was empty.

I waited for Dad to explain why we were sitting there. Maybe there was an explanation in the story he began to tell me, about the night he and Mom had first met. I cringed but also wanted to hear. It was at a dance in Newark, he told me, a Portuguese dance in the crowded basement of a church, of all places. She was small, with jet-black hair, like a lot of the girls there, but unlike a lot of them she sat quietly alone, with a controlled smile like she was laughing to herself or daydreaming of somewhere else. He felt out of place himself, strangely, and so he thought they might hit it off, sharing that feeling of being alone in the middle of a crowd. So he asked her to dance. She hesitated, but he could tell she wanted to; he pulled her up off her chair and they danced through song after song. It turned out they were the best dancers there. She hadn't been shy, she told him later, just selective—she'd liked his face and the way he'd stood and moved.

"You know," he said, "maybe it sounds corny, but I think I knew right then and there we'd be making a life together, and that it would be in another place, a much better place we'd find together."

It did sound corny. But somehow reassuring. He continued to stare up at the house as he had all through this detour down memory lane, in which he still seemed to linger.

"You know who built it, right?" he said after a while.

"Sure," I said. "Albert Bultmann, 1885."

We had probably gone through that question and answer before. He gave me a sharp look, then laughed. "Yeah," he said. "You'd know."

He resumed looking at the house.

"It must have been satisfying, don't you think?" he continued after a while. "Taking clay out of the ground and making something with it. Something valuable, useful, maybe even beautiful. Solid buildings. Strong houses."

"I guess so."

As he gazed up the hill, his brow wrinkled as if the loud music had returned.

"And what do they do with the land now? Pile garbage on it. And what do they build? These ugly cardboard boxes, one on top of another."

I resisted the urge to say the obvious: that we lived in one of those boxes. Instead I said, "They were destroying the land back then too, Dad. People had their land taken away, too. Indians. And black people."

He looked at me. "Black people's land? Where did you get that idea?"

"I read about it."

"Well, you can't believe everything you read. And if your grandfather told you that, believe it even less."

I shrugged. I didn't want to argue, certainly not about my grandfather. The air in the car was getting warmer. I rolled down my window all the way.

He turned to look up at the house again. "Anyway, it's a grand old place. Imagine living in it."

Of course I had already imagined it, many times. But who knew that my father harbored these secret desires? Who knew he had an imagination?

"You never know when you're going wrong, that's the problem," he continued, as I attempted to follow as if tracing a winding, tricky path in dark woods. "You end up doing things you don't really want to do. Banking. What is that? Shifting money around. Not even money. Things that represent money. At least my father worked with his hands. Avo did too. Where can you work with your hands today that's dignified?"

I tried to think of an answer but quickly picked up that

he wasn't expecting one, at least not from me. He was still staring at the rambling relic.

"My father didn't want me to do work like he did. Heck, I didn't want to. So I started as a teller after college. Spent a year or so smiling at all kinds of people through bars, like I was in the zoo or jail, or they were. Quickly moved up and out of there. Eventually became an assistant vice president. Sounds impressive, hmm? It isn't really. You know how many assistant vice presidents there are in a big bank? It wasn't so easy with a name like mine in that bank, either. Mostly WASPs with Ivy League degrees, and no matter how incompetent some of them were, they always walked around with that smug sense of superiority. Whereas we guys with the exotic names, we had to work twice as hard to get anywhere, and the assumption always was that we weren't quite good enough, we didn't really *belong* there. Nobody said so, of course, not in so many words. But we got the message. And the women there—well, they were even worse off, no matter what their background." He was quiet for a moment, continuing to look up at the old house. "I mean, I enjoy the work some of the time. But it often feels so, I dunno, so unimportant. Am I really doing anything of value?"

I felt almost panicked by his question, which he seemed this time to be really asking me, as if trusting me to understand. I felt a kind of terrified joy that he was talking to me in this grown-up way. I hesitated before answering, because any response seemed weighty, important.

"Sure you are," I said at last, trying to sound certain, trying to stop the hurt and distress in his voice. "People need banks."

"Yes, they do." He seemed relieved, as if I'd given him a convincing argument. "And we need the money they pay me. Anyway, there's no going back now. And God knows I want you to have a good job someday—you and your sister both, if she ever gets her head on straight. But there are so many ways you can go wrong, and you don't even know it. Can I help you know it? I hope so, but I'm not sure. You take that Jimmy, now."

And so it came back again to Jimmy, the ambiguous object lesson.

"Such potential in that kid. And so many opportunities! He could march right in there and help run his father's company. Build things. Transform the land here. And make a very good living, too. He could have something like that house up there, a grander life than his father. But what is he doing? Racing around in that flashy car, getting into all kinds of trouble. Big trouble now."

He paused again, still gazing up at the mansion. I felt like pushing the door open and running through the woods until I got to Claytown.

"All that freedom to do what he wants. And the girls falling for him, falling all over him, or his money maybe, I'm not sure which. And he changes his major every month in college, it seems. Yeah, sure, the old man's paying, so why settle on anything, why graduate on time. Spend your free time do-gooding, even if you're helping out people opposing your own father. Maybe that's the attraction."

All this sounded nasty and stupid and confused, and I didn't want to hear him talking that way. What happened to all that stuff about building flimsy boxes? I couldn't tell anymore what Dad really thought; sometimes he was pushing me toward Jimmy and other times trying to get me to hate him. Now it seemed like a warning or an accusation. I felt confused sharing this obsessive interest with him, even if part of me wanted to. It no longer seemed like gratifying, proto-adult confiding but something crazy, disorienting. Shouldn't my father have bigger, more important things to think about? Yet somehow the important things swirled around this subject of Jimmy—his privileges, his freedoms, which I was less and less sure about.

"But you can't just let people tear down every tree, ruin the land," I said. "Jimmy knows that."

Dad laughed. "He doesn't know beans, lemme tell you. It's his father's hard work that allows Jimmy to be so idealistic. His father's money. Idealism is a wonderful thing—I used to be that way, too. But you get older and you realize the world doesn't work that way. You gotta get what you can, look out for yourself and the people close to you. These kids like Jimmy will realize that, one of these days. They'll learn."

He started up the car engine, and we pulled away with a screech of tires as he made a quick U-turn, and I gripped the door handle, startled and giddy. We drove back home, as if my father had forgotten where he'd intended to go or hadn't intended to go anywhere in particular.

NINE

Near the end of July, Jimmy was released from the hospital. We got this news from Dad, who heard it from Gerthoff Senior. It seemed Jimmy's repentant mumblings had begun to diminish, and he was recognizing people again. My grandfather was convinced that Dad was in fact making up or wildly exaggerating Jimmy's post-crash confessions. "Feels guilty too, maybe," Avo said, puzzling me.

The morning of Jimmy's release, Dad asked if I'd like to go and see Jimmy leave. I didn't dwell on why Dad would want to do this, or why I wanted to, I just said yes. I'd wanted to visit Jimmy earlier, but I was told they wouldn't let me in, and besides, a fear, even horror, of seeing him in the hospital had held me back anyway. I figured maybe Dad now thought it would make me feel better to go there, or maybe it was intended as another life lesson. If I had thought more about it, I might have discerned my father's mixture of resentment, admiration, envy. I might have understood how his ambivalent desire for Gerthoff Senior's friendship spilled over into his attitude toward Jimmy. Or maybe I couldn't have seen all that then.

Dad insisted we should stay in the car and not make our presence known, so we wouldn't "intrude on Jimmy's family." We didn't tell Mom. It all seemed daffy and conspiratorial, but also like a bonding secret between Dad and me.

We parked across the street from the hospital, and it turned out that we weren't the only observers. A few feet down the sidewalk stood Sebastian Ward, in a blue seersucker suit and straw hat, grasping his walking stick and gazing toward the hospital's entrance. When Dad spotted Ward, he told me "the old kook" had been visiting the hospital almost every day, only to be turned away by Jimmy's father.

We waited a long time, this odd trio of watchers, until the hospital's front doors opened and Jimmy emerged in a wheelchair. He looked passive yet restless sitting there, as if invisible restraints kept him from jumping out of the chair or rolling it at high speed. It seemed to me that he was miraculously himself, wounded yet surviving, as if he'd escaped the clutches of some devouring monster. A candy-striper was pushing the wheelchair, and walking alongside was Jimmy's father, carrying a basket of flowers. (His mother wasn't there; she would be home, of course, maybe lying in bed with the shades drawn.) Both son and father wore shorts and polo shirts. Mr. Gerthoff looked tanned and relaxed, smiling and leaning over to say things to Jimmy that got little response. Gerthoff went to retrieve his car from the adjacent parking lot while Jimmy sat waiting, suddenly cheerful, flashing a flirty grin at the candy-striper. They both laughed at something Jimmy said. Gerthoff drove up, got out, and Jimmy raised himself from the wheelchair. He hugged the girl and walked the short distance to the car, limping slightly. His father reached out and grasped his arm, but Jimmy shook him off and got into the passenger seat. Even at a distance I felt the tenseness between them.

Ward observed this scene even more carefully than we did—he leaned forward expectantly, as if he wanted to bolt across the street. My father noticed Ward again and said, "Look at that guy," and then returned to watching Jimmy himself.

As we drove home, I waited for Dad to say something about what we'd seen, why we'd gone there, why it was all so secretive. He didn't, and when we got back, something else took over: my mother was sitting on our front steps with her head down in her hands. My father zipped the car into the driveway, jumped out, and ran to her. She was crying softly. At first she pushed Dad away as he tried to calm her by putting his hands on her shoulders and speaking directly into her face. He sat down, and she let him put his arm around her. Curious neighbors, watering lawns or taking in trashcans, looked our way. Their looking seemed intrusive yet detached, a vague and abstract concern. No one had come over.

Slowly, a story emerged. Diane had been caught stealing a pair of jeans from the Pateras' clothing store. Mrs. Patera herself saw my sister walk out the front door with the pants; she quietly confronted Diane, who at first said it was a mistake but then called Mrs. Patera a crook. Mrs. P, enraged, threatened to call the police, further inciting Diane. Words like "pigs" and "fascists" were spat in our neighbor's face. Doris's mother's face. Mrs. Patera grabbed the jeans from Diane, tearing them in the process, and told my sister to get out of her sight and never come into the store again.

"This is the thanks we get," my mother said. "Like she needs to steal clothing. Doesn't she have all the clothes she wants? What's wrong with these kids?"

She looked at me—accusing, angry. There's nothing wrong with me, I wanted to say, but I couldn't bring out the words. My father persuaded her to go back inside the house and ordered me to my room. He assured me that Mom would be okay.

"Where is Diane?" I heard him ask as I paused in my doorway, listening. I wanted to hear the facts, even as I felt a fear for my sister that was like the floor opening up to swallow me.

"Out. God knows where. After I talked to Marty Patera on the phone, I confronted her in her room. She screamed at me, threatened me. She called me stupid. If I'd ever said those things to my mother, let me tell you, I wouldn't have a tongue left to say anything else. I slapped her and she tried to hit me back. She ran out the front door screaming at me, and I just collapsed there."

I wanted to do something, but I felt powerless and alone. I closed my door, sat on my bed, and looked up at Christ and that mercurial angel, who seemed to loom over the blond boy—protective and menacing.

That evening after dinner the Pateras came by, including Doris, who was dispatched to my room to hang out while the adults talked. I was feeling calmer, after listening to loud music (better than mantras) and working out with some small weights my father had bought me that I'd only started using that summer. I turned down the volume on *The Rise and Fall of Ziggy Stardust and the Spiders from Mars* in the middle of my favorite song, about the starman waiting in the sky. I'd been playing the song over and over recently, imagining and reimagining the starman. Sometimes I wanted him to come and get me, sometimes I was terrified that he would. Other times I yearned to soar into the night sky to find him.

Doris was filled with information about subway murders, muggings in parks, and racial conflicts in the city. She had taken to watching the local TV news every night, and she saw disturbing patterns. The night before, she'd dreamed of gang members breaking through her parents' bay window and setting fire to the sofa.

"Maybe you shouldn't watch the news," I said.

"Oh, and bury my head in the sand? My father says the city's going to pot. The suburbs, too. He's talking about moving to a farm town in New Jersey."

"What, and grow chemicals?"

"He'd still keep his job, wisenheimer. But my mother's getting tired of hers, with the store losing money. People would rather drive to the malls than walk to her shop, she says. Your sister's little escapade didn't help."

We were silent awhile, listening to the muffled conversation from the living room. I couldn't make out much, especially over Doris' explanatory chatter; she thought that her father felt sorry for Diane but also knew something had to be done. It was a result of the surroundings, according to Mr. Patera, all the bad influences.

"And it'll only get worse," Doris went on, "once they start busing those colored kids down from the North Shore."

"Black," I said. "Not 'colored.'"

"Well, whatever it is. I'll be going to high school next year, and it scares me. And what if we have to get bussed up there?"

Of course, Doris had a point: the North Shore schools were pretty bad and sometimes violent. But the North Shore kids I'd met were okay, and my own school had plenty of nasty students who beat up and bullied puny kids like me or anyone who was different. I didn't much care about North Shore kids being bused down to our schools, but I didn't like the thought of having to ride a bus way up there.

It became clear, though, that Doris didn't know much about the stuff she was parroting. I got antsy listening to her little-girl voice faking grownup knowledge, when it had begun to seem we didn't know much about anything. I went into the hall to hear for myself what the Pateras were saying, and Doris followed me. Mr. Patera was speaking pretty loudly. My parents' responses were quieter, but we could still make them out. Mrs. Patera didn't say a word.

"I don't like to interfere, but I think your daughter has a problem," Patera said. "She's full of anger about something and she aimed it at my wife, who is trying to run a business. We're not social workers or shrinks. But she seems out of control. Have you talked to her?"

"Talk, talk," my mother said, with a sort of tense laugh in her voice. "We talk till we're blue in the face, it doesn't matter. People always say talk to your kids, but what if they don't listen? Maybe there's a point where you're paying too much attention."

"Libby's right," Dad said. "Talking only seems to backfire. I think we're going to try professional counseling again."

"Well, it couldn't hurt," said Patera. He lowered his voice. "Again, not that I want to be a buttinsky, but is she still spending time with that Gerthoff kid? Is her behavior because of his accident maybe?"

Doris and I exchanged looks. She stood very close to me and the hall was warm with our bodies. I moved away from her, closer to the kitchen. I didn't want her to know how sweaty-scared I was.

"Well," Dad said, "she feels bad for him, but it's all over with between them, thank God. I put an end to that."

His attempt at toughness seemed to convince Mr. Patera, who didn't say anything else about it. I wished he had, because my father's words were like a further dark hint about Jimmy and our family. And about this other side of Dad, revealing itself in piercing flashes. A strange feeling came over me, like when you look at some object that you've seen a thousand times and notice it doesn't look the same, and you wonder: Was it always like that?

"You think it's all because of Jimmy?" Doris whispered. She'd moved nearer again, and our arms touched.

"Get away from me," I said, and rushed back to my room.

Diane was grounded for a while (so she had to miss a Neil Young concert, among lesser things). The Pateras agreed not to press charges, but only if Diane would re-enter therapy for what my parents called her "self-destructive behavior." She did begin counseling again, with a different doctor this time—a psychiatrist rather than a psychologist. I could tell from the way everyone talked that this was a significant and worrisome difference.

A few days after the Patera incident, I went to see my grandfather. The House Judiciary Committee had just voted articles of impeachment against the president (we heard this phrasing over and over). Avo was somber and mostly silent. We sat on Adirondack chairs together at the beach, looking out at the trash left amid the rocks and driftwood. Nobody used this beach much except for walking, and it was another juvenile delinquent hangout I was told to stay away from. Avo had once had a small boat, which he'd take out on the calm bay to fish and relax, but he'd stopped using it because he couldn't venture out far enough to get past the pollution. He mumbled a few words now, about the piers that used to be there, back when the water was clear.

I'd thought he might somehow help me deal with my fear and puzzlement about Diane, but we didn't talk about her. I wondered what Avo was thinking. Maybe he felt vindicated, about both Nixon and Diane, as if it was all exactly what he'd foreseen, an unheeded prophet proven right. He'd always believed that Diane's form of rebellion was selfish and useless. Or maybe it upset him too much to talk about it.

"Plants and trees," he said, out of nowhere. "Only as good as the soil they grow from, Papa would say." His papa? I wondered. I tried to imagine someone so remote in time and space, who had actually lived in that green, hilly country of clustered seaside villages and stone farmhouses that seemed to exist only in Avo's stories and my imagination. Someone long gone, who would be impossibly old now. It felt equally impossible that Avo had been young way back then, back there.

Avo had nothing else to say, so we looked out toward the ocean for a while and I wondered if he was thinking about the other side.

Biking home, I pondered contamination. I imagined the dump grown to a dark mountain, with Claytown right under it, like Pompeii in the shadow of Vesuvius.

Despite her protests, Diane soon began taking a doctor-prescribed, mood-altering drug. She sensed a plot, though, to force her into a conventional life and take away her freedom. She pointed to the police, schools, mainstream churches, and the Swim Club, among other dark forces, all of which wanted to stamp out premarital sex, drugs not controlled by the medical establishment, and alternative religions. Diane had, of course, talked to me now and then about this oppressive cabal, but I'd thought it was some crazy joke. Now it didn't seem much farther out than some of the things Avo was saying, or that I was thinking myself.

One night I passed by Diane's room and heard her crying. I stood watching at the door: she was bent over her desk, head pressed down into her arm. She looked up quickly as if sensing me, and I felt a stab of panic at meeting her bleary gaze. But she gave me a tepid smile and asked me to come in. I sat on her bed. It seemed to calm her to have me there. I asked what was wrong, and she said she didn't know, but it felt like someone had died. Like she was in mourning. She'd been feeling that way for a long time, she told me. Then she joked about being morbid and laughed. She asked me how I was getting on with my reading. I said fine, wanting to say something else, to help her or ask questions, but it was all too large and baffling, and saying anything might make it worse. We sat awhile silently. I felt embarrassed, helpless. I asked if she was okay. She said yes, and I got up to leave. "Sometimes things just hurt," she added. "But I'm all right." I only nodded, full of thoughts and feelings like a flood that would burst the tight confines of words. She never explained what she'd meant about mourning.

My father had been insisting more and more often as July became August that I shouldn't spend time with Jimmy, even though Dad had taken me to see him released and couldn't seem to stop talking about him. Jimmy had started physical therapy. He was at the Ward house a lot, Dad said, and I certainly shouldn't be hanging around there. Of course, this warning further fed a curiosity that remained unsatisfied—since he'd gotten out of the hospital, I hadn't seen Jimmy around at all and hadn't heard about him from Bentley or Solomon. Without Jimmy, it didn't seem we'd get any closer to discovering why all those trucks were grinding through the night toward the landfill and back. I saw them now in my dreams, weird life forms creeping across stark, prehistoric, otherworldly landscapes as I viewed them from above, clasped by my spaceman angel. Jimmy, it seemed to me, had gone much farther into these mysterious places.

One early-August evening we all sat together in the living room watching President Nixon's resignation on TV. My grandfather sat at one end of the sofa, sinking down into the corner, hand to his head. He didn't say anything until after the speech, when he announced that he had to go home. "Nixon's not the only one who's got some packing up to do," he said. Nobody paid much attention to this, since it was the sort of puzzling thing Avo was always saying now, when he spoke at all.

A couple of evenings later, Bentley called and told me that there was something he wanted me to see out near Ward's place. He'd found Jimmy, he said, as if he'd been lost. It was like some teasing riddle, like one of Jimmy's, in fact, but I didn't question it.

We got off the bus and walked together down the quiet street, past the hospital. Trees and telephone poles cast long shadows onto the brick entryway where I'd seen Jimmy emerge in a wheelchair. The humid evening air had a stagnant, fishy smell as we crossed the street to Ward's property. The side of the house facing us receded in deep shadow. I pictured all the rooms inside locked in that distant parallel world I'd glimpsed in the antique mirror.

Bentley led me past the house, toward the marina, and rows of small boats appeared—masts and cabins and raised outboard motors silhouetted in the late light. I'd been silent, but now I asked Bentley where we were going. He smiled without looking at me and said, "You'll see."

So I followed him as we picked up speed, energized by anticipation I didn't know the source of, moving past the bayfront perimeter of Ward's property and on to the woods at its other end. Here the docks gave way to rocky sand between the woods and the narrow channel to the bay. Two or three cars were parked there, at the edge of the trees, facing the water. Reflected lights shimmered on its surface, and across the bay more lights were blinking on in the gray outline of the Atlantic Highlands. I remembered the view from over there, how small our neighborhoods had looked.

"This is where they meet almost every night now," Bentley whispered, so close to my ear I could feel his warm breath.

"'They' who?"

This time he laughed, in a deep, almost malicious way, and clapped his hand over his mouth. He walked ahead and waved me on to follow. He disappeared into the woods, already dark because there were no streetlights that far down, and I hurried to catch up. We scrunched through twigs, thick grass, and weeds, and Bentley crouched down amid the clumps of green. Despite glimpsing some poison ivy, I got down beside him and put my hand on his shoulder. I looked where he was looking, at the car parked nearest the woods, apart from the other cars. It was Jimmy's father's Lincoln. Two figures were outlined in the front seat, close together, looking out at the water—Jimmy and Theona. Music thumped from the open car windows: disco with some squealing female singer, stuff I couldn't stand and figured Jimmy wouldn't listen to. Must be her choice, I thought.

My face felt hot even amid the cool trees, and there was a tugging pressure in my crotch. The car door opened, and both of them got out the same side, the passenger side, facing away from the other cars and the boatyard. I felt Bentley's shoulder tense and I squeezed it as Jimmy and Theona lay down together on the sandy soil and started kissing, stroking, undressing. We stayed very still, but we were both breathing hard, and I wondered how and why Jimmy was doing this two weeks after getting out of the hospital and why they weren't at least doing it in the car like in the movies. Dad's words about physical therapy came back to me, and I tried not to laugh.

Then the unbelievable happened: Jimmy yanked his

pants down and his underpants as he got on top of Theona. His ass was round and muscular, a man's ass, and on his lower back shone a purple bruise, slick with sweat. Bentley swallowed hard, and he tensed again. Jimmy lifted himself, and pulled Theona's top up and off. She wore no bra, and her breasts were fully revealed—globes of skin with impossibly huge dark circles at their centers. Jimmy began stroking, squeezing, kissing them.

"Holy shit," Bentley said, and I could hear his breathing as quick as mine.

I still had my hand on Bentley's shoulder as we watched the couple moving in ways that seemed alien yet familiar, like it was happening far outside me yet inside me at the same time. I stared at Jimmy's ass, tensing and releasing, and his balls darkly outlined between his flexing thighs, and I felt his motions in my own body. My dick tightened against my pants, and I could smell sweat. Bentley shook me off with a sharp, low "quit it," and I realized, with a jolt of bliss and terror, that I'd been squeezing him harder and pressing against him. It was like the air all around was sweating and breathing, like something alive. The excitement scared me—inside us, surrounding us—but I didn't want it to stop. Jimmy and Theona's loud, quick breaths became low, urgent moans that also seemed to encircle and fill us until they lessened into sighs and murmuring. They were lying still now, and I could hear Jimmy's voice, deep and strangely sad, repeating some phrase over and over. Theona answered him in a whisper, and she laughed softly as he kissed her cheek, nose, forehead.

Slowly Bentley stood up, and motioned for me to follow him, hinting there was more to see. I couldn't keep my eyes off the hard-on visible through his shorts. With that and my own stiff cock, I was stumbling as I tried to keep up.

Bentley abruptly stopped, and I nearly bumped into him.

"Wait," he said. "Look over there." Pointing, he laughed again, a nasty seen-it-all laugh. I followed his finger's direction out over the road toward Ward's property. And there on a tree stump, holding a pair of binoculars to his eyes, stood the lord of the manor himself. I jumped back, thinking at first he was watching us, but Bentley corrected me, still laughing.

"Them," he said.

Of course, of course, he was watching them.

TEN

My grandfather spent more and more time with us in those first weeks of August. He seemed to want company, despite his increasingly narrow communication. He would sit shaking his head as if at some thought that had invaded his mind, or he'd be reading books on politics or history and let out laughs and phrases in agreement or annoyed dissent. Sometimes he'd work on his map. The more he was with us, the further away he seemed. He drifted into distances. He'd look up with that squinting but sharp gaze, briefly startled at his surroundings, at the immediate world—including us—beyond his thoughts. It frightened me to look back at him.

We all watched the new president address the nation, informing us that our long national nightmare was over. At the end of the speech, Avo exclaimed "Ha!" and called Ford a moron. Nobody defended the president, although my father said, not exactly to the point, "And McGovern would've been better? Begging the North Vietnamese to give back our prisoners?" My mother expressed the hope that we could all now look toward happier days for our country. This brought out another "Ha!" from my grandfather.

The governmental purgation didn't change much in our lives, it seemed. By mid-August I was writing things in my religious instruction journal that I knew I'd never show to Sister Michael Mary (or put in the school paper). It seemed I was writing to someone else, although I couldn't see or name who it was. This silent confidant might exist in some distant unseen world, so far away it could be at once the past and the future, and yet might perceive my secrets. I toted the journal, my portable thought-catcher. I wrote a lot about Jimmy, as if working through the confusion about him would somehow clear up everything else. I tried to explain my pendulum feelings, how Jimmy sometimes seemed like a smart, cool, caring guy and other times like a reckless jerk. I described his sex with Theona down by the water, and I could feel again the thick night air, the wonder, the hypnotic, fearful lust—for Jimmy, for Theona, for Bentley, all mixed. I put down my thoughts about Claytown, how it felt like another home, like a memory of someplace I'd never actually seen before, and how people there seemed to be gradually, scarily disappearing. I asked questions about Claytown and Ward. I described my grandfather's situation and his crazy ideas, which I couldn't get out of my head.

There was no way I could make sense of all this, or say how it was teaching me anything, or how I was doing any good for anybody. But it didn't matter, since—at Sister M's bidding—I'd gone way beyond the original assignment and was writing freely, without a point or moral, exploring strange territory. Only the describing mattered for now. Anyway, doing good things in the world seemed like something you told children to do until they no longer believed it, like Santa Claus. Or until they discovered how complicated such a task could be.

I'd been spending a lot of time in the house, so when Doris asked me one morning to join a softball game, I jumped at the chance. It was a weekly game in an empty lot. I hadn't been part of it for a long time, but I needed to get out again, away from murky thoughts about Jimmy, my family, Claytown. It would be great to play in a game whose rules were clear as the bright day's sky and air. Maybe, I thought, we'd have fun the way we all used to. Maybe I could outrun all the changes and fears. But as I walked with Doris ("slow down," she said, "what's the hurry?"), I felt how much it wasn't the way it used to be. I was uncomfortable with her. I felt like a bundle of things all competing, affinities clashing, thoughts about guys and girls and sex like electrical wires tangling. Doris, even with her social fears, seemed a calm contrast, as if she knew exactly who and where she was.

Once we started playing ball, though, things got better. That afternoon was charmed, and I hit the ball nearly every time I came to bat. Maybe it was built-up tension, maybe it was watching Bentley play: his blade-sharp focus, his taut arms gripping the bat, his strong swing. I tried to imitate him, and in one blastoff moment in the fifth inning, I felt the bat contact the ball in just the right thudding way and watched it arc free of all reaching gloves, all obstacles, and land somewhere between second and third base in the outfield. The fielder flubbed his throw, and I ran and ran, the grassy wind in my face, around to second. It was a great view from there. All threats seemed far away—except for that of third baseman Joey De Julio, who tagged me out on the next play.

All this fun pretty much dissolved by dinnertime. In one way, the meal seemed fairly normal, that is to say unusual: Diane was there and actually in a good mood, at least for a while. But my mother was distracted and silent. So was

Dad. After we'd finished, Mom said, "Your father has something to say."

The "your father" thing was not a good sign. Diane rolled her eyes but I couldn't share her peevish amusement. My muscles, pleasurably achy, tensed.

"It's about your grandfather," Dad began, in a strangely toneless emotionless voice. "He will be coming to live with us. He can't stay in his house any longer. It's going to be torn down."

"What?" Diane said. It was as if she'd suddenly awakened to Avo's plight for the first time. "They can't do that. Don't we live in a free country? What about property rights?"

I thought Dad would yell at her for that last question. But he only sighed. "Take it easy, Diane," he said. "The fact is your grandfather doesn't own that house. He rents it. When we bought this place, he and your grandmother wanted to move down here, too, but they couldn't afford to buy. I know, he treats it like his property and we all sort of came to think of it that way, but it isn't. The owners, the ones who started that little commie colony over there, live out in Basking Ridge now and accepted an offer from the developers. A lotta money. Who can blame them?"

"*I* can," Diane said. "Greedy hypocrites. Jimmy's father is like the Gestapo. It's evil."

There was a sudden silence, a collective jolt, as if there'd been a loud boom or the lights had flickered. Dad stared at Diane and his eyes blinked a few times; he was holding something back, it seemed. He took a long breath and calmly explained that Avo wasn't paying market rent and couldn't afford a new place, and he wasn't so healthy anymore. As my father spoke, my mother kept nodding in agreement, her face tight as if she was afraid to loosen it.

Later that evening, lying on my bed, I thought again of all the things that Avo had told me about his life, the story they made: the farmboy in breeches throwing rocks at priests and bigshots, the merchant seaman laboring his way to New York on an antique cargo ship that reeked of oil and bilge; the greenhorn finding fellow Portuguese, mostly from New England, on the Newark docks, then conniving jobs, reading American newspapers for their everyday English, hauling crates of produce with splintered hands; stashing meager money to become, finally, the respectable store-owner, newly middleclass in his shirt and tie. Living now in a leafy corner of a New World city but feeling he'd come full circle, the lording landowners still asserting their privilege. After all he'd gone through, Avo would now be thrown out. His life would shrink to one upstairs room, without the ocean and the beach and the woods outside his door. He'd be confined there, it seemed. And of course the whole colony would crumble. The few people still living there would be forced to leave those fragile, obsolete bungalows.

I felt like jumping up to do something, fight someone. But what, who? It wasn't like some heroic tale. I could hear Diane spitting the word *evil*, as if an obscure deadly threat were spreading over all of us.

The word itself stayed in my mind after my flash of anger faded, so I decided to look it up, to clarify it. I wrote down the definitions in my journal: 1. a) Morally bad or wrong; wicked; depraved. b) Resulting from or based on conduct regarded as immoral [an "evil" reputation]. 2. Causing pain or trouble; harmful; injurious. 3. Offensive or disgusting [an "evil" odor]. 4. Threatening or bringing misfortune; unlucky; disastrous; unfortunate [an "evil" hour].

These definitions did seem to lurk in the occurrences around us, as if buried in them like a secret substance, much more than *good*, the supposed opposite, the thing we were told to strive for. But even though I felt these extremes strongly and knew lots of people I'd have called "good," neither word fit, really. It was like people and events were sliding away from explanations, from the labels anyone tried to put on them.

Once again it seemed that Diane was exaggerating, but those exaggerations were like a sudden eruption of feelings long hidden.

In the days that followed, when the subject of Avo's house came up, my father went on defending the builders and their need to make money (often arguing with Diane), while my mother tried to ignore it all, preferring to focus on the upcoming luau, maintaining her hope for one perfect late-summer party.

I began to wonder again about the puzzling connections among things and people. The common denominator in all of it, for me, was still Jimmy. He worked for his father's company, after all, and they were the ones destroying the house, and they were building houses near the landfill. He had a new car already, a brand-new Camaro in bright red, and I would see him flashing by sometimes, with Theona, with kids around my age, once with Eddie Randono. Jimmy had resumed his many-sided life, it seemed, his intense work and play. And yet there were so many contradictions in him, so many conflicting forces. It still seemed to me that all the conflicts would smooth out. Yet often now the sight and sound of his car only made me imagine some dangerous, hungry thing in swift pursuit.

I took the bus out to Claytown one afternoon later that week. Bentley came with me; I still didn't want to go alone, much as I liked being there. I guess Bentley liked something about the place, too, about Solomon and the other people there, despite his outward cool and bursts of nastiness.

As we rounded the big hill with the grand house, I recalled my father's almost trancelike words about

Bultmann. I wondered again if Bultmann ghosts might be wandering through all those rooms, reliving corrupted lives or violent deaths. Or maybe the ghosts were far below, in the former clay pits. Unacknowledged ghosts of forgotten victims.

Solomon met us at the bus stop. We walked to the house on a different road, winding deeper into Claytown. It was mostly trees on both sides, with houses half-hidden among them. Solomon pointed to a house on the right: two stories and an attic, shaped like the simple triangle-atop-square houses that we drew in kindergarten, but with a wide front porch framed by carved wood railings and trim. It was freshly painted and had a deep green lawn and bright flowerbeds out front. Solomon told us it was the Woodrows' house. "You should see the inside," he said. "Filled with all kinds of stuff they bought on their trips. They used to travel a lot, all over. It's just the two of them there, no kids."

A little farther up the road, Solomon gestured to the opposite side, to a house like a concrete cube close to the street (there were barely any sidewalks). A brick path led up to the house, whose stucco façade glistened in the sun. In fact, the whole house seemed to reflect the light.

"Dalton's house," said Solomon. "That's all glass. Pieces of glass stuck in the cement. All kinds of bottles, broken up and pressed into the surface."

He explained that Dalton's father had built the house and put in most of the glass—an old African tradition. Dalton had continued the decoration, and now he had a huge collection of fancy jars and bottles, all kinds of glass stuff.

"My gran says there's so much glass in there you're afraid to move."

We walked past the house. As the sun caught different bits of glass, varied colors sparkled out like a kaleidoscope. I figured there wasn't another house like that anywhere, and it made me think of Dalton differently from the way he'd seemed at the picnic.

We shortcutted to Solomon's place through the woods between two houses that looked almost derelict. Solomon said nothing about them. We heard a hammering sound as we approached the back of his house, and there, nailing loose clapboards in place, was Jimmy. I felt a rush of excited shame and couldn't look at him. I had a lot of questions, but it seemed impossible to ask them.

"Didn't know you were here," Solomon said. This sounded disapproving, a little anxious, as if Jimmy hadn't followed some schedule or plan.

"Been meaning to come over," Jimmy said. "I had some free time from the construction sites. Does that meet with your approval?"

He smiled, and got Solomon to smile back, then resumed his work.

Feen welcomed us, offering ham sandwiches and lemonade. This time Solomon's grandfather sat at the kitchen table, smoking and coughing. He leaned his thin arms on the table, as if to hold himself up, and watched us through glasses too large for his hollowed face.

"Won't give up those cigarettes, this man," Feen said. "Doctor told him they'll kill him, but does he listen? Won't listen to me, either."

"Argh, the doctor," said George in a phlegm-rattled voice. "Takes away all your pleasures, so who wants to live, then?"

This sounded like a familiar routine between them, but George was aware of a new audience. "Can't have that stuff, neither," he said, pointing a shaky finger at our sandwiches. "Might as well feed it to white boys."

"Hush now," said Feen.

"We don't see many white kids over this way," her husband said. "That Gerthoff boy sometimes. Outside there now, hammering away. Had a close call, that one. Lucky he wasn't killed."

"I invited them, Poppa," said Solomon. "They're my friends."

George examined us. His eyes were milky gray. "I used to have white friends," he said. It was spoken flatly, a neutral observation. He began to say something else, but the words were sliced off by another coughing fit.

Solomon got up and walked over to his grandfather. He patted his back and reached for a small inhaler sitting on the table next to an ashtray in which half a cigarette burned. He put the inhaler in his grandfather's hand and nudged his arm; the old man raised the device to his mouth and pressed on it. It made whooshing sounds as he repeated the motion. Solomon took up the cigarette and pressed it into the ashtray until its smoke stopped rising, then he took the inhaler and set it down on the table.

"It's good this boy has friends," George said once the coughing calmed. "He's a good kid. But alone a lot. Not many kids his own age here. Mostly it's the old here now. The old ones and the dead ones. In a way you can't blame his father for hauling ass out of here."

Solomon looked up at Feen, who had been watching silently with hands on hips. "You boys finished?" she said. "Why don't you all go out and get some air. I need to clean up in here."

We drank the last of our lemonades and went out through the kitchen door. I was wondering about Solomon's father.

Feen followed us. She watched Jimmy working, told him he'd done enough for a hot day, that he was still recovering and shouldn't overdo. "Come inside and have a cold drink," she said.

He nodded. "Just a few more minutes. Almost done."

She went back inside.

"Where you guys headed?" Jimmy asked.

"Woods," Solomon replied.

"Careful," Jimmy said, with an odd laugh, some oblique comment on his own warning. I still couldn't meet his eyes.

Wet with pond water, stripped to our shorts, we sat in a patch of sun on warm, bare earth. The only sounds were those of the forest itself, alive around us: the hammering of a woodpecker, the rustle of chipmunks, pond-life plopping into the water. I could almost believe we sat in wilderness, and that time was suspended, not moving us toward summer's end. Not taking us back into society.

Solomon and Bentley both lay on their backs in the dirt with their hands behind their heads, looking up at treetops and sky. Both of them had rounded muscles on their upper arms; mine were punier but expanding. I lay on my side, facing them.

"So how come you don't have friends here?" Bentley asked, out of the sky's blue.

"I got friends," Solomon replied. "In school."

"But they're white."

"Mostly," Solomon said, unfazed. "There are some black kids here I know, too. In church and Sunday School. But most of them don't live here. They're not around all that often."

This opening-up only emphasized how much Solomon kept to himself. He had never mentioned his parents. We had never seen his room because he'd never invited us in to see it. Our visits were always in the kitchen or outdoors: the woods, the pond, the tree house.

He told us he'd never really liked the North Shore boys, with their fighting and smoking, their need to act tough. They all wanted to be cool, but all in the same way—same clothes, same talk, same music, same everything. They didn't like difference or deviation. Loners were losers. "You pick up a book they call you a fag," he said.

That was a fearsome term, although I think we all had pretty hazy ideas of its meaning. Solomon looked at me, and I stared back, a little queasy, shaky. He blinked nervously and looked away. I lay back, and after a while turned my head toward him. He was looking at me again. His hand was very close to mine, and he moved it so that we were just touching. My shakiness became a kind of current that gathered and tightened in my crotch. He looked at me fixedly, as if scared to move, and we stayed like that, in trembly contact, until he pulled his hand away. I wasn't sure what had happened, but I knew that was the end of it, and that we wouldn't talk about it. He looked up toward the sky again, hands at his sides.

I glanced at Bentley, who didn't seem to have noticed or didn't care.

We lay on our backs silently awhile longer.

"Got any brothers or sisters?" Bentley asked Solomon.

"No," Solomon said, after a few seconds. We were sitting up now. I could tell Solomon wanted to say something else. Saying was hard for him, as if the words wouldn't be good enough or would pull him away from what he actually thought or felt. I knew what that was like.

We didn't force it with more questions, and he continued, telling us about his mother, who lived in Virginia and didn't come up to New York much. She'd had a lot of troubles, and she thought he was better off with his grandparents. He used to go down there in the summers but hadn't been for a long time. She'd gotten married again.

After this outpouring, like a sudden brief rain, nobody said anything for a while. It was pretty clear that Solomon didn't like his mother's new husband. But it seemed like that had to be left unsaid.

Solomon asked us if we'd had fun at Ward's place, and we said yeah we had. He told us that usually there weren't more than ten kids at a time there. It went on in the winter, too, with fewer kids: all those neat things in the rec room, chess or reading by the fireplace in the parlor, in soft wide armchairs. Ward would serve hot cocoa and he'd talk, mostly about the house and land, their history, and the people from Claytown who once worked there. "I had the feeling he was trying to explain something," Solomon said. "Like I needed to understand. But I didn't get it. And I didn't really want to hear about things that were so long over with. That's all the old people talk about around here. But Ward seems all right. I like him."

"What about Jimmy?" I asked.

Solomon sat up, drew his knees up toward his chest and clasped his hands in front of them. He looked at me awhile, as if trying to gauge what I'd meant by the question, but the question itself didn't surprise him. He recited facts, most of which we knew: that Jimmy worked for Ward, and part of that was coming to Claytown to fix up houses and otherwise help people out. He organized games there sometimes—softball, touch football, soccer. And of course he gave rides in his car, mostly over to Ward's house.

"Jimmy's fun, but he can be sort of bossy and stuck-up and sometimes it's like he's just pretending about things. It's hard to explain. But he's a good guy."

"He is," he added, as if I'd objected.

I was about to ask what was going on between Ward and Jimmy, but I wasn't sure I wanted to know the answer. The *fag* word and our silent touching still lingered, as if in the air around us.

So I asked about Theona.

"Well, she's not from here," Solomon said. "My grandmother calls her a harlot."

I looked at Bentley, who was lying on his side, grinning.

"What's that?" I asked Solomon.

"You know, a woman who sleeps around."

"We saw them screwing," Bentley said.

"You what?" Solomon said.

Bentley laughed and Solomon laughed too, but as if he didn't want to.

"And we saw Ward looking at them with binoculars," Bentley continued. Solomon's laughter ceased as if a needle had lifted from a phonograph record. He stared at Bentley.

"You're crazy. You're making that up."

"Luke was there. Ask him."

Solomon turned to me. He looked confused, almost panicked. I nodded. My belly gurgled and I felt I might be getting sick. I wanted to tell Bentley to shut up now.

"No," Solomon said. "That can't be true." He got up. Dirt caked his back and shorts. He started walking in swift strides toward the empty, quiet road. We followed him to the spot where Jimmy's car had crashed. I looked at the scarred tree and felt it rush toward me. I flinched, as if dodging it.

We all just stood there, and nobody said anything else about Ward's behavior or Jimmy and Theona.

We walked back to the house, where Solomon abruptly stopped again. He pointed to something ahead. "I guess Jimmy hasn't fixed that yet," he said.

A large X of tape partially covered a jagged hole in one front window. I'd noticed it before but hadn't thought much about it, since so many Claytown houses had patched or even boarded windows.

"Scary stuff going on," Solomon said. "You know that truck that chased Jimmy, well, I didn't tell you that same truck came by here like a week later, and the guys in it threw a rock through our window."

"Holy shit," Bentley said. "Anybody get hurt?"

"No. It was late, like eleven. No one was in the front hall. I was taking out the garbage and I heard the glass breaking, then I saw the truck speeding away. Couldn't see it too well, but I'm sure it was the same truck."

How could he be sure, I wondered. I asked if they'd called the police.

A brief smile bent Solomon's mouth. "Yeah. But like gran said, 'Claytown is a low priority.' And we had no proof."

I tasted forced-up lemonade in my throat and tried to re-swallow it.

"There was a broken window," I said.

"That doesn't prove much," Bentley said.

"No," Solomon said. "And, well, my grandparents don't like to make trouble. Lots of people here feel like that. Nobody's really sure what's going on."

Solomon told us what he'd been thinking: that it was all connected to the landfill, and it was mostly happening after dark. He had seen red and white lights in the darkness like ships on some angled sea, gliding up and down the barely visible trash hills, and he'd heard, louder against the night's silence, the steady mechanical hum that we could sometimes hear during the day. And even louder sounds: the crack and thud of trees falling. In the daytime, he'd found the knocked-down trees in a large cleared space just outside the landfill, on lots Claytown people laid claim to.

He had also seen Jimmy again, driving up to the end of the road, parking, walking through the woods. Solomon wouldn't dare follow in the dark, but he figured Jimmy was there to find out something. And he had the feeling that Sebastian Ward was involved, too.

We went back to Ward's house a couple of days later, on another warm afternoon. The place kept drawing us back, despite our misgivings. On the way, Solomon started talking about Ward's spying. He didn't believe what we'd told him, or he had other explanations for it—maybe Ward was just looking at boats, or birdwatching (notions that made Bentley laugh). I didn't want to talk or think about it, but of course I thought about it. I knew we'd been gawking at Jimmy and Theona, too, but an adult watching them was something else altogether.

There were only a few kids there, including Daryl and Beth and a quiet, thin-faced boy named Mark we hadn't met. Ward was welcoming, even though we'd come there without Jimmy—it seemed Solomon could visit anytime he liked. Jimmy was in the yard. He stood watching Daryl shoot baskets, shouting encouragement like a proud older brother, although Daryl looked skilled and sure and wasn't paying Jimmy much attention. Jimmy's chest was pale and shrunken and stitches traversed his torso like rusty tracks. I hadn't noticed them in that dusk when we saw him with Theona or when he was working in Claytown.

When Daryl saw us, he asked Solomon to join him.

"Not much good at basketball," Solomon said.

"But I am," Bentley said.

Daryl gave him an unsure, sizing-up look, and nodded. "Okay then," he said.

They started an intense one-on-one; the shifting ball, the dodgy jumping moves, the clash and interplay pulled us all in and charged us up, Jimmy especially. He clapped and whooped and mirrored the moves of the game like he was in it. I kept picturing him naked, oblivious to pain, immersed in the rhythms of sex.

Solomon and I meandered to the swing, where we found Mark gently rocking. He said, "Hello," in a lilting, British sort of voice. We joined him and talked about Claytown, where he was visiting his aunt, his dad's sister. Mark lived in Brooklyn near Daryl and Beth. He told us that his aunt's house was falling apart, and she had no money to fix it, so she was selling it. Some men had come by and offered her "a fortune." They were a little scary—fancy clothes and cars, big muscles, loud talk—but after thinking about it for a few weeks she took the offer. So she was going to Brooklyn, too, near his parents and him.

"I guess this is my last visit here," he said.

After a few silent minutes, we heard shouting, and all of us ran back toward the house. Daryl was pointing and yelling—at Bentley, I thought. But in fact he was pissed at Jimmy, telling him to quit watching them like he was their coach or their father, and that he had no right telling them what to do. Jimmy raised his hands in a calm-down gesture and walked off, away from them and us. Daryl and Bentley stared after him awhile and resumed their game. We didn't interfere and left, too.

We played some tennis, swam in the pool near the bay-side road (Jimmy was lifeguard for a while). The wind off the water cooled our slick skin. Ward took Solomon, Mark, and me down to the marina and guided us aboard his yacht, which was tethered and bobbing in its dock. He let us sit in the captain's chair before seating himself there, sipping a drink he'd carried down from the house. He watched as we leaned over the side, looking at small fish and tadpoles. He asked if we'd like a ride, but before we could answer he laughed and said, "Not today." I wouldn't have gone anyway—the thought of Ward at the wheel scared me for reasons beyond that drink in his hand.

On the way back to the house, with Ward walking ahead, I asked Solomon if he had ridden on the boat.

"Sure," he said. "It's fun. Out there in the bay, like the middle of the ocean. And we fish."

"Does he drink booze out there?" I whispered.

Solomon stared. "But Jimmy's there. He steers the boat. He's got a license."

"Oh," I said, not convinced.

For a while that afternoon, Ward seemed like the world-wise, eccentric but benevolent aristocrat I'd sometimes imagined him, offering us a sort of safe place to be whatever we were—or fancied (or feared) we were, however different it might be. He strolled around, pausing to watch kids competing on the tennis court or playing catch or throwing Frisbees. Or improvising games that had no established form. He'd call out to some by name, asking if they were having fun, giving gentle warnings, shouting compliments and encouragement. He seemed happy watching them, with an eager sort of look, almost as if he'd like to be out there, too, running across the broad lawns. But there was always a distance, even when he briefly put a hand on some kid's shoulder or head, like he wanted to connect but couldn't really. After an hour or so, he returned to the cool shadows of his house to sit amid the dimly lit relics of another time. Solomon, Bentley, and I joined him there later, sweaty-exhausted in a way that felt good, while Mark and Daryl went off to find Beth.

Jimmy wandered around the property, too, looking for things that needed doing. Apparently he didn't find many—before long he sauntered, shirtless, into the parlor, where we were sipping cold drinks while Ward talked. He did love to talk.

"Why don't you go lie down upstairs?" Ward said to Jimmy. "You look flushed and tired. You still need rest."

"Not a bad idea," Jimmy replied. As he passed by, Ward reached out and patted his arm.

Ward told us that Jimmy spent a couple of afternoons a week there, when he needed to get away from "that environment" at home. He didn't say anything more about Jimmy's family or what was going on around Claytown. Instead, looking from one object to another in the room, he returned to his favorite topic: history. "The past determines so much of what is happening now," he told us, like some professor or TV narrator. "You can't escape it. Patterns repeat."

Bentley and I shared a small sofa while Solomon had settled into a wingback chair that he seemed to find comfortable and familiar. Ward faced us as he leaned back against the plump cushion of a large armchair, his fingertips pressed together as he spoke. He wore a white shirt open a couple of buttons, loose black pants, sandals. Occasionally he'd take a sip from that same glass he'd been carrying (and refilling) all day, it seemed—a rum and Coke, he'd told us, a "Cuba Libre." The parlor was warm (Ward shunned air-conditioning), but a large ceiling fan swirled the air wafting through the tall windows.

I sat sipping rumless Coke from a crystal glass that I feared I'd drop and break. Ward gestured as he spoke, wide dramatic motions, and I thought of his hands touching Jimmy and grasping those binoculars as he watched Jimmy doing it with Theona. But the thoughts felt less frightening as I sat there watching and listening.

Ward's voice charmed and lulled us. The ticking mantle clock and the breeze billowing the long curtains were the only sounds aside from his easy cadences. He used big, old-fashioned words, as if talking to adults of some earlier era. At the same time, he seemed like a clever, strange child trying to form some bond in strangeness. I was happy, just then, to respond with my silent attention.

He talked about his family in the nineteenth century, as if they shared those many uninhabited rooms with him now. They were mostly good people, he said. But then he described one ancestor who seemed to especially fascinate him—to obsess him, even. Cornelius Ward, his name was—a ship owner, who had lived in the house in the 1840s and '50s. He had many important friends with estates nearby where they escaped from the city, people like William Cullen Bryant and Frederick Law Olmstead. They rode back and forth on Commodore Vanderbilt's steam ferry. He was another friend. (I wrote the names down and looked them up when I got home.)

Ward coughed, face flushed, and took a gulp of his drink. He continued: these people were friends only up to a point. Most were abolitionists, and Cornelius Ward had, if not slaves exactly, servants whom he treated like slaves. They worked on his boats or on the property. Some he had brought back from Caribbean islands, but most came from Claytown—mainly people who couldn't support themselves by farming or oyster harvesting. Cornelius would work these people hard, including the women and children. Mercilessly hard, he added, leaving the details for us to picture.

Through all this, Solomon had a distant expression, as if he'd heard it all before, which he likely had. But it seemed Ward wanted him to hear it again. It felt like a ritual of sorts, into which Bentley and I were now being initiated. As though three adolescent boys of a lower class sat as judges, an audience for some sort of unburdening. Gradually Ward's voice grew quieter; he stopped gesturing and almost seemed to be talking to himself. He described how Cornelius Ward, increasingly alone, took to sitting awake all night, drinking, in that very room we sat in now, frightened that his workers would rise up in a gang one night, kill him in his bed, burn down the house. He began to imagine them at the windows—angry, grasping knives and guns, smashing their way inside. Eventually he went crazy (*mad* was the term Ward used), and he died in an asylum in the city.

"A kind of justice," Ward said. "But the exploitation continued. We continued." His voice had turned somber and woozy, and I started getting restless, eyeing the doorways, as if Ward's darkening story were no longer cocooning but entrapping us; it was like we were all stranded in that house, on some farther-out island a long way from the mainland. It almost seemed like Ward couldn't leave that place, or that past he was reviving in words.

Solomon spoke now too—sudden, startling. He asked Ward outright what he and Jimmy were doing around Claytown and the landfill, and if that's why Jimmy was being chased that day he crashed. Solomon's boldness thrilled me, like he'd exploded that thing enclosing us.

"My," Ward said, "you boys have vivid imaginations."

"I saw it," Solomon said.

Ward smiled. "Ah," he said. "Well, yes. Jimmy had fled from the dump, and that truck was following him. He panicked and turned the wrong way. He was driving too fast."

"Why was he running away?" I asked, emboldened too.

Ward turned to me, no longer smiling. "I can't tell you, because he hasn't told me." He swirled the dark liquid in his glass. "You see, he's trying to find things out. *We're* trying. Maybe he'd seen too much."

After a pause, as if to let these ominous statements linger like the musty warmth in the room, he told us that one of his restaurants, in an old ship captain's house near Claytown, had been vandalized—windows shattered, vicious words scrawled across the front door. He blamed people with projects in and around the landfill. They knew he wanted to protect Claytown and save old buildings near there. Now even the Bultmann house might be demolished, and that house meant a lot to him, was part of his own family history—the Bultmanns, too, were family friends.

"Some say I'm doing all this for money," he said. "But sensible people know that I want to preserve the past. Keep memory from fading, what's left of it. And I'm trying to stop the greed and hatred."

Now we'd gotten into even murkier territory, way beyond us. It was like Ward was leading us toward the risky zones he had entered by asking Jimmy to snoop around the landfill—even though Jimmy's father was working on a project there and Jimmy had been threatened. Of course, Jimmy hadn't really been forced, it seemed. And no one was forcing us, either; we'd plunged in, wanting and fearing to know the whole story.

This time it was Bentley who mentioned the police. Ward shook his head and told us, no, the police did not trust him and he didn't trust them. He needed someone he could rely on to help, someone who genuinely wanted to find out the truth himself. Someone who could get in there and see what was happening. A witness. That's why he'd asked Jimmy. He and Jimmy had a lot in common, shared some of the same ideals. Some of the same burdens, too, he added.

Before Ward could further explain these baffling things—if he was going to—a door slammed, and footsteps sounded in the hallway. Ward looked toward the sounds and sat up suddenly in his chair. "But I shouldn't be talking to you like this," he said. "I forget how young you are."

As he spoke, Daryl and Mark raced into the room. Walking behind them was Beth. When the boys noticed us, they stopped short, breathing hard.

"Children," Ward said, a term he almost never used. "*What* are you doing? There is *no* running allowed inside the house."

"Sorry, Sebastian," Beth said. "They ran ahead."

One of the clocks chimed five, others overlapping and echoing it, and I said I had to leave.

Daryl asked Solomon if he was leaving, too.

Ward laughed. "No one has to leave. You can all stay," he said, sounding like a favorite uncle who isn't bound by the rules, dangling fun and adventure instead.

"No thanks," Solomon said. "I've gotta get home, too. My gran's waiting."

"Gotta leave, too," said Bentley.

"As you wish," Ward said.

The other three walked outside. "See ya, man," Daryl said to Solomon, who answered "Yeah." Daryl and Bentley said nothing to one another; their hoops camaraderie had vanished.

"Why should you take the bus, though," Ward continued. "I can get Jimmy to drive you."

"No," I said, too quickly and loudly. I wasn't exactly sure why I'd said it. Solomon and Bentley threw looks at me but didn't object.

On the way home, I asked Solomon about Mark.

"He comes from some island in the Caribbean. Trinidad I think. Part of his family ended up in Claytown like a hundred years ago, so he visits there. Cool accent. Usually hangs out with Daryl and Beth." He looked out the bus window awhile and added, "Mr. Ward really likes them, says they need his place more than I do." He sounded both proud and peeved.

He started talking again about Jimmy, and how we had to find out what was really going on at the landfill late at night, what Jimmy was doing there, almost getting himself killed like that. I wanted to find out, too, but Solomon seemed more anxious about it--maybe more was at stake for him than I could know.

Eleven

As August shifted into higher heat, things around our house turned even more Hawaiian. Currents of South Seas fantasy seemed to pour in with the air-conditioning, relief from our New York sweat-bath, which the TV weatherman, pointing to a triple H (*heat, haze, humidity*) on his hand-marked map, told us had no end in sight. We had no vacations planned, so we were all there together, mired in dog-day inertia. In contrast to this sticky closeness was distant, breeze-washed Hawaii, far beyond even California, out in the open Pacific miles and miles from anywhere. So it was tempting to lose ourselves in my mother's luau dreams. Even my father got back into the spirit—for a while. He resumed working on cardboard Tiki-god figures in the backyard. He'd discovered an old ukulele in the garage and would strum it while singing Don Ho novelty songs. This was his looser, funny side and we all enjoyed it, even if it emerged now only after he'd downed a couple of mai tais.

Through behavior modification, Diane was relearning to obey the Eighth Commandment (while she continued to break several of the others). Sometimes she'd try to pierce the palmy bubble in which my mother was enclosing us. On one otherwise tranquil Sunday, a tense discussion erupted on the subject of the patio: Could it accurately be called a *lanai*, as my mother had begun (half-jokingly) to do? Arguing against this usage, my sister spouted information about Hawaiian architecture, history, and culture with a confidence that made it all sound like bullshit. As it all got sillier, they both burst out laughing—they hadn't laughed together in a long time, and it was a relief to everyone.

One afternoon, I again saw my mother with her box of old photographs opened and emptied onto the bedspread. But this time she wasn't looking at them; she stood at the side of the bed with her arms raised and her head tilted to one side, eyes closed. She lifted one knee, then the other, in a pattern like a jig. She was dancing. I thought at first it was some embarrassing luau thing, but as I watched, I realized it had something to do with the photographs. A sort of high spread through me, a disorienting giddiness. This lone dancing was crazy and comical, but she was enjoying it. She went on, as if unaware of anything except her body moving, her bare feet making muffled thumps against the carpet until, abruptly, she stopped and slowly lowered her arms. She opened her eyes, blinking. Before she could notice me, I hurried away, still caught up in the daydream of a woman I knew as my mother but also hardly knew at all. I felt like I'd invaded some private refuge, and I wondered why she hadn't closed the door. If she was happy in that moment, it was a moment isolated from her everyday life, a time and place apart from all of us.

A few minutes later, in my own room, I heard her go down the hall, and then I heard her talking to my father. I sneaked back into their bedroom to see what photos she'd been looking at this time. On the bed was a single small picture: a girl of maybe twelve or thirteen wearing a brightly colored dress and blouse and a long scarf-like headpiece. Her arms were raised above her head, which was turned to one side. She was smiling but looked a little embarrassed, awkward. It was my mother, dancing. My mother as a foreigner, the child of foreigners. She stood on the top front step of my grandparents' row house in Newark.

I wanted to take the photo and keep it with the one of my young grandfather, but since she hadn't yet put it away, I knew she'd miss this one immediately. I left it there on the bed.

After dinner, my parents told me they'd received a note about me from Sister Michael Mary. They weren't used to correspondence from a nun. Their attitude about Sister M was ambivalent: they wanted me to have some religious education but not so much that I'd get serious about it. My father in particular didn't like the fact that Sister was still meeting with me over the summer. He knew I liked her, and he suspected I had a sort of crush, and he found this altogether too peculiar: a boy and a nun as friends. Growing up, Dad always had nuns and priests around and still had a sort of arms-length respect for them. And of course Mom had learned piety from my grandmother and Church-aversion from Avo and never talked about religion. So when, after the table had been cleared, they announced that they'd gotten the note, it was with an odd mingling of disapprovals.

"She says," my mother told me, "that she'd like to speak to us about you."

I was still thinking about my mother dancing, in the old photograph and in her very bedroom only a few hours earlier, so her parental sternness seemed to lack its usual heft and command.

"What would she want to talk about?" she asked.

"I don't know."

"Can you guess, maybe?" my father said, as he poured a generous amount of anisette into his espresso. (He drank this "black" coffee, while my mother preferred the weaker "American" brew.) "What have you been talking about with her? What have you told her?"

"He doesn't have to tell you that. He has some rights." This came, of course, from Diane, still at the table. I felt a rush of love for my big sister, the "public defender," as my father called her, even as I resented her for talking for me.

"Diane, maybe you should leave the room while we talk to Luke," Dad said.

Diane got up, giving our parents a venomous look and slamming her chair toward the table. She walked past me, pausing to lean in and whisper. "Don't you tell them anything you don't want to," she said into my ear, as if our parents were the secret police.

This only ratcheted up my fears: maybe Sister M wanted to talk about my interest in Claytown and Jimmy; maybe she'd make it all sound weird or dangerous, a matter for doctors, like Diane's kleptomania. But I couldn't believe Sister M capable of such betrayal.

"I've been talking to her about Avo," I said, keeping my voice steady even if my brain wasn't. "Things he's said to me."

"I've told you a million times," my father said. "Don't listen to everything your grandfather says. You let it go in one ear and out the other and believe maybe 10 percent of it. What's upsetting you now—the business with the house?"

"I guess so," I said. I wasn't sure that my parents were even aware of Avo's poisoning theory. It couldn't be true, I told myself, but if it wasn't true then my grandfather was in even deeper trouble. They'd lock him away somewhere in one of those loony houses I'd seen in late-night movies:

people screaming, tearing their hair, wandering around like zombies.

"Your grandfather will be okay," my mother said. I recalled the way she'd looked at Avo's photograph, and her own photo, and I tried to reconcile (again) what seemed like her clashing feelings about him.

"Yeah," I said.

No one spoke for a moment. The hum of the refrigerator seemed louder than normal.

"Is that all you were telling the Sister?" Dad said.

I looked down at the tabletop. "I talked to her about Jimmy," I said, and it felt good to say it.

"Oh, fine, fine," my mother said.

My father leaned closer to me, with a look of keen interest. "What exactly?" he said.

I repeated Sister M's hints about Jimmy's family, that their troubles had affected him.

"Oh, yeah, typical social worker thinking, blaming the parents," my father said. "Problem is he has no sense of responsibility. Something needs to be done. Racing his car around these streets like he's on the damn turnpike, no worries about gas prices for him, right? No worries about anything."

"John," my mother said.

"And taking up with black girls from the projects. Getting them in trouble, I bet."

"John!"

"Well, it's true. The nun isn't gonna tell Luke that. The worst part is that Jimmy thinks he can just fool around for the rest of his life. He's out there like a loose cannon. Rich kid with a draft deferment. Can't take orders from anybody. Won't settle down to anything. Making his father crazy, spending all that money on Hill College, and for what? So the kid can live a fantasy life? You can't have endless freedom, you can't go on trying to find yourself forever. You've got to face the world of reality sometime, tedious as it might be. You'd think crashing the car would've stopped him, but it didn't."

I stared at my father as he got more and more agitated and off the point. When he finished talking, he looked at me with a sort of angry confusion, and I looked away. Mom told me to go and stay in my room for a while, saying we'd go see Sister Michael Mary together and work this out. I got up, glancing at my mother and now avoiding my father's face.

Ward and my father weren't the only adults monitoring Jimmy's life, I discovered. He was becoming more and more a focus of attention around town, the way people sometimes do in small places. I learned that a particular group of men had been setting their sights on him, a group whose discontents had gradually tightened into anger. It included several fathers of Jimmy's former girlfriends, although that connection wasn't clear until later, and Jimmy wasn't the first or sole target. This club of sorts had formed years earlier at a local bar, the Underbridge Inn, so named for its location beneath the ramp of the bridge to Jersey, and they continued to meet there. They labeled themselves a community watch group but had become increasingly focused on "cleaning up" Wardville, fixing what they considered its social problems.

I knew all this because one of the newest members, it turned out, was my father. At first I couldn't believe it—although he had joined or lent his name to some community protests (opposing a highway or the location of a prison or a polluting industry nearby), my father had never been part of anything like this. Dad had never cared much what other people did with their lives as long as they weren't impinging on his or ours. But that had changed, it seemed. Maybe he was thinking differently about who and what was impinging.

The guys who met at the Underbridge mostly weren't in the luau-planning crowd. They were more working-class, more outspoken about their fears and hatreds, things the Swim Club people would rarely talk about openly. Several worked for Jimmy's father's company. Others were city workers—sanitation, police, fire.

Around the third week in August, I was spending a lot of time at my grandfather's house, helping him box up his things. It was definite now: the house would be torn down. He had resigned himself to the fact of it, and so he was packing his belongings once again for a new home. But he remained defiant in other ways. Ever attuned to the doings of the town "Neanderthals," Avo in fact told me about the threat to Jimmy, the meetings at the Underbridge. He had no great love for Jimmy, of course, but his dislike of "the crew" my father was suddenly socializing with was much stronger. In fact, they provoked another long outburst.

"Democratic turncoats, the bunch of em," he said as we placed some of my grandmother's knickknacks into cardboard cartons. "They get a little money, buy a house, all of a sudden they're Republicans. Better than everybody, out to protect the town from the colored invaders. And the hippies who'll steal their daughters. Meanwhile they vote for the crook Nixon. Drinking every night at the bar while preaching to their kids about pot."

He paused, gesturing with a ceramic robin, part of my grandmother's bird collection, housed in one antique étagère. Often when she had sighted and identified a bird in the yard or on her walks in the woods with my grandfather, she had added its miniature ceramic version to her aviary, along with European birds she distantly remembered. The Bird Lady of Wardville Beach, Dad had named her.

"What gets me is your father being involved with all this," he continued. "You know we've had our differences, but I always thought he was smart. We don't like what happened with Jimmy, none of us, but this goes too far."

Before I could ask what had happened with Jimmy (I hesitated, not eager to ask), Avo abruptly shifted from Dad and the Underbridge guys to an attack on President Ford for thinking about pardoning Nixon. Ford's action just proved they were all in it together, Avo concluded.

He paused and looked down at a plaster blue jay in his hand for a few seconds, as if he were trying to figure out what it was.

"Gerthoff boy got himself in deep," he said, shifting back. "Can't just be about those Underbridge jerks. Got in with bigger fish. Sharks. The kid must know things."

I stared at him, trying to connect his scattered dots. He had slipped back into his habit of speaking in fragments about larger patterns. I wondered what Jimmy could know that would make those men want to hurt him. I didn't say anything. I continued stowing objects into boxes—my wandering grandparents' portable property.

Avo went on talking: somebody was riling up the ignoramuses to turn on Jimmy. "And that parasite Ward. Wants to protect his buildings near the dump. They can't throw *him* out. Can send him a message, though, and Jimmy, too. One hell of a confrontation coming."

I figured this was only Avo wanting his own confrontation. But I learned otherwise, from Bentley. His father, who like most cops and firemen thought the Underbridge guys were a bunch of troublemaking clowns, had told his mother that the group had plans to converge on Jimmy's house sometime very soon.

Meanwhile, of course, there was my meeting with Sister Michael Mary. It was no longer a topic of discussion in our house, since my father was coming home late nearly every night, slightly drunk, and rambling about Jimmy toying with people's lives and how he was a good-for-nothing bum who spent his life cruising in cars and living it up at the Ward mansion with that fat, perverted pig who never did a day's work in his life but lorded it over everybody anyway. Naturally this led to more arguments, with my mother even defending Ward if not Jimmy. Ward brought "class" to the town, she declared, and he supported all sorts of charities, even if he was a bit eccentric. And what had he ever done to us?

I tried to get away from Dad's sharp words—in my bedroom, or out in the woods. I felt like running off again to Claytown. I hadn't seen Solomon since we were together at Ward's place, and the plans to follow Jimmy to the landfill hadn't gotten much further.

When the conference with Sister M did happen, it wasn't what I'd expected. Sister called my parents to ask if we could all meet at the convent house, an old brick pile a couple of blocks from the church and school. I had never been inside it, and that was fine with me.

My father, it turned out, refused to go, muttering something about his nuts freezing at the thought of going in there (rough language for Dad, at least in front of me; Mom frowned at him and I laughed). So Mom and I went alone. I carried a fragment of my journal, the parts I dared show her, just in case she asked about it.

A surprise came when Sister M opened the door: her head was bare, and she wore a shorter skirt than usual, with a short-sleeved blouse. Except for a fringe along her forehead, I had never seen her hair, which was short and light brown and made her face look very different—it was the face of a pretty woman as old as my parents. Her pink skin looked less artificial, less like a doll's or a statue's skin. It had creases, even pimples. It looked slightly moist and would be warm and soft to the touch. Blood ran through it.

She welcomed us in with a distracted smile and motioned us into a room that resembled the waiting room of our doctor's office. A leather sofa with a metal frame faced two matching chairs. Above the small mantelpiece hung a portrait of the pope, but otherwise the walls were bare. A low table stood amidst the sofa and chairs; a few magazines were neatly stacked—topmost was *Time*, from which Gerald Ford's face looked up at us.

Mom and I sat on the chairs while Sister perched on the sofa, leaning in towards us. She asked if we'd like a cold drink. My mother declined for both of us and immediately announced that she didn't have much time, that she had lots of errands. All of which, I knew, involved the luau.

"Well then," Sister M said, with a flicker of annoyance. "Let me get to the point."

She told us she wanted to meet with each of her pupils and their parents before the year of their Confirmation. "It's an important time," she said. "Spiritually, emotionally."

I could feel my face stiffen and flush. I already wanted to crawl under something, given the way my mother was acting, the opposite of her usual eagerness to please (which could be awful, too). I tried to stop my reaction, which made it worse.

"Maybe," my mother said. "But you know, we aren't the most observant Catholics."

Sister M looked at my mother as if she were a student. She began to explain—she had training in psychology and knew I was at a complicated age, especially for boys. And these were confusing times, she continued, with all the discord, the rapid changes. Cocooned in our little town, we thought we were apart from all that, but we were not. We shouldn't be. And some young people felt this acutely, especially if they were different from the crowd. Sensitive, aware, rebellious. Often they were looking for a role in the larger world as they broke from the small worlds they'd known. Or they wanted an alternative world, a different place altogether, someplace better. She knew this from experience, having grown up here.

"We all want someplace better, don't we, in a sense?" she said.

My mother was at first nodding impatiently, like she was about to interrupt and maybe yank me out of there, but as Sister spoke Mom seemed to relax, sitting back a little, considering Sister's words, if not assenting.

Sister M went on: Confirmation involved reaffirming faith with some of the knowledge of an adult. We begin to understand what we are asked to believe. This can lead to a lot of questioning, a lot of exploring. We were born into the Church as into a family, which we didn't choose, and there could be an urge to break away. We were asked to commit ourselves, but there were different kinds of commitment. Deeper kinds sometimes. Different ways to take on life's responsibilities.

My mother let out a small laugh. "A lot of weight to put on kids."

I tried to get in some words for myself, but they weren't listening to me. It was almost as if they'd forgotten I was there. I began to feel I wasn't in the room at all.

"That might be true," Sister M responded to my mother. "But it's not too early to think about choices. And the weight is on them already. There are more troubles around here than you'd think, and kids sense them. People can feel so alone. Sometimes thoughts and feelings can overwhelm. You look for guidance, and not always in the expected places."

The two women sat awhile and watched one another; it seemed that each was about to say something but couldn't get it out. I looked around the room, which seemed suddenly very small and constricting. The talk had turned somber, obscure, a sour mix of dull and frightening, and it no longer seemed to have much to do with my classmates or me.

"Things get buried," Sister continued. "And it can be difficult later if they are buried too deep. It's so easy to fritter away potential, waste one's energy."

My mother leaned closer and began talking to Sister M earnestly, confidingly. Her words seemed to reach me through some heavy, deep curtain; only intermittent sense came through, emphatic words and phrases. "Anxieties" and "tensions" in our home, "conflicts" affecting everyone. "Guilt" and "regret." She kept glancing at me yet continued talking as if she couldn't stop herself. Her tone was flat, cheerless—it seemed to lack her usual hopefulness, that implicit belief in betterment that underlay even her doubts and disapprovals. Sister M listened, occasionally responding with a "yes" or "I understand," which made me feel even more distant, more dense.

After a while I felt as if I shouldn't hear what I was hearing. They were like conspirators now, and I imagined them prisoners in that stuffy house we sat in, plotting to break out.

My mother finished talking, and Sister M turned back to me. She looked unsure and impatient, as if considering what to say. She told me to keep up with my journal, and that I should share some of my thoughts with my parents. There was great opportunity for learning, for everyone, she said. There was too much hiding, and people needed to connect.

I nodded as if agreeing (and comprehending), but I felt like something was being pulled away from me, or as if I'd been coaxed from behind a screen to be shamed. As though she were asking me to reveal my thoughts about Jimmy and Theona, Ward and Jimmy, Ward and those kids, my curiosity about people's bodies, even her own. My face again felt like a burning mask. But I knew she wouldn't ask me to describe all those pictures behind my eyes—even though she was looking at me as if we shared a hugely important secret. My embarrassment was, strangely, for her, too. Sheepish and amazed, I knew I'd glimpsed some of Sister Michael Mary's own discontent and uncertainty— because she had let us glimpse them.

As my mother and I walked home, she said nothing. She stared ahead as if she had to concentrate just to make her way. As soon as we got inside the house, though, she asked me what was going on, what was bothering me that I'd told Sister about. She seemed more confused and curious than angry. Maybe also embarrassed, exposed.

I told her, in a barrage of colliding words, about Solomon and Claytown and the shadowy evil forces threatening people there. They might have tried to kill Jimmy, I said, and they might try again.

But it all sounded crazy, or like some thriller tale or boys' adventure, and I felt suddenly like a confused, over-excited little kid. My mother's face signaled bewilderment and dismay. And now she *was* angry.

"Jimmy," she said, almost forcing the name through her teeth. "Who would be threatening him or anybody else?"

I looked at her: was she kidding? Didn't she understand the danger? "Mom," I said, stretching the word into two exasperated syllables. "Maybe they want the land."

"Who's 'they'?" she shot back. "And why? If people want land, they buy it. And what would Jimmy have to do with it? Really, your imagination gets out of control sometimes. And your grandfather feeds it, doesn't he? He thinks everybody's against him, yet he does all he can to attract the wrong kind of attention."

I could tell she wouldn't listen; I had provoked some sore-spot fury. I didn't argue but went to my room and closed my door. My father wouldn't be home for a couple of hours. I couldn't focus on the Tolkien book; the words refused to become transporting images and remained entangling black marks. I couldn't pay much attention to the *Bob and Ray* radio show either, not even "Mary Backstage, Noble Wife," which didn't seem as funny as usual.

I went downstairs to the rec room, where I'd left my weights in the corner near the sliding doors, the side of the room with the stacked-up board games, the musical instrument cases, my old chemistry set. I picked up both weights and raised them to my chest in rapid motions.

When I heard my parents' voices, I put down the weights and went to sit on the top step, in the vestibule. They spoke quietly at first. Mom asked Dad why he had taken up with "lowlifes." My father said something about Jimmy and Diane, and my mother answered, louder, that two wrongs don't make a right, and that I should be kept from seeing Jimmy and from any further involvement with Claytown. And she insisted that my father too stay out of it all. "Let Gerthoff worry about Jimmy," she said. "We just want to be left alone. We don't want any more trouble."

Twelve

On another sunny, hot afternoon a couple of days after the meeting with Sister M, I stood beside my grandfather watching bulldozers demolish his house. He stared ahead, no readable expression on his face, no words, no signaled emotion. Rapid and regular breathing came through his nose with a tight, rough sound that was soon lost in the din of destruction.

I thought about the times I'd visited that house; I thought about my grandmother who'd lived and died there. I wanted to somehow stop it all, push back the bulldozer. But I was also thrilled by the sound and force of the giant machine as it smashed the side of the bungalow, pulled back and rammed again. It boomed in my chest. I was awed at how swift it was: the house just collapsed like one of the shoebox garages my father used to make for my Hot Wheels cars. It fell in on itself in clouds of debris and dust, with a cacophony of shattering glass and crunching wood.

The bulldozer left dust-clouding rubble and moved on to the empty Alvarez cottage. The Cruz house would be next;

the old woman had already packed her things and left. All the other houses looked similarly abandoned. My grandfather turned away and said, "Well, that's the end of it."

Later, he moved the last of his possessions—clothing, some books—into our house. He'd stayed in his own until the last possible moment. In fact, that was one reason I'd been there with him: my parents had dispatched me to help him and, I suspected, to make sure he left before the bulldozers arrived. It didn't surprise me that neither of my parents went there themselves. My mother had come to pick us up in the car, but only after it was all over. The duty made me feel anxious, alone, burdened—what if he hadn't left?

My grandfather entered a household where things were still out of balance. Diane had her thievery under control, as far as we knew, but spent a lot of time in the woods, near old Van Todt's house. She made no secret of that. I'd followed her back there one sticky afternoon, the salt-fish smell of the bay and the tickle of ragweed in my nostrils, and observed her lotus-positioned at the edge of a wooded bluff , facing the water, chanting. She seemed remote there, unapproachable. She was often that way at home, too. Diane had moved a little further outside our family's enclosed ring, and we communicated now mainly through notes she left me, filled with cryptic Zenlike phrases. ("I'm letting darkness move through me and waiting for the light," one note read.) She repeated that we should talk, that she had to help me find my way, but she never actually sought me out. The door to her room, like the door to mine, was usually closed.

Mom continued practicing her songs, wearing her bird-of-paradise shirt, refining menus. We were all getting tired of teriyaki and fruit. Since the truncated meal of *bacalhau*, nothing Portuguese had appeared on the table again. The day my grandfather moved in she told him not to expect any more of her mother's recipes because she really had to perfect her Polynesian dishes. Avo laughed so hard it seemed like he'd pass out. He went to his new room, where he continued laughing. He hadn't said a word.

My father had been sullen for several days and had gone back to ignoring the Labor Day plans. He watched TV a lot, commenting on commercials, especially the ones for expensive cars. "Look at the way they're driving that thing," he'd say. "Like there's no one else on the road. I guess if you've got a shitload of money you can drive like that. Me, I'd get arrested." My mother would sigh and look up from the book she was trying to read (that month it was a fat novel about the matriarch of an Australian frontier family). "It's only a commercial," she'd tell him. "Why don't you turn the sound off?"

I was relieved, the day after Avo's arrival, to get a call from Bentley. He told me he'd just talked to Solomon, who'd asked if we could come over to Claytown because he thought Jimmy might be out near the landfill and we could follow him.

I wondered why Solomon had called Bentley and not me. It bothered me and scrambled my thoughts.

"I don't know," I said, lowering the volume on the Stones' *Sticky Fingers*. It was my first Stones album, already a four-year-old LP. I'd stared at its cover with the close-up of a guy's bulging blue-jean crotch many times at E. J. Korvette's department store, where I got my records, but until that summer I'd never dared buy it. That cover was too distressing, exciting, fascinating.

"But Solomon said he'd take us right there, to the edge of it," Bentley insisted.

I pictured us alone at the gate to those evil-smelling hills.

"I'm sort of grounded, though," I said. "I'm not supposed to go to Claytown or see Jimmy. There's a ton of shit going on. You know about these Underbridge guys?"

"You mean the ones who hang out at that bar?"

"Yeah."

"My dad knows em. All losers, he says. Cops with gripes, things like that. Why?"

"They have this thing about Jimmy."

As of course did my father. As of course did I.

"Yeah, I know. Not just Jimmy. Anybody they don't like. It's niggers this and spicks that and fags. Big brave men when they're in a gang, my dad says."

Normally *my* father would have said that, too. Silence stretched like a widening pit as I thought about how to answer.

"Actually, Bentley, my dad's been hanging out there too," I began.

"With *those* guys? No. You're shitting me."

"I'm not. He's been spending a lot of time down there."

As I said this I felt, bubbling up through my shame, something else: satisfaction, pride almost, as if I was impressing Bentley with this information. He was a tough cop's would-be-rebellious son and now I was the son of an outlaw.

"Jeez," he said. "Wow. So you don't think you could get out?"

"Well, I'll try," I said. My glance fell on the album cover with its outline of a big guy's hard dick as Bentley laughed and said, "Cool." Jagger was singing about wild horses.

I did get out. As we rode the bus that night, my mind was on Solomon. I hadn't seen him in a while and I'd missed him, even though I barely knew him. I thought about the fun at Ward's house, the tennis game and our walk around the property. The brief touching in Claytown, the fear and thrill of it. And it felt daring to have a friend from that set-apart place beyond the edge of town. But our friendship only existed there and at Ward's house. Back in Wardville it seemed almost like something I'd imagined. I would've liked to be in Feen's strange-familiar old house again, even more so now that Avo's house was gone. But we wouldn't be going to the house that day: Solomon had told us to meet him in the woods—our refuge, it seemed, from towns and houses.

It was a hazy evening, and the sun blazed orange through the gray-blue Jersey air to the west. We rounded the last bend in Riveredge Road before Claytown, and in the near distance rose the landfill's three huge hills, reddish brown in the declining light. From our vantage, the hills looked barren, like the surface of Mars.

We walked up the road past Solomon's house, and I got that strange feeling again as we approached the site of Jimmy's accident, like the woods were racing toward me. On the bruised tree, someone had painted a large red arrow directing vehicles to the right at the curve. We stopped where the paved road became a dirt path, with a gate blocking the way. A sign on the gate read PRIVATE.

The woods were dense here, the light dim, and you couldn't see very far down the private road. Bentley pointed toward the darkening trees and said that Solomon should be waiting for us up ahead. He figured we could ignore the gate sign. We walked past it, onto the grassy, hard-soil path rutted with tire marks. It was quiet except for bird chirps and the occasional flutter in the brush.

After a while the trees thinned out and the ground gradually dropped. We skirted the edge of a ravine whose sides descended in uneven copper-colored terraces. Small trees clung at precarious angles in the crumbly, unstable soil. At the bottom snaked a stream. These were the old Bultmann pits, the ones that gave Claytown its name. I could picture, down in the darkness, bodies buried in the walls of the pit and piled deep under years and years of accumulated clay at the bottom. I could see them rising up, staring from vacant sockets, permanently grimacing as they reached out dead arms to pull me down.

A hand gripped my elbow, startling me. A voice said, "It's okay, you won't fall in." I turned around. Solomon was looking at me with a sort of baffled concern. I looked down at his hand grasping my arm, and he pulled it away.

"No, I . . . thanks, I'm okay," I said.

"It really isn't that deep," he said. "I've climbed down and back lots of times." It wasn't bragging, more like reassurance.

"Why?" I asked.

He didn't answer at first, then said, "Just wanted to see what's there."

"So what did you find?"

"Branches. Mud. Stuff thrown in there."

"Oh," I said, afraid to ask any more about it. "And where were you just now?"

He cocked his head toward the trees. "In there. I know the place. Thought we'd better meet here, since Gran would ask questions, and I don't like lying."

We started walking again, then abruptly stopped. Not far from us, amid the trees closer to the road, stood Jimmy and Theona. They didn't seem to have noticed us. She had her head down; he brushed her hair away from her face and stroked her cheek with the back of his hand—slowly, gently. He brought his face close to hers and pressed his mouth against her cheek, and she looked up at him briefly before turning away. His hand moved toward her face again, but she grasped it, keeping it from her cheek but not letting it go. Their gestures and the way she stood not quite facing him suggested mysterious things, more complicated than the sex we'd spied on.

Now Theona let go of Jimmy's hand and stepped away. He reached out, maybe to pull her back toward him, but he stopped and put his arm down, slowly, boyish again, less like the confident, comforting lover. He said something to her in a low, tight voice.

"I am not sulking," she said, loud enough for me to get the gist. "I'm not a fool or a child. You're the one who spends his time around children."

He near-whispered something else.

"No you haven't explained," she said. "Why are we standing here watching these holes in the ground? You think they need your help down here, these backwoods Negroes? Your charity?"

He put a finger to his mouth.

"Who'll hear me?" she said. "And so what? Maybe they should know the truth. First you parade me around, then we're supposed to hide. Couldn't even visit you in the hospital down here cause I didn't want trouble."

"I don't want us to hide, but I don't want you hurt," Jimmy said, forgetting to be quiet, and he took Theona by the shoulders. But they were distracted by something and turned to look at the road; two trucks were advancing, with rumbles and gravelly dust.

Solomon started running toward the woods.

I was about to call and maybe run after him when Bentley said, "Look," and pointed up the road. The trucks had stopped and some men were getting out—two from one truck, three from the other. On the sides of the green trucks lettering had been partly concealed by tape.

"Stay quiet," Bentley said.

"Who are they?" I whispered.

"Shit, Luke, Underbridge guys."

I looked again. A couple of the men looked familiar. Most likely they couldn't see us standing there, sheltered by the trees. Jimmy and Theona, meanwhile, had hidden themselves behind a thick oak, where he held her tightly, as if restraining her.

•

One of the men, a tall guy in jeans and a baseball cap, waved the others toward him and pointed in our direction. Jimmy said something to Theona, and they both began walking toward us. I mouthed "Hurry," anxious for Jimmy to get away from those men. I looked at the pursuers again to confirm what I'd first seen: my father was not among them. I was relieved.

"Let's go," Jimmy said to Theona. "That way—toward town." They began circling around the end of the paved road, through the woods. Bentley and I followed, neither of us really knowing the way. We ran back past the clay pit toward Solomon's yard, the direction we'd seen him running. Jimmy and Theona cut across the yard and ran into the next street, the one with Dalton's and the Woodrows' houses. We rushed after them, cracking twigs underfoot, shoving aside bushes and branches, and I looked behind to see the men still chasing.

Ahead, Jimmy pulled Theona into Dalton's front yard, and they tried to conceal themselves at the side of the house where a bay window jutted out. The entire window was filled with multicolored, sunlit jars and bottles. Bentley and I dashed to a fence alongside the Woodrow house and hid ourselves behind it, looking out through the broken slats interwoven in the chain-link.

The truck guys soon appeared out of Solomon's yard and started crossing the street toward Dalton's house. The front door opened and Dalton came out, waving his arm and shouting at the men, who stopped in the middle of the street and began gesturing and shouting back. Dalton screamed that he had a gun in the house and was ready to use it. The guy with the baseball cap yelled his own threat at Dalton but was pulled back by the others, who seemed eager now to get away. They all turned and started down the road, the long way around toward their trucks; the baseball cap guy hurled a few more taunts at Dalton.

As the men were walking away, the Woodrows' front door opened and Seth emerged, followed by Reverend Wilson. Dalton had crossed the street after the retreating men, and he stood watching them, near where we were hiding. Seth and Reverend Wilson came up to Dalton and asked what was going on. Dalton, still shouting, told them the guys had come looking to destroy his house—they'd already broken some of the glasswork and maybe they were coming back to finish the job.

The reverend put a hand on Dalton's shoulder and tried to calm him. Seth questioned how Dalton knew it was the same men. Dalton pulled away, pointing to where the truck guys had disappeared around the corner.

"Trying to force us to leave, that's what it is," Dalton said.

"And maybe we should," said Seth. "Maybe it's time."

"You mean time for *you*. I'm not going anywhere. You just want the money."

"Is there something wrong with that?" Seth gestured toward his house. "It's my property. I've worked to keep it all these years. I have a right to do what I want with it."

"I can't believe this," Dalton said. "Whose side are you on anyway?"

The reverend raised his hands, palms outward, like some pastor-referee. "It's not a matter of sides," he said.

"Damned it isn't. They want us *all* to sell out or run away, and the more people who do it, the harder for the rest of us to fight em."

Seth shook his head. "We've had this talk before, Dalton. It's a pointless discussion."

"Yeah, well, it sure is pointless talking to *you*. You'd sell your children, if you had any."

"Enough," the reverend said. "Let's not have talk like that."

Dalton made a dismissive motion with both hands and turned away. He strode back across the street into his house. He hadn't noticed Jimmy or Theona, and now they came out from behind the rainbow glass, cautiously.

"Well, what do we have here," the reverend said. Jimmy had stopped when he noticed the reverend and Seth, but now he approached them, holding Theona's hand, almost pulling her along. She held back, looking around her.

The reverend asked Jimmy what had happened, who the men were and why they were chasing him and Theona.

"Why in hell do you think?" Theona said.

The reverend glanced at her.

"Oh, they're just some local redneck creeps," Jimmy said. "*I'm* not afraid of them, but I didn't want them near Theona. I was just showing her around. I don't want her involved."

"Then you shouldn't have brought her here," the reverend said. "And isn't she already involved?"

"Say again?"

"I mean, aren't these people taking out their hostilities on you because of your work in this community? Especially with Sebastian Ward."

"Ward has nothing to do with this."

The reverend looked at Jimmy but didn't answer. I knew that Jimmy's statement wasn't true—it was a sort of boasting, as if he enjoyed having everything revolve around him.

Theona hooked her arm under Jimmy's and took his hand, as though their argument had never happened. "They can't stand seeing us together," Theona said. "White trash idiots. Jimmy's breaking their rules, so they hate him. They'd like to ignore you people completely, or get rid of you, and they sure don't want us ghetto folks coming down here."

As Theona spoke, the reverend's squeezed lips pulled his thin face closed like a drawstring pouch.

"'Ghetto folks.' Makes you sound superior to us, doesn't it?" he said. "Of course there is hatred and bigotry here. Maybe it's better if you see each other someplace else, where those things don't exist, if you could find such a place."

Theona laughed. "We should stay away so you won't seem threatening to your racist neighbors?"

"That wouldn't be the worst thing you could do." The reverend spoke quietly, but he wasn't calm. He again looked away from Theona. People were exaggerating, he said, and there was no real danger. After all, we didn't have Jim Crow here.

"Certainly not," Seth said.

Theona let out another laugh.

"No," the reverend continued. "There are other things going on, having to do with our land, our houses."

I looked toward Jimmy, waiting for him to explain, vaguely wondering if he had something to do with this crow named Jim. "You're right," he said. "It's not because of Theona and me. Not mainly. It's not just good guys and bad guys and, well, people want to make money and build things and there's nothing wrong with that, I guess, but it's just some of it has gone too far, much too far." He started to say something else but checked himself.

"I'm not sure you know what you're talking about," Seth said. "We don't really need Sebastian Ward here looking out for us, like the master. We can handle our own problems."

"Not if you can't see what's going on," Jimmy said. "With all due respect, you're mostly elderly people here. You want to keep separate from the world, but it's closing in. If you don't wake up, your little town won't be here much longer."

"'The world'?" Seth said. "I've seen more of the world than you have, I'm sure."

Reverend Wilson had drawn his head up, almost as if he'd been struck. "I have to agree on that," he said. "Our little town. So we're some white do-gooder project for you and Ward? Or maybe fieldwork for your sociology class?"

Jimmy shook his head and repeated "No, no, no" with a long, exasperated sigh, but the reverend ignored him.

"All this fighting," he continued. "I don't understand. For years and years we lived here peacefully. Now we have such violence and anger on all sides. We should follow the example of our Lord, as Dr. King did. Resist injustice with love."

"Yes, but King fought back, too," said Theona. "He wasn't an Uncle Tom. And they killed him for it."

"That's enough," Reverend Wilson said, again with a sort of forced calmness, looking only at Jimmy now. "I'm not going to stand here in the road having this discussion. If you want to come over to the church, you can stay as long as you want. But maybe you should think again about all the trouble you're stirring up."

"*I'm* stirring up?" Jimmy stared at the reverend. The pleading and urgency in Jimmy's face had causes: property damaged, people pursued. He was in the middle of all the trouble, of course, but the trouble was—who knew for how long?—already there.

Thirteen

Feen was fretting. She sat looking through the *Vantage*, clicking her tongue. "Dear Lord," she said. "This place is on the road to ruin." There was a lot in the paper to fuel her worries: muggings at the mall, car thefts from driveways, even murders and rapes. North Shore demonstrations for more police protection and garbage pickup, for access to better schools, nicer stores. Some Wardville people, especially newcomers, were resisting the school changes, and some Claytown people were, too. More highways would slice through woods, more new houses would accommodate the mostly white hordes still escaping the inner city. Identical wooden frames rose everywhere like giant matchstick models. And there were protests against all that, too. The city was running out of money; jobs and services would disappear. ("Guess who's gonna be hurt by *that* most," Feen said.) New drugs swept through schools, and some whites blamed North Shore blacks for dealing them, although everybody knew the higher-ups were white.

But what concerned Feen most was the way all these problems seeped into Claytown, affecting the people she was closest to. She'd heard about the men chasing Jimmy and Theona, and she knew it must have to do with developers and the landfill. She also knew that Solomon was mixed up in it all somehow, although he wouldn't tell her what had caused him to run home in such a panic.

It was a couple of days later, and Bentley, Solomon, and I sat in Feen's backyard with cold drinks, pressing iced glasses to our cheeks. The air that afternoon was so moist you couldn't tell your clothes from your skin. We hadn't seen Solomon since that day he ran off, but he'd met us at his front gate and told us what we should and shouldn't say to his grandmother if the subject of Jimmy and Theona and their pursuers came up. And it had come up, after Feen's commentary on the *Vantage* news. Feen's reaction to what had happened was complicated: she thought the truck guys were ignorant thugs, but she didn't like Theona's kind, either.

"Lots of delinquents up on the North Shore, lemme tell you," Feen said to us, putting down the paper. "Roaming around the city, cutting school to take the ferry. And now in the summer—too much time on their hands. The devil does make work. Should get those kids out of there. Like my friend on the next road, she used to take in kids for the whole summer. Give them some space, some nature, work to do, get them out of that environment. Wish I had the energy and money for that. Wish more of us could do it here, rather than leaving it up to rich people."

She was addressing most of this to Solomon. His attention seemed elsewhere. But he perked up as Feen began describing how hard it was keeping up the house now that George was so sick and couldn't do much work. They'd even thought of selling the place, she said, but then where would they go? They didn't want to leave, this was their home—but sometimes it all felt like too much to handle.

"I try to help," Solomon said.

Feen smiled. "You do what you can. And I have to say that Gerthoff boy has been a big help, too. Fixing things and yard work. But, you know, he's not so reliable, and he has his own problems. And there's too much needs doing around here. Of course, it isn't his responsibility. Isn't yours either, really."

"Sure it is," Solomon said.

Feen ignored this, told him to be careful around that Jimmy. She wasn't even sure he should be riding in that boy's car or taking trips to that Ward house. She didn't want to deny Solomon the chance for some fun and learning, but she had her doubts.

Solomon mumbled something and Feen ordered him to quit the backtalk.

Once Feen had gathered up our empty glasses and brought them inside, we started whispering about when and where we'd meet to go into the landfill. Solomon told us that Wednesday nights his grandmother had her Bible study group at the church, and his grandfather sat watching the fights on TV, so he could sneak out. Getting back in would be harder, but he'd manage. It was going to have to be earlier than we'd planned, since Bentley and I too were under closer observation.

Things did not go well between my grandfather and my mother after he moved in with us. Of course he'd never really wanted to be there. He wanted his own house, which wasn't possible, and he dreaded living alone in an apartment. (Even more dreaded was an "old-age home," as he called it.) He and Mom argued over domestic details: the level of the air-conditioning, my mother's cooking techniques, allergens in the shag carpeting. Not arguments, really, since Avo barely spoke except to register a brief and broken complaint to which my mother, frustrated at his sneak attack and quick retreat into silence, would respond with a long, defensive monologue. Usually these exchanges would end with my grandfather muttering throaty Portuguese curses and retreating to his room, where he'd often confine himself like his own jailer. Later I would hear my mother in there, speaking to him gently.

My hopes that Dad had left the Underbridge club were demolished—he was still going out almost every night and coming home tipsy. Mom felt angry and humiliated, especially with the luau fast approaching. She harangued; he mostly listened. Themes recurred: Dad was supposed to play an important role, not only by strumming his ukulele and putting up sets, but also by keeping track of donations. They needed to keep careful account of the money raised for charity. People should be properly thanked for their generosity, and all the rules of nonprofit fundraising had to be followed, especially after all the trouble with the Fourth of July event. It seemed bizarre and awful for her to be lecturing him about things he was expert in, as if she thought he'd forgotten.

One night, as I sat in the kitchen, I heard them talking in the living room. Their low, intense voices were somehow worse than shouting.

"Is it so important, this luau thing?" Dad said. "I'm sick of hearing about it. You'd think Jesus Christ was going to show up to announce the Kingdom."

"Hardly," my mother replied, calmly but with a sort of quiver. "It will be a happy occasion with all our good friends, and maybe a chance for the family to be together enjoying one another for a change."

Dad was now standing against the railing above the stairway down to the front door. He was focused on Mom, across the room, so he didn't look into the kitchen. He said something about Diane not going to the party and having to force me to go.

I wanted to tell him I didn't need to be forced; I liked swimming and it might be fun. It seemed Dad was trying to pull me into his frustration about the whole thing. But I sat silent, listening.

"Silly outfits and weird food won't make everything all right," he said.

"Every family has problems," my mother answered. "Every community." She invoked festive traditions, good causes.

"Right," Dad said. "Like some after-school programs would change things. Kids getting high, having sex like monkeys, blasting music from their cars after midnight."

Mom asked Dad when he'd gotten so crotchety, so low-class opinionated. She mentioned Archie Bunker, and Dad tightly laughed.

"Yeah, we're supposed to be better than that," he said. "Have our community-events bullshit while the whole society falls apart. Like those Short Hills muckety-mucks throwing parties while Newark went down the toilet."

And then he brought up Sebastian Ward. "Hypocrite," he said, his voice lowered, tense. "Helps kids so he can have boys around him."

Now my mother strode over and stood face to face with my father. He stepped back, coming close to the top of the stairs. She told him to stop repeating disgusting rumors, and he shot back that the rumors were true, that Ward was after Jimmy, too, and that's why he'd hired him in the first place. Except Jimmy liked chasing girls, especially black ones lately. Mom said "What?" and Dad didn't answer at first. I was glad she'd challenged him, and I also wanted to know what he was talking about. She asked what Ward or Jimmy had to do with it. Dad growled something about Jimmy running away, disrespecting his father, about Diane and a baby.

My mother put her hands to her mouth. Dad was staring at her like some frightening man I didn't know, and he said, louder, that if my mother thought it was all in the past she was mistaken, that Diane wasn't doing well at all. He turned away, stumbled down the stairs and hurried out, slamming the door behind him.

My legs felt stiff and I wasn't sure I could move. Pictures were appearing in my head that I couldn't control: Jimmy and Theona grappling naked on the ground, only it wasn't Theona, it was my sister; Ward's hands on Jimmy's chest, only now it was Solomon's chest, and both he and Ward were naked, Ward like a huge, pale kid. I stared down at the front door, terrified now that my father, this angry unfamiliar father, would return and open it, and that he'd see me there in the kitchen. He'd grab me and vent his rage about Jimmy, our uneasy connection with him, and I half felt he'd be right to be angry, since Jimmy was a no-good liar who did nasty things. Or were they Dad's nasty ideas? I rushed to my room, where I closed the door and sat on my bed. As I tried again to stop the pictures in my mind, I spotted Diane's last note on my night table. I grabbed it and read it over again. The shapes of the letters, my sister's neat orderly writing, unchanged through all her changes, brought back our closest times—after I was no longer a threat to her only-child status and before I was the unhip little brother. Back when she would read to me from books without pictures as I followed her guiding finger and tried to correlate her voice to the half understood marks on the page, their meaning wondrously emerging, the world opening.

But my father's words still seemed to reverberate around me, and I tried to make sense of them. Did Diane have a baby? How could I not have known that? Where was it now? I focused again on the note I was holding, as if it contained answers.

And then I remembered something, with the double-edged force of feeling stupid and seeing from a sudden new perspective: Diane had been to the hospital the previous fall for some "operation" that no one fully explained to me. At the time, I hadn't cared about the details, as long as she was okay, and I hadn't thought much about it since. But now it seemed clear, or partly so. Diane had in fact been pregnant back then, but there had never been a baby.

That night Dad did not come home for dinner and didn't call. He had never done anything like that before (even when he'd disappeared for whole evenings). My mother seemed oddly calm, maintaining a dazed serenity. I tried to read Tolkien again, but all the characters had my father's face, elves and wizards with dark hair and glasses. So I joined my family at the kitchen table, keeping a sort of vigil. Diane was softly crying; she kept repeating "Daddy, Daddy," like a little girl. I could feel her anxious, confused sadness with a new urgency, but I was unable to ask her about it. It wasn't the time to ask anyone about it, even if I could have formed the questions out of my wispy comprehension. Avo told Diane to calm down and mumbled something about poison pills. He started quizzing Mom eerily: Had Dad been to the doctor recently? Had he had a blood test? If he had one, they'd find a chemical change. And that Gerthoff big shot and his cronies were polluting his brain, too. My mother responded only with an empty look. Her eyes seemed to focus on something not in the room.

She'd had the presence of mind, though, to phone Bentley's father—not to notify the police but to seek advice. From what I could tell, she was being told to sit tight and not worry. She had also called someone else earlier that evening but had spoken so briefly and quietly that I had no clue who was on the other end. After a while, I couldn't stay any longer in the kitchen listening to Avo, whose disconnected discourse had somehow linked my father's corruption by rich guys to the secret history of the United States government and the capitalists who controlled it.

I went out the front door and sat on the steps. In the streetlight glow, clouds of cigarette smoke drifted from a car parked in front of the Alessandros' house next door; they were upstate for the summer. I got up and walked toward the car. It was Mrs. Velman's Mercedes, with the teddy bear in a Gucci-logo T-shirt looking out the back window. Two people sat in the front seats. I walked closer and recognized them: Eddie Randono and Andy Velman. They were talking loudly. I stood still.

"Yeah, well," Eddie was saying, "that's the point. This could be really big, the biggest thing the company's seen in years. So we can't let some shit-ass guys who really have zilch to do with it fuck it all up. I never trusted em, really. They're not family, if you get my drift. Not really family like us, I mean. Your dad and my dad, man, they go way back."

"Oh, they sure do," Andy said. He was behind the wheel. Cigarette tips flared red and smoke columns wafted up. "My dad remembers when he was like the first Jew around here, and your old man was one of the first Italians. Everyone looked down on them, all the white-bread shits like Gerthoff in their crummy old houses."

"Yeah. They thought big, our dads, and we're thinkin' even bigger."

"Yep. You got it. And if we have to break a few rules . . ."

"Or even a few legs . . ."

They both laughed.

"Well," Eddie continued. "It's necessary sometimes. But we're the heirs, you know."

"Princes of the dynasty."

"And we're not fucking it up like Jimmy."

"Yeah, he's become a real do-gooder. A hippie going nowhere." They laughed again and one of them belched, and I heard a metal crunch. A crushed beer can arced out the passenger window and landed on the Alessandros' front lawn. A few more puffs of smoke plumed up before Eddie spoke again.

"So where is the spic asshole?"

"He's not Spanish, he's Portuguese."

"Oh, excuse me. Same fucking rice and beans, ain't it?"

So now they were talking about my father. It was like they'd whacked me in the chest: a short-breath, dizzy feeling of anger and humiliation. Why wasn't Dad coming home? Were they waiting for him, like we were? I wanted to pick up the beer can and hurl it back at Eddie.

I heard another car approaching and watched it slowly pull up in front of our house, behind the Mercedes. Eddie and Andy quit talking and looked back at the other car, an old station wagon. The driver opened the door and got out—it was Sister M, alone. She wore slacks and a short-sleeve top, and her hair looked as if she'd combed it hastily after a nap.

As I walked over to her, wondering if she was there about me, the Mercedes started up and screeched away. We both looked at the retreating car and back at one another, and it became clear: she was the one my mother had phoned. Yet I had the feeling she was in the wrong place.

"Luke," she said, putting a hand on my shoulder. I was almost crying but I held it back. I couldn't talk, though. She asked if I was all right, and if my mother was at home.

I nodded "yes" to both questions and we walked into the house together, her hand still on me.

My mother came up to us in the vestibule, and Sister M grasped her hands as they stood looking at one another. Mom looked weary and uncertain, but she allowed Sister to guide her up into the kitchen. Sister sat her down and got her some water, moving without hesitation, as if she'd been there before. My grandfather wasn't in the kitchen now, which was a relief—no telling what he would have said to the nun.

Sister turned and gave me a quick smile. "I think your mother wants to talk with me alone now," she said.

"Okay," I said and went downstairs to call Bentley. He told me that his father had gone out to look for my father, just to have a talk with him. I no longer felt any pride in Dad's Underbridge associations; Bentley's father as my father's rescuer, as if Dad were a runaway child, was too shaming to think about. At the same time, I was hoping Bentley's father could help.

A half hour later Bentley and I were walking together on the beach, stepping across driftwood and garbage. He said it would be okay, my father would come back. He mentioned Solomon and going to the dump but I didn't want to talk about that, so we trudged along without speaking. I looked out at the rotting remains of the old pier, half-visible in the light from the beachside road. The prow of a capsized motorboat stuck out from the brownish water. We skipped some stones off of the lapping waves. I thought about Eddie and Andy; the conversation in front of my house seemed to confirm that my father was involved with Randono and Velman. It was all mixed up together: the threats to Claytown, the landfill activities, the Underbridge guys. I didn't tell Bentley that my father might be in a deeper mess than I'd thought. The father I really wanted back was the normal, steady one, with his guarded, guarding love.

When I got home, I walked up from the downstairs door very quietly, and I could hear Sister M talking in the living room. "Yes," she was saying, "they do behave strangely sometimes. He'll come back, of course. Sometimes they have to have their tantrums, assert their control. But they need us. It's the same in the Church. They can act like childish tyrants, yet they know we do most of the work. And we can't even give Communion. Sometimes it can be hard. You can feel things too deeply."

I stood on the staircase watching them. They sat close together on the sofa a few feet from me, looking at one another. Sister M was holding my mother's hand. Strands of hair had fallen across Sister's face, and her arms, like my mother's, were slick with sweat. She squeezed my mother's hand and said, "We have to take care of ourselves." My mother nodded.

My father did come home, but not until the following evening. He had gone directly to work from wherever it was he'd spent the night: his clothes were wrinkled and he was unshaven. I'd never seen him in a state like that on a workday, despite all the nights he'd gone out. No one expressed relief that he was back. He discouraged these feelings by more or less ignoring all of us. Dinner that night was silent torture.

For the next few days, my father was somewhere else even as he walked around the house. He had completely abandoned the luau duties, the more so as Mom clung to the approaching event more and more tenaciously. He was still leaving the house every night and stumbling in around eleven.

After several such nights, though, there was a change. Dad was calmer and more present, and spoke to us in complete sentences. He did not have a drink before dinner or one after. He watched the evening news and seemed to follow the stories. But then he softly announced he had to go out. My mother sighed a fed-up protest, and (unlike previous nights when he'd said nothing) he told her he'd be home in less than an hour, that Stan Velman had asked for some accounting advice. I'm not sure my mother believed this, maybe she just wanted to, but she didn't object any further.

After Dad left, we all tried to keep busy. All of us sat in the kitchen except Diane, who was listening to Buddhist-themed self-help tapes in her bedroom with the door open. "Our bad habits are a result of attachment to things and people that we must lose," a woman's gentle voice intoned. Mom was reading the sheet music to "This Nearly Was Mine" and weakly humming the melody, which seemed like a fragile bird attempting to fly. I was trying to get back into *The Fellowship of the Ring*. My grandfather had spread across the table his elaborate map of Wardville and its environs. He added new red dots every day to chart the spreading toxic menace, following some pattern no one else could see. Black dots, also growing in number, indicated green space and old homes lost to development. Some of the red and black dots overlapped. (My parents had barely taken notice of Avo's obsession, as if they thought it was just another example of his contrary nature.)

About half an hour after my father had left, we heard shouting and laughing outside in the street. Not the usual teenage fun-and-games; these were adult male voices—harsh, edgy. My mother and I hurried to the front window. A group of men were walking quickly down the street on the opposite sidewalk. Some were holding sticks.

"Oh my God," my mother said. "I know where they're headed."

She started down the stairs to the front door. My grandfather, standing in the kitchen doorway, called after her to stop, saying that they would hurt her (as though he knew who they were).

"Pop, I have to go over there to see what's going on. John might be out there. I'll be all right. They aren't looking for me."

"Looking for all of us," my grandfather said. "Don't kid yourself."

Ignoring him, Mom told me to keep an eye on the front yard, that she'd be back soon. I asked what was happening, although I pretty much knew.

She hesitated. "It's probably some trouble over at Jimmy Gerthoff's house. I think your father might be involved."

"Of course," Avo said. "Taken his brain. Turned it to mush."

"Pop, please."

She walked out the door and I watched her cross to the other side of the street. I knew I would follow her. Her candor had almost given me permission, even as she had warned me not to. After a few minutes, I headed out. Avo had lost himself again in his map and didn't try to stop me.

Once my mother had turned the corner and was headed for Jimmy's street, I began to walk after her.

I heard the crowd before I saw it: a low murmur of deep, mingled voices, like a restless male audience before a ballgame but tenser, more menacing, with the occasional shout of a single voice or a few voices together screaming. Only then could you make out words. One name was repeated: Jimmy's, sometimes just his last name, sometimes the whole thing, sometimes a drawn-out, taunting "James." And other words: "Come out here." "Coward." "Punk bastard."

And then my mother turned the corner onto Jimmy's block and stopped. "Jesus Christ," she said, fists clenched at her sides. I came up behind her and she turned: her face looked frightened and confused. I felt my own courage spiraling away.

Seeing me sharpened her. "I told you to stay home."

"What are they going to do? Where's Dad?"

"I don't know," she said. "We can't go near them, they're all crazy drunk. We have to get help." She turned back to look at the crowd. "Oh, where *is* your father?"

The men, maybe fifteen of them, were standing on the sidewalk, sitting on the wall of Jimmy's front yard, grasping the bars of the gate. All of them were watching the house. In the front windows, lamp light filtered through drawn drapes.

The shouts continued. "We got business with you, come on out here." Then a different, hoarser voice: "We ain't leaving till you come out." And another, deeper: "You got that black girl in there? You fucking her in your father's house?" A loud "whoa" followed, and laughter.

My mother stepped closer to the men, and I tried to pull her back. She was searching among the backs and profiles, looking for my father, and I began searching, too. He didn't seem to be there. That calmed me a little, but the shouts and mocking laughs, the manic faces of the men, their vicious energy, still rattled my insides like close thunder.

I continued tugging at my mother's arm and reminding her we had to get some help. They'd burn down Jimmy's house, I said, and kill him.

She drew herself up, her control and authority returning, and put her arm around me. "No, no," she said softly as she walked me away from the men. But I ran ahead of her, ashamed and mad at myself for my childish exaggeration, while still unsure, still horrified.

We hadn't reached the corner when a big tan car came speeding around it, with siren and spinning light. It was followed by a standard blue police car. As the first car passed by we looked inside: the driver was Bentley's father, and sitting next to him was mine.

My mother cried out, "John!" and she began to run after the car, which came to a halt across the street from the Gerthoff house.

My father and Mr. Riley got out of the car, but with all the noise and commotion I wasn't sure they had noticed us there until my mother called my father's name again.

He turned, looking baffled, a little frightened, and we walked up to the two men. My father and my mother looked at each other without touching, until a sound of glass shattering startled all of us and we turned toward it. One of the men had hurled something through Jimmy's front window.

Riley pulled out a gun; I'd never seen him hold a weapon before. He fired a shot into the air—a loud, explosive sound, not at all like the popping bursts on TV. The sound itself seemed to rip through me. Dad now held Mom, his arm around her waist, and she leaned her head into his chest. The shot hushed the crowd, and they were all looking at us.

"What's going on here?" Riley shouted.

"We want that kid," one of the men yelled. "We want to talk to him."

"You want to beat him up is what you mean. Come on, now, break this up and get yourselves home. You've got no right to trespass here. You've already smashed a window. I could throw you all in jail."

Some nasty laughs erupted. I recognized one or two cops in the crowd as well as the guys who'd chased Jimmy and Theona through Claytown. One of the cops told Riley he could go to jail himself for shooting a gun in the air. Riley repeated his warning, and this time it seemed to have an effect: a low-voiced grumbling spread through the assembled men, and they stopped moving toward Jimmy's house. The voices seemed confused and ominous, like the babble in dreams just before waking, when you're not quite sure what you've heard yet it's full of dark meaning. The men looked unreal on that familiar street, and once again I had that weird feeling that some other version of our town existed, some shadowy duplicate, creeping into the one I knew. I watched my father as he stood behind Riley, who looked so bold and resolute. Expressions flickered in Dad's face, combining alarm and something else, a faint version of that cynical half-grin he'd lately been giving us. Mixed with my relief was that sense that he, too, had a double who would appear there among the crowd of angry men.

One of them stepped forward now and came up to Riley: he was a stocky man in a Mets championship T-shirt and shorts.

"Let me tell you, buddy," he said, pointing a finger at Riley. "We bust our asses to pay people like you. And then we gotta do things ourselves. Otherwise the whole town would turn to shit like the rest of the city. People like you and that punk in there"—his finger now aimed toward the house—"need to understand what the score is. You tell that boy to wise up."

"I'm not in a position to tell him anything and neither are you, Phil," Riley said in a calm voice. "Maybe *you* need to wise up. First maybe sober up."

"Yeah, sure, stick up for the draft-dodger. Meanwhile our sons went to Nam to die."

"Not your sons, Phil. You have two daughters, as I recall."

Riley told them again they should all get home. Phil didn't answer, but he lowered his gesturing arm and backed off, with a sneering smile. Slowly the whole crowd began walking away. A few chucked beer bottles like glass grenades, shattering.

One of the men turned and shouted back toward the house, "What's the old queer paying you to suck your dick?"

My mother gasped as laughs and hoots went up from the others. The words were like my own whispery thoughts suddenly blaring in electric, violent distortion, and I felt like laughing too, from a kind of sickly-scared excitement, as if exotic and dangerous creatures had been released onto the tame, tended sidewalks. My head was like a throbbing balloon.

Once the crowd had disappeared around the next block's corner, the front door of Jimmy's house slowly opened and he stood there, with his mother behind him grasping his T-shirt and imploring him to close the door and come back inside. But he didn't move. Even from the sidewalk I could see he was trembling and pale. One leg jiggled frantically. He opened his arms wide in some gesture of invitation or surrender.

I started to walk toward him, and my mother yanked me back. I pulled myself out of her grip again but stayed where I was.

Mr. Riley went up to the door and spoke to Jimmy and his mother, who was still pleading, still holding on to his shirt. Jimmy lowered his arms and seemed to be calming down. He answered Riley, but they spoke too quietly for me to hear. Riley returned to where I stood with my parents, at the foot of the walk, and the front door began to close. I tried to catch Jimmy's eye, but he was looking away now. I wanted him to tell me something, a jumble of things: about Diane and what had happened, about the landfill and Claytown, about Sebastian Ward and things I didn't want to picture clearly even if I could. And maybe something deeper about Jimmy himself, and myself, and the confusion in and around us, that he probably couldn't have told me anyway. As I watched the door close, I was hoping Jimmy would be safe inside, but I also wanted to rush up there and force that door open so he could run from the house, escape from town.

"He's alone in there," Riley said. "With his mother. She's frantic."

"Where's the father?" my mother asked.

Riley shrugged. "Out, the kid says. Working by the dump."

PART THREE

Fourteen

After that night, Jimmy was nowhere to be seen, at least within my limited range. I figured he might be hiding out—as, in a sense, I was. Suddenly our quiet streets seemed menacing, and I kept seeing the faces of those guys converging on Jimmy's house. Men you were supposed to look up to. Bentley told me that his dad was mad as hell at the Underbridge guys and was keeping tabs on them.

I was content to stay in my own house, for the moment. Alone in my room, I kept thinking about what was going on and tried to work some of it out through my journal. A few things seemed clear: they'd targeted Jimmy because of his connections to Claytown and Ward, and it all seemed linked to work at the landfill. Jimmy's freewheeling behavior irked people, too. But all that didn't really explain what Jimmy was up to, or why. I felt sorry for him now but also more confused and angry and let down. And words kept coming back that I couldn't bring myself to write; they created blurry, disorienting pictures, thrilling and terrifying feelings: *queer* and *suck your dick* and *fucking*. And the stuff about black girls. All of it shouted with such aggression and disgust that I wanted to stop myself from recalling it even as I was obsessively recalling it. Why did all this anger and violence seem to focus on Jimmy?

I still wanted to believe that he would get it all together, that what he really wanted deep down was to find some free, fair, harmonious place where his life, and somehow everyone's life, would be better. I needed to keep hoping it was possible, so I could go there, too.

Around me, in our house, things were seriously gearing up for the Labor Day party, now only a few days away. My mother gathered strength and took charge, pushing other concerns aside. My father eagerly went along— too eagerly, it seemed, as if he was also trying to distract himself or make up for the bad things he'd been doing. All day Saturdays and Sundays he wore his hula-girl shirt from the fabled Honolulu trip, and he'd resumed his uku-lele strumming. He drank at home again rather than at the Underbridge, which had become a forbidden subject, along with both James Gerthoffs, Junior and Senior. Dad told us to forget about what had happened with Jimmy, that it was a bunch of frustrated jerks out of control. He didn't explain how he'd gotten mixed up with them but implied that they'd crossed a line he would never cross. I gratefully clung to that difference—for Dad it was all talk, I told myself, whereas the Underbridge guys had acted, shocking my father back to his senses. He no longer reported what was going on in Jimmy's household; when Mom raised the subject of Gerthoff Senior, Dad said he hadn't spoken to him in a couple of weeks and that was just fine.

Avo spent a lot of time now in his small garden off in the corner of the yard, tending his new plantings. Indoors, he alternated between his reading, his map, and occasional fragmented outbursts on subjects that my parents didn't want to hear about: his lost house, the continuing threat from all those powerful conspirators, and how much it all reminded him of the Salazar dictatorship in Portugal.

Diane had begun confining herself to her bedroom. Once she'd learned about the confrontation with Jimmy, she had stopped talking much to my parents, not even to argue. She spoke mainly to Avo, when their self-enclosed worlds briefly intersected—at meals, say, or passing in the hall. She left me no more notes or books. But that break in our long relationship, with its intensities of love and battle, didn't bother me as much as I would've thought. She now seemed part of a boundless, daunting adult life, no longer my childhood companion, and I wasn't sure that I wanted to know what had really happened—I was afraid of what I'd feel about her, about Jimmy, about this place we all lived in, and, somehow, about the world beyond it where my future would be.

My strange dreams continued, but now I was alone in them. The spaceman angel, fluctuating center of those shifting dreams, had disappeared, and I was left in the dump. It now seemed such an overwhelming presence, so near us, in a way it never had been before—almost as if we lived in Claytown. Those towering heaps of waste, rotting away in summer heat and frozen under snow in winter, were taking over my thoughts (awake and sleeping), sort of the way sunny visions of Hawaii possessed my parents—or at least my mother. In the dreams, I'd be standing below one of the stinking mountains, imagining all the random rejected things trucked there from all parts of the huge and complicated city. Things desired and consumed, providing pleasure or nourishment, or having served some purpose but now broken, worn out, or obsolete. Somehow a key to the larger world was buried there, something more than local secrets. I would have to climb the mountain to find that key, which would admit me to some greater awareness, a higher understanding, even a heroic power. But as I began climbing, I'd hear a low rumble, and the giant hill would begin to erupt and break apart, rolling all its filth and stench down toward me in a hellish avalanche as I turned to run, but I couldn't run fast enough and the ground would dissolve into lava-like mud and I knew I would be stuck there and buried.

I soon went back to the library to find other books about Claytown. The library's tall-columned, dark-wood entry-way seemed, even more than usual, a sort of gateway to solace and wisdom and wonder. Mrs. Foy took down an old volume and opened it on one of the big mahogany tables. It's the best history of our local towns, she said. She thumbed pages and scanned columns of tight print. She asked me what exactly I wanted to know. Why did so many people leave Claytown, I said, in such a short time? She peered at me over her half-glasses a few seconds before continuing to read. Finally she turned the book toward me and slid her index finger down some paragraphs. They described how, by the mid-twentieth century, farms could no longer sustain themselves. Fishing became harder because the nearby waters were polluted.

That much I already knew. But this book told more: the Bultmann factory had mined much of the land and disposed of industrial waste around Claytown. Houses were bought out and torn down to dig the pits, and a burial ground was dug up, too. The bodies were "relocated." On top of that, a huge fire at the factory spread through the woods and burned down twenty-five houses. Lives were lost, and those left without homes moved away. Afterward, only a dozen or so houses remained.

The book said nothing about fights or murders.

I asked Mrs. Foy about the landfill. She asked why I was so interested in that godforsaken area. I told her the same fib I'd tried on Bentley's dad and got a similar skeptical look in return. But she brought me another book, a much newer one that confirmed what Feen had said: the dump began as a small one, covering up swampland, which was considered a useless health hazard. There was a lot of swampland, though, with a long creek running through it, and the city had a lot of garbage. There were no significant communities nearby, the book said.

I walked out of the library in a time-warp daze, thinking about the different versions of what had happened in Claytown: the history in the books and the hidden, bloody history in Ray's tense telling at the picnic. I wondered which history was truer, but more than that I was scared that these awful things weren't only history for Claytown but still there, right now. So close.

I sat in the garden with my grandfather that evening as a hose at his feet dribbled water into the recently planted soil.

"Dry summer," he said. "Plants aren't doing so good. Put them in late. The sun is good for the tomatoes, though."

"Yeah," I said.

"Summer went fast, no?"

"I guess so," I said. In fact to me the summer had seemed endless. Spring felt like ages before. It seemed so much had happened.

"It all goes fast. Faster and faster."

I shook my head (a sudden inner protest clutched me), but he looked me in the eye, adamant.

"People do, maybe," I said, trying to match that sureness. "And machines and things. But not time. Time only exists according to how we look at it. It's how we use it that matters." This was a mixture of science and Sister M.

"Well, people try to run away," he said. "But it all catches up. I like gardens. No restlessness. Every year the same way. They don't forget in the winter. Life in there like memory."

He seemed to be thinking out loud, so I didn't answer. I wasn't used to this kind of wise-old-man philosophizing from him. It was peaceful there, but it was also lonely, and I had never thought of my grandfather as lonely when he lived alone. I had never thought of him as old, either, not the way other people were.

For a while we sat silent. I didn't ask Avo about the landfill and Jimmy and Claytown. The garden was tranquil: the breeze brushing the willow in one corner, the trickling water. I didn't want to get him started again. And he had already answered my questions as far as he could.

The next day we learned that there'd been another incident in Claytown—this time an assault. The *Vantage* told us the story, and I could see it happening: a man past sixty, alone at home watching a ballgame in his living room, hears a thud and hurries to his front door whose screen, he notices, is warped inward. He opens the door and sees a large stone on his wooden porch with a note tied to it. He reads the note, which warns him that his days in the house are numbered and tells him that if he wasn't such a backward fool he'd sell and get his black ass out of there. The man looks around, doesn't see anybody but reaches for a walking stick he keeps on the porch and makes his way into the front yard. Two men in T-shirts and shorts and bizarre dime-store masks jump out from behind his front hedge. They grab the stick, knock the man down, and he feels a searing blow on his shoulder, then on his legs and arms as he tries to shield himself and push the men away. But one strong stroke contacts his head, and he screams in rage and pain as the blows continue, until the men drop the stick and run away laughing, like harlequin demons. Summoning strength, he crawls back to the house to phone for help.

The man was now in critical condition in South Island Hospital.

This news briefly pulled my parents out of their tropical reveries. My father repeated over and over, "I can't believe this, I can't believe this." Neither he nor my mother suggested any connection between the beating and the near-attack on Jimmy. Only my grandfather raised that possibility, but he expressed his ideas in nefarious-plot phrases warning of impending doom for us all. He was ignored.

After a day of speculation and head shaking, my parents were back into Labor Day planning. My mother told us that the festivities would be even more important now to get the community back to normal. This prompted Diane to point out that the luau wouldn't make Claytown people feel any better, even if they'd been invited.

After I hadn't heard from him in a while, Solomon called and asked me and Bentley to come over. I was glad he'd called but reluctant to go back to Claytown. He really wanted to see us, though. He'd heard about Jimmy and was pretty freaked out about it and about the assault in Claytown. Also, Reverend Wilson had asked to talk to him. He wanted Solomon to come by his office on Sunday after services. Solomon figured it had to do with all the stuff that had been happening, and maybe the three of us, too, and so he wanted me and Bentley to go with him. Bentley agreed when I asked him, with his usual shrug-shoulder attitude. It seemed peculiar that we'd all go, but Solomon had convinced me.

So we (gladly) skipped Mass and got to the Claytown Church as the service was beginning. At 10:00 a.m. it was already hot and the weather seemed likely to follow the month-long pattern of humidity building into late afternoons of incipient rain that, as Avo had reminded me, rarely arrived.

As we walked up to the church, we could hear singing. I felt apprehensive and a little guilty, like the time Doris took me into her synagogue: it seemed I shouldn't be there. But the flip side of that unease was curiosity.

I looked up at the arched wooden doors; above them, in old-fashioned lettering, was the full name of the church: Claytown African Methodist Episcopal. This explained the A.M.E. but still left a mystery, since to me Methodist and Episcopal were two different Protestant churches.

Inside, the singing hit us full force. The whole congregation was singing, a huge sound filling the small space. It was so different from hymns in our church, where the congregation mainly mumbled along with the wobbly-voiced ladies of the choir: four or five women dominated by the screechy soprano of ancient Mrs. McCloskey. Here everybody sang like they meant it, with shouts and claps, and words like joy and pain felt joyful and painful, and my self-conscious feelings dissolved in the praise of God washing over us. It was like the voices were swaying me from side to side, lifting me up toward the wooden beams. I looked at Bentley, who looked startled, amazed, like he'd been pulled out of his habitual no-big-deal.

No one in the church really noticed us—the few people who glanced our way quickly returned their attention to the service. Once it ended, we stood in the vestibule as the congregation, mostly older women, filed out past Reverend Wilson. Everyone was dressed up; the men wore suits, the women dresses and big hats—much fancier than people at Mass. Among the first out were Solomon and Feen, who looked surprised but nodded hello. Solomon had on a white shirt, gray tie, gray slacks. They stopped and waited with us; Feen wasn't going anywhere. Solomon hadn't told us that the meeting would include her, but now it seemed obvious: of course Wilson hadn't arranged a meeting with Solomon alone. And I felt glad Feen was there.

Reverend Wilson greeted each person leaving, and a

few gave Bentley and me the once-over as they passed us. When everyone else was gone, we all stood looking at one another.

"Are you expecting your friends to join us?" Feen asked Solomon.

"Well, I thought maybe they could."

"Oh, did you?" Feen said. She looked at Bentley and me and then at the reverend. "Might be a good idea."

Wilson smiled tightly. "All right, then, come with me." He led us to his small office in the dank, warm church basement and switched on a noisy old air conditioner. We sat on folding chairs in front of his desk.

"So," he said, clasping his hands. "I asked Mrs. Peek to bring Solomon here with her, and it's just as well you two showed up also. I'm sure your parents don't know half of what's really going on. I know you boys have good intentions, but you know what they say about that pavement on the road to Hell. I think you might also know what generally happens to people who play with fire."

Maybe we didn't get all the references, but the warning seemed clear. He turned toward Feen and began explaining: when Ward had first approached him with the idea of helping out youngsters in Claytown, the idea attracted him. But he was also suspicious. He told Ward that the few children in the community weren't in need of outside help. They had families—extended families, plenty of people looking out for them. And most children who visited didn't actually live in Claytown anymore. But Ward thought it would be good for them to have open space near the ocean and all the things he could offer—a large library, all kinds of recreation. So the reverend had decided it would be unfair to deny kids all those opportunities. Ward seemed sincerely eager to do good. There was even talk of financial help, although the reverend was uneasy about that.

"So I became involved, I set up the programs here and over at Ward's house. Mainly over there. And by and large the kids loved it."

He paused, took a large white handkerchief out of his pocket and wiped his wet face. He had already been sweating from his sermon and singing. I had the feeling that this was another sort of sermon; he always seemed to talk that way, as if giving a lesson, like Ward but harsher, without that sense of dreamlike storytelling. Maybe he was trying to work things through, feeling stuck in the middle of a situation he didn't fully understand, and maybe he was struggling with what he should be doing as a minister. I could sense some of that as I sat listening to him, but mostly it seemed he was reviewing his actions, as if to explain or justify them—to us, to himself, to someone or something else that wasn't clear. He was like a lot of people that summer—trying to make sense of things, aloud, to all who'd listen.

He turned up the air conditioner, creating more rattle, then swung his chair toward Feen. "But certain things began to occur that disturbed me," he said, in a louder voice. "I heard about rides in James Gerthoff's car. On Ward's boat, which is dangerous and possibly illegal. There were other things too." He paused, looked at us a moment.

"Then I found out," he continued, "that Ward had asked James to go wandering in a restricted and dangerous area after dark and, well, I had to ask myself, why would a grown man send a teenager on such an errand?"

"Good question," Feen said.

"And I still don't know the answer, but I don't think children should be further involved. James shouldn't be either, but that's his choice. If Ward thinks there are bad things going on in that foul Gehenna north of us, he should report it to the authorities. We're already doing as much as we can here."

Feen cleared her throat and told him she'd been worrying over some of those same things herself. "Maybe
I should have done something sooner," she said. "I can't
tell Mister Sebastian Ward what to do, but I can forbid my
grandson from visiting him."

Solomon protested, but Feen talked right over him.

"And I don't want Solomon anywhere near that garbage
dump," she went on. "Jimmy and that Ward, they're rich
folks, and they've got some ulterior motives, I'm sure. Like
you said, we can take care of our own here. Always have."

Solomon looked from me to Bentley and back, as if we
might speak up now. We didn't.

"But they hate us," he said. "And they make us hate
them. It's like they want us to all just die or leave. That's
why that old guy was beaten up. And Jimmy almost was
too. Somebody should stop them."

The reverend and Feen both stared at Solomon, who
looked trapped and confused. I could see now that his fear,
his confusion, his sense of himself as different and targeted,
went way beyond anything I felt; his insecurity was like a
deep crevasse between us, and I was on the safer side.

The reverend suggested that Solomon wasn't thinking
clearly, that he was overexcited, that there were things he
was too young to deal with.

"You might have a wise man's name," he said. "But it
takes years of living in this imperfect world to begin to
understand it. Who is this enemy, do you really know?"

"Jimmy Gerthoff does," said Solomon. "Mr. Ward
does."

"Do they? Why, because they're white? Wealthy? What
can they know about us here? James is impulsive and has a
lot of growing up to do. And Sebastian Ward has his own
difficulties. He lives in the past. Feels guilt about the past."

Solomon didn't respond. He was staring at Wilson
now, intently, as if he'd suddenly noticed or understood

something. What Wilson said about Ward seemed true, but I was wondering why the reverend hadn't spoken in any forthright way about the beating or what had happened to Jimmy.

Feen stood up. She hadn't said anything about the incidents, either. Now she too was giving Wilson a quizzical look. "I can't say I share your faith in the authorities," she told him. "And there certainly are nasty things going on around that landfill. I don't know what the truth is."

She and the reverend looked at one another in silence. He seemed suddenly at a loss for words.

"But my grandson is my main concern," she went on. "And you're right that he's too young to be involved in all this. Children want to run before they can walk today, that's the problem. I'm grateful for your advice, Reverend, but I've got this boy under control. Things are going to be different. Let's go, child."

She pulled Solomon up from his seat and toward the door.

"I want to talk to my friends," Solomon said.

Feen turned back to look at Bentley and me. She examined us awhile, almost as she'd done that first day at her house.

"I want you home in half an hour," she said. "I'm timing it."

Outside, blinking in heat and sunlight, we followed as Solomon made his way through the woods beside the church. On the other side of the trees, the graveyard came into view. Its gate was open for Sunday visitors. Old and new headstones stood together, the leaning and the worn away next to those still sharply etched and solidly in place, and I wondered if some of the bodies had been "relocated" here when the clay quarries were dug. Solomon walked through the gate, headed toward the far side of the small cemetery, and finally stopped at one corner, shaded by a huge sycamore tree just outside the fence. He sat on the ground. We caught up and sat with him, at the edge of a neatly tended plot with blooming geraniums and dwarf pines. On the stone was the name Hadley, one of the ancestors' names Feen had mentioned. Solomon told us that this was another place he liked to come sometimes to think. He began scooping up sandy-clay dirt and running it through his fingers.

"I'm not listening to the reverend," he said, in a quiet voice. "I want to see what's going on. Who's trying to hurt us."

"But your grandmother doesn't want you to," I said. And she had a point, I thought; maybe we shouldn't go any further. Maybe we were just kids getting in over our heads. What could we find out, after all, and what could we do about it?

"She doesn't understand. She thinks if she hides it'll all go away. But it won't, it just gets covered up."

Solomon continued to sieve soil through his fingers, almost as if looking for something there. No one spoke for a while. A breeze rustled the sycamore leaves and birds chirped their coded messages in the woods.

"We really need to talk to Jimmy," I said. "He's part of all this, too. Maybe he can help us."

"Talk to him?" Solomon said. "We don't even know where he is."

"I know where he *probably* is," Bentley said, in a low voice as if the dead would overhear.

We all defied orders and went to the Ward place that afternoon. Bentley felt certain Jimmy would be there. It still seemed to all of us like Jimmy had answers, even if our questions were foggy.

We made our way directly through the open back gate and found Jimmy gently rocking on the swing in the garden. The thick air hummed with insects and smelled of late blooming trees and, when a gust blew, the grass and the bay.

Jimmy wore only cutoff jeans. His arms, legs, and chest still looked paler and skinnier than usual, but his cuts and bruises had begun to fade. He was fiddling with his binoculars, moving them around and focusing on things from different angles. (I wondered if these were the ones Ward had used to watch Jimmy.) He pointed them toward us, and I lifted my hand reflexively, as if to protect myself. As we approached, he lowered the binoculars and gave us a secretive, uneasy smile.

"Hey guys," he said. "So you found me."

"Wasn't hard," Bentley said. "Me and my dad saw you walking the other day near the marina."

"Yeah? Your father spying on me?"

Bentley and I exchanged a quick look. "We were going out fishing," Bentley said.

Nobody spoke for a few minutes. I looked over at the house, whose open windows framed darkness, which seemed to be watching.

"Actually, I don't think it's a good idea for you guys to be here," Jimmy said. "Things are getting hairy."

His eyes flitted nervously behind his smudged glasses, which were askew. He looked a little clownish and perplexed. His foot pushed forcefully against the ground with each swing, as if he wanted to launch himself away from there. None of us seemed to want to ask him directly about the confrontation with the Underbridge gang.

"You know, we saw you near the clay pits a couple weeks ago," Solomon said. "We saw those guys running after you and Theona."

"Yeah?"

"So what were you doing there? Why were they chasing you?"

Jimmy laughed, still nervous, but with a cockiness creeping in.

"Whoa, Solomon, you've got a lot of questions," he said. "And you're not even the detective's kid or the boy reporter. I could ask the same thing. Why were you there?"

"Looking for you," I said, and I couldn't keep the sharpness out of my voice.

He laughed again. "So I *am* being spied on," he said. I wanted to grab him, shove him, because now he seemed to be making fun of us, as if he'd been playing some cruel, teasing game. I felt foolish and weak, his ex-girlfriend's little dorky brother once again. But I was also confused, frightened even, because he no longer seemed so strong or wise or hip, no longer such an exalted contrast to me.

Without answering Solomon's question, Jimmy leaped up from the swing, leaving the binoculars on the bench, and told us to follow him inside the house. He took us in through the back door into the gleaming kitchen (no food piled on the table now), to the parlor where Ward sat reading a book, sipping a drink—another Cuba Libre, it looked like. The room was hot, despite windows and fan. Ward had on safari-style pants, a white short-sleeved shirt with epaulets, and his straw rancher's hat. He smiled but didn't get up.

"Well, well, what a pleasant surprise," he said. "We were concerned you had forgotten all about us."

I looked at Ward, not much liking *his* jokey tone either. I thought of all the different people he seemed to be. The encyclopedic gentleman with lots of hidden problems. The sinister snob. The admired survivor of an old family. The community leader trying to help his home town. The smooth storyteller who made us feel like equals and friends. There were benign Wards and creepy Wards, all of them there in that room which itself seemed to exist in multiples, in many different times.

We all sat down, except Jimmy, who was hanging back by the doorway like some servant who'd turned us over to the boss. I was still seething at him, or just seething without knowing exactly why. Ward gestured for him to sit in the chair next to his own, which he pulled closer. Jimmy obliged, and Ward reached over and put a hand on Jimmy's thigh. I felt it on my own skin like electric rippling. Jimmy spread his legs wide and sat back. But he wasn't relaxed: he kept scratching the stubble on his chin.

"They told us not to come here anymore," Solomon said. He sounded a little pissed, too.

Ward smiled. "Yes, 'they.' You mean the nice preacher. Don't look surprised—I don't read minds. I talked to Reverend Wilson yesterday."

He eased into that confiding tone that made me feel satisfyingly mature but also uncomfortable, because it didn't seem right somehow. The reverend, Ward explained, had asked him not to invite any more young people over to the house, and Ward had agreed to end the whole arrangement if it wasn't what Claytown wanted.

"Reverend Wilson, however, doesn't speak for the entire town," Ward said. "Obviously he wants to discourage contact between our communities. As far as I'm concerned, you're welcome to stay."

"You mean hide here?" Solomon said. "Like him?" He gestured toward Jimmy, who sat up and gaped at Solomon but didn't say anything.

Ward took his hand off Jimmy's leg (I'd kept looking at that hand there, resting, the fingers sometimes stroking Jimmy's skin). He continued explaining in a sort of indignant shorthand. *Awful mob. Collection of lowlife puppets. Big shots pulling the strings, resisting the law, not fighting fair. While Jimmy went after the truth.*

"Wouldn't want to see Claytown destroyed," he insisted. "I'm willing to fight back. Not like that reverend. But I don't want my children here, any of you, directly involved—you're another part of my project. The next generation. Things will, I hope, be different."

Ward had lost me now. *His* children? What project? We were suddenly included in the group here, it seemed, what Jimmy had called Ward's "family." Jimmy leaned forward, straightened his glasses. He told Ward that it was all their fault for trying to force people together. He glanced at us. "Maybe I should take them out to the Kills tomorrow and show them what's going on there," he said.

Ward shook his head. "Dangerous."

"Everything's dangerous," Jimmy said. "Might as well let them see it all."

"As if *you've* seen it all," Ward said, with a quick sharp laugh. He gulped down the rest of his drink.

FIFTEEN

On Labor Day, it rained—the first real rain of the summer, a gushing-from-gutters rain all morning. Frantic phone calls were exchanged among the luau organizers, and my parents shifted from telephone to radio to window, gauging the downpour, hoping it would end before the two o'clock start of the festivities. Diane snidely suggested an appeal to the Hawaiian gods whose tiny representations sat on tables and shelves around the house—souvenirs of the long-ago honeymoon or new acquisitions in the luau spirit. Dad laughed, but Mom was too tense for joking. Only Avo was glad about the rain, balm to his ailing garden.

Bentley and I had told Solomon we'd meet him out near the landfill. Jimmy had never acted on his offer—or threat—to take us there. My parents had said I could invite Solomon to the luau ("a kid from school," I'd told them), but he'd said no. It wasn't hard to figure out why: although he wouldn't have been the only black kid, he would have been the only one from Claytown, subject to curiosity and condescension even from the two black families (headed by professionals) in the club.

At noon, the rain still hadn't stopped. My mother opened the refrigerator and stared at luau food. "Maybe we should just eat all of it now," she said. Dad took her hand and reminded her about the tents waiting to be set up, maybe already set up, around the Swim Club's main pool. She didn't look reassured.

When the rain let up around one o'clock, then, all of us were relieved—except Avo, who lapsed back to the blank expression he seemed to have more and more now. After the rain stopped, he walked out the back door and sat on a wet lawn chair. He looked at the plants expectantly. "Where is it?" he asked. He continued looking, as if the plants might answer this question.

I told the parents I'd go to the Swim Club later with Bentley, and once they left the house, he and I headed to Claytown. We rode the bus through pothole puddles as damp, drooping trees scraped the windows. Around Claytown, the air took on a muddy smell. We hopped off the bus into sunlight that sparkled on the tall wet grass along the roadway. We bypassed the church, in case Reverend Wilson might be watching, and we avoided Feen's house. Solomon met us at the top of his road, where it joined the larger road leading to the landfill. This was the opposite end from the site of Jimmy's accident, so we were reversing the route he took that day as he fled whatever he was fleeing. The main road was much better paved than Solomon's—fresh asphalt leaked its pungent oil in the sun.

Up ahead, the road ended at a large closed gate with an adjacent gatehouse, the landfill's main entrance. We were still a long way from the dump hills, but you could smell them now in the breeze. Solomon said it was a good day for the stink, meaning it wasn't too bad, since the prevailing winds took it elsewhere. There was something strange and lonely, though, about the fenced-in wooded area ahead of us; it seemed abject yet menacing, a scrap of neglected nature jacketed in steel. It was like the fence was holding in something awful. My grandfather's warnings welled up again, and I was almost afraid to breathe.

I asked Solomon why we were there when there wasn't any way we'd get in. He stopped walking, and so did I. He looked at me as if I'd said something disappointingly stupid. We'll wait outside, he told me.

"For what?" I asked.

"To see who comes out, or what goes in," he said, like he was explaining the obvious.

We continued walking, and I felt that we were being watched from the gatehouse, although there was no sign of life in or around it. As we approached the imagined sentry, Solomon gestured toward the grass by the road and told us we should hide ourselves there. Bentley balked and said he'd rather be at the luau, and Solomon answered, "Fine, if you're too scared, go. Who needs you." He turned away, and Bentley, fired up, ran ahead into the grass. "Yeah, *so* scared," he mocked.

Solomon had been acting strangely the whole time—not talking much, snapping at us when he did speak. It was like we were in the way somehow, as if he had an urgent task to carry out and wasn't sure we were committed to helping, even though he seemed uncertain himself about all this crouching and spying in the weedy mud. I'd first noticed this change toward us the afternoon we met with Reverend Wilson, as Solomon sat amid the gravestones. He didn't want to believe what the reverend had said about Jimmy and Ward, yet he seemed to be taking out his mistrust partly on us, maybe because it was his community there, his ancestors, his continuing battle—not ours.

After a few minutes sitting in silence, with only the rustle of trees and grass and the low hum of an airplane high above us (or was it a truck nearby?), Bentley got restless again and I did, too, picturing the Swim Club's cool, clear water.

Solomon, though, kept staring toward the gate and, as if by the force of his looking, a Mercedes with dark windows appeared in the road. The car stopped at the gate and two men got out. The driver was Dom Randono, and the other man was Stan Velman, short and stocky, wearing a tropical shirt and swim trunks. Dom, too, was dressed for the luau: polo shirt, shorts, deck shoes. The two men were talking and laughing, Dom's voice a bass line under Stan's higher tones. Without a word, Solomon began moving through the weeds toward the gate. Bentley hung back, saying we should let him get caught if he wanted to, but I felt an obscure, insistent duty toward Solomon, and I figured maybe he wasn't thinking right. I wouldn't try to stop him, though.

Closer to the gate, Solomon crouched again. Now we could clearly hear the conversation.

"Where the fuck are they?" Dom said, looking at his watch. "I wanna have a drink and get my ass in that pool."

"These kids got no real work ethic," Stan said. "The money they'll take but when it comes to helping out, they're not so eager."

Stan walked out a little and looked up the road. "Here they come. Finally. Thank God. My feet are killing me in these sandals."

Two giant dump trucks, their contents hidden by canvas, hulked into the road. Dom went inside the gatehouse, and a few seconds later the gate slid open. The trucks stopped very close to us, and we heard their brakes whining above their engines' steady growl. In the cab of the first truck I saw the profile of Eddie Randono. I ducked lower down, but he continued looking straight ahead. The ground rumbled as he drove the truck through the opened gate, followed by the second truck. I looked up to see the driver, expecting Andy Velman. But the driver was Jimmy. His truck roared past, shaking everything.

"Shit," I said. Jimmy wasn't supposed to be working here, driving a Randono and Velman truck. His father's construction site was a mile or so down the road.

Bentley had come up next to me. He stared up at the passing truck, as did Solomon, as if they'd never seen a truck before. The vehicles disappeared into the wooded road beyond the gate. Dom came out of the gatehouse and stood beside Stan. They looked toward where the trucks had gone.

"Sometimes I wonder what's gonna happen to this business," Dom said. Stan shrugged.

We all looked at one another but none of us spoke.

A few minutes later, Jimmy and Eddie appeared, walking along the road out of the woods. They approached Dom and Stan.

"So he's back," Dom said, cocking his head toward Jimmy.

"He decided to come," Eddie said.

Dom gave Jimmy a long look and said something in Stan's ear, and Stan nodded.

"He ain't supposed to be there," Dom said. "Not tonight. For one thing, his old man's getting all Nervous Nelly about him being there. So Andy will help out tonight. And some other guys, too, making sure you're doing what you're supposed to."

He took Eddie aside, far from Jimmy and closer to us. I tried to silence my breathing.

"Eight o'clock," Dom told Eddie in a low voice. "We'll still be at the club. This one has to be done fast. Got it?"

Eddie nodded while Jimmy stood looking at the ground. Stan walked over to the car, and the teenagers followed. They all got in and drove past the gate. Dom went back into the gatehouse, and the gates clanked shut: there was something final and hopeless about the sound. After locking the gatehouse behind him, Dom got in the car, too, and it sped past us. Eddie was driving; Jimmy had climbed in back. The only other time I'd seen Jimmy get into a passenger seat was the day he left the hospital with his father.

Solomon watched the car head out, speeding through Claytown. He gave us a look you didn't want to look back at and said, "They're all creeps." It was as if something had zoomed up from the marshes and stung me.

"You guys can go to your party and stay there if you want," Solomon said as he started walking fast back toward the woods. "I'm coming back here before eight." We followed him. I figured his statement was a backhanded sort of invitation: he wasn't going to ask us outright to be there, and yet it seemed that he wanted our help, our involvement. But with what? I wondered. What would we do here?

When we got to the pits again, instead of making his way along the edges, he trudged down into one of the ravines, sure-footed as if he knew the way.

"Where you going?" I shouted.

He didn't answer, just kept climbing down. I looked into the pit, fear and dizziness wafting with the mud-smelling breeze, but I could see the path Solomon had followed and I started down, pressing my sneakers into his footprints. Bentley yelled after me that he'd had it and was heading home. I turned, briefly tugged by an urge to go back with him, but I only shouted up that I'd see him at the Swim Club later, and then I continued tracing Solomon's steps. I could see him way at the bottom near the creek, standing, looking down at something there. I half slid the rest of the way, grasping branches jutting from the sides of the bluff, muddying my hands.

Solomon stood staring into the shallow creek.

"You see it better when the water dries up," he said. He hadn't turned to look at me, but he knew that I'd followed him.

"See what?"

He pointed. "There, next to that rock."

I looked into the red-tinged water where it gurgled around a protruding boulder. Beside the rock lay a narrow, cylindrical white object, half buried in the mud.

"What is it?"

I looked up, and met his tense, somber eyes. He said nothing, as if he knew what I'd been imagining, what I feared it was.

"No," I said, with a sort of laugh, as if to dispel the dread that suddenly seemed to be filling that ravine.

"It's human."

I shook my head. I looked back down and, yes, I saw that it could be a bone and could be human. But it could also be lots of other things.

"Why don't you pick it up and find out?" I said. The words made me tremble,

and they set Solomon off.

"No way," he shouted at me. "It has to be left alone. They're all over the place here and they have to be left alone."

I stared at him, and his sudden panicky rage made me panic, too. I wanted out of there. Without a word, I started clambering up the steep bank, this time ignoring our blended tracks and slipping as much as I made progress. But I got to the top and I didn't look back.

On the bus ride home, I gazed out the window and saw only Solomon's face and that long white thing in the water. It eclipsed my thoughts about Jimmy in that truck. Even if it wasn't a human bone, there were bodies buried where they shouldn't be, and Solomon was right to be scared of what might happen to Claytown. Right to be mad at Jimmy, too. I felt ashamed that I'd left Solomon there with his fear and confusion, but I didn't know what to do to help him, and I didn't want to go back there. Not yet.

I ran to my house to get my swim trunks, eager to forget the things I'd just seen and try to enjoy myself. My parents had already left for the club, and Diane was gone, too. I found my grandfather shuffling around the garden, tidying up after the rain. He was muttering to himself as he worked—how they were all off celebrating while everything fell apart. Whole country in a mess. Fiddling while Rome burns, he said. Need a little honesty and hard work. Some attention to the working people. Labor Day, isn't it? I asked if I could help. He looked at me as if he hadn't understood, so I repeated it. No, he said, just get your feet out of those shrubs, I just cleaned them out. Go enjoy the big *festa*, he said, the summer will be over before you know it.

She stood looking out over the blue-green water in which flowers floated, lit from beneath, reflecting the oil-lamp torches and the people all colorfully dressed around tables adorned with orchids and tropical fruits, sipping after-dinner coffees with their coconut desserts, all of them smiling at her, the whole area framed by darkness, as if they were all in some remote and enchanted place, gathered around a turquoise lagoon, and she herself were some native princess, spotlit there on the stage flanked by American flags and flamboyant ferns, under a bower of ti leaves and heleconia. The music was already playing, the gorgeous strings behind her, slightly out of tune but lovely anyway, of the Wardville High School Orchestra. She had felt a pang of regret seeing them there, or rather not seeing her daughter Diane, who'd given up the viola for that strange Indian instrument, but the feeling quickly passed once the music started, the soaring melody. Everything was all right, the world had not changed so much after all, the summer had reached this joyful culmination. She began to sing.

It was hours since I'd fled the dump, and I sat directly opposite my mother, at a table with my father watching her over the pool and through the smoke from Dom Randono's fat cigar at the next table. Randono looked relaxed and sated, taking in the music. I felt he was keeping an eye on me, as if he knew I'd seen him earlier. Next to him sat Mrs. Randono, plump and serene, like a worldly Buddha with spirally hair and diamonds. My mother's face showed a nervous sort of happiness, as if she were surprised at it, and her voice sounded clear and strong in the quiet evening. As usual when I saw my mother perform, part of me felt proud and part wanted to disappear. My father watched her with a smile and an expression in his eyes like wonder. When she looked back at him, I felt centered in their love, but I also felt I wasn't there between them at all. Diane was wrong—we'd leave them long before they'd leave each other.

I'd had fun that afternoon with Doris and Bentley, swimming in the pool and eating the kalua pig and the laulau, which seemed far out to Bentley but by then almost ordinary to me. At the corners of the pool stood Dad's palm trees interspersed with real plants and flowers, and the large cutout gods gazed at the revelry. Along one side of the pool stretched a bar with a palm frond roof. More fronds formed walls around the tents sheltering the tables. There was recorded music from the loudspeakers—Hawaiian music, of course, but also mild fifties pop with summer themes, as well as some livelier mambo stuff and Brazilian jazz, courtesy of my father. People mingled in shorts or bathing suits; some men wore tropical shirts and some women had on long colorful skirts over their swimsuit bottoms. Everyone wore leis, which were handed out at the gates. High school kids, some looking eager, some bored, walked around with trays of exotic hors d'oeuvres—"horse duffers," Dad joked. People sipped pastel drinks from plastic cocktail glasses; a few took their drinks into the pool, reclining on rafts or floating pool chairs. Some of us younger boys had skimmed nets along the water to clean away debris after the rain. The sky had turned crisp blue, and the sun sharpened the bright colors in the clothing and decorations and, it seemed, brightened the people, too. Everyone was having a good time. It did seem we were all in some place apart from the troubled world, in some isolated idyll.

All the while, though, I was thinking about Solomon and what had happened earlier in the day and what might happen later. I saw Randono, Velman, and Gerthoff Senior huddled in one corner near the cabana, smoking cigars, holding drinks, laughing. They didn't look concerned about anything; they were friends having fun. My father seemed to be avoiding them. He was arranging tropical props on the stage and trying to calm my mother's performance jitters. Mom hadn't sat down all afternoon. She drifted from conversation to laughing conversation, wearing her muumuu the whole time, like some goddess of parties.

To our surprise, Diane had said she'd come by after dinner for the music and the dancing. A rock group was promised—not Randono's Warlock boys, but some "nice kids" my mother had selected who performed at weddings and high school dances.

Diane did show up, just as my mother was finishing her *South Pacific* medley, which had built up to "This Nearly Was Mine." Mom's voice cracked a little on "paradise." When Diane made her way to our table, it was clear she was high on something. She sat glazy-eyed and giggly, shooting sarcastic zingers about the food, the décor, the clothes, the music. She asked when the bride and groom would show up, so we could see them stuff each other's mouths with cake and throw the bouquet and the garter. Everyone was tipsy and sated enough to laugh at these jokes, the kind of thing they expected from Diane anyway. By this time, my mother had made her way to the table, fanning her face and looking like nothing could be wrong in the world. We all applauded as she sat down. She kissed my father briefly on the mouth, then bent to kiss me and Diane. I felt happy for her but a little uneasy; Mom's giddy triumph seemed precarious. Diane pulled away from our mother, and Mom's expression fell, and I wanted to scream at Diane to go home. Mom turned from her as if from a bad smell and sat down, smiling again, chatting with her friends, but she kept giving Diane sharp, pained glances.

Dad did some ukulele numbers and told a few bad jokes, making everyone laugh, which was a relief. The rock group took the stage, and after some show-offy guitar tuning that lasted too long, they launched into some Beach Boys songs. My mother bobbed her head back and forth to the tunes. This was stuff she could half enjoy. Midway through "Surfer Girl," Diane spoke up again, picking up where she'd left off but in a louder voice that slashed through the smooth music. (Now people were giving Diane alarmed, even hostile looks.) She would never have a tacky conventional wedding, of course, she declared. In fact, she had once pictured a very different kind of ceremony. She could still imagine it: dawn on Wardville Beach, everyone dressed in white cotton robes, standing around a big fire with the gentle waves of the morning tide sliding up the sand. A Hindu priest would preside, and everyone's face would be colorfully painted. It would be a combination wedding and birth celebration, welcoming her soon-to-be-born baby. Or maybe it would just be a ritual for the baby, because who needed a goddamn husband anyway.

At this point, Mrs. Randono invoked the names of Jesus, Mary, and Joseph while glaring at Diane, and my father leaned toward my sister and put his arm around her. He whispered something in her ear. She stood up, pulling herself away, and shouted, "I can't let it go, I can't." My father stood up, too, and this time he grasped her arm and told her to calm down and come with him. She let him guide her away from the table. The band stopped playing a few bars into "Little Deuce Coupe," and now everyone was looking at our table. A silence dropped over the party like ash. My mother sat with her hands over her mouth and didn't move. I got up and walked past the gaping Randonos toward my father and my sister, but Dad waved me back as he walked Diane slowly toward the lantern-strung cabana. She leaned her head on his shoulder, and they disappeared inside.

I stood there amid the plywood deities and palm trees, watching the lights trembling in the crystal water. I looked back at the table. Even as the conversation and the eating and the music slowly resumed, it felt like something had ended. My mother had not moved from her place, and she wasn't talking to anyone. All the festive brightness receded into unreality as I watched her. It was as if she were suddenly immobile and alone. She was staring at the cabana.

Sixteen

So there it was ahead of us, closer than it had ever been: the southernmost of the trash hills, where the private haulers piled their loads in the area bordering Claytown. I'd read the facts: the world's largest dump, over two thousand acres, the largest of the mounds two hundred feet high. The one directly in front of us was smaller, maybe fifty feet, but it seemed immense, and obscurely malicious. In the distance to the east and to the west, lights blinked through the swaying trees, but otherwise everything was dark, especially the massive hill itself, darker than the faintly glowing sky. The hill was cone-shaped, tapering to a flatter top. As we approached it, proportion was lost and it loomed above like an actual mountain, almost like the volcano I'd imagined. The book facts faded before it.

We'd met Solomon at the gate entrance and taken the long way through the woods. He'd nodded hello but then forged ahead as if he were alone, and we'd trudged after him across the clay pits, down muddy paths, stepping on rocks when we could, past the swampy low points and back up—me grasping tree limbs for balance. I hadn't said anything about that strange object Solomon had showed me in the creek, and he hadn't mentioned it either.

Now, in the distance, at the base of the hill, we could see a chain-link fence with a gaping gap—torn away or left open. Between the hill and us stretched a cleared space ending at the edge of another pit. There had once been trees there; fallen trunks lay in a stack as if tossed by destructive giants. This was the spot Solomon had told us about, the trespass on Claytown land.

We made our way along the rim of the pit, at the bottom of which lay a pool of dark water, not a stream or a creek like the other pits. The smell was fierce—a sweet-sour stench of rotting garbage mingled with an oily chemical odor. The pit ran up to the base of the mound. We glimpsed dark shapes scrambling away.

"They're rats," said Solomon.

I stopped.

Solomon looked back at me and laughed. "It's okay, they're afraid of people. Just keep walking."

Actually I thought it would be cool to see a rat—at a distance, and not in a pack. I followed as Solomon and Bentley continued ahead, and soon you could discern in the scant light the green patches growing partway up the hillside, which mostly looked brown and slick.

Now Solomon stopped and looked around. I caught up to him, and my sneakers sank into the mucky earth. I suddenly felt overwhelmingly alone in that barren place. I looked up at the few faint stars emerging in the dusk— white, impossibly distant, granting no wishes. No sign they were the home of any nighttime transporter, any starman angel.

Solomon seemed alone there, too, apart from us somehow, caught up in his own thoughts and feelings, the way he'd looked in that graveyard sifting sand, in that clay pit staring into the creek. I wanted to say something that would put us back in sync, bridge the gulf—some joke, maybe—but the words wouldn't come out.

Bentley had stopped a few feet ahead of us, and he was pointing up. "Look," he said.

Atop the mound stood a thin male figure I knew was Jimmy, a silhouette against the declining light, hands on hips, head down, maybe looking at something below on the other side of the hill, beyond the broken fence.

We approached slowly, and the smell got stronger. I still felt like I was walking through some unearthly place, or someplace deep within the earth. Soon the ground began to rise and the tall grass brushed our legs, which made me think of those slithering rats. We started climbing the mound, which was drier than it looked, cracked and crumbly. I held my breath as long as I could, then sipped air through my mouth.

Jimmy was now holding his binoculars to his eyes and seemed to be focusing on an asphalt-paved area past the fence, eerie in dim amber streetlight, where some trucks were lined up, their engines grumbling in unison. Slowly, one truck moved through the fence gap, guided by a man waving a flashlight, and made its way toward the pit, passing below where we stood concealed (I hoped) by the darkness. Now the truck turned around and backed up to the edge of the pit, where it stopped. With a loud grinding, the huge dumping mechanism began to tilt, and a mass of gunk slid into the water. The rotten, chemical stench saturated the air.

And I noticed now that Jimmy had something else around his neck: a small camera, which he now pointed toward the dumping truck. A flash went off.

"Damn," said Bentley, beside me.

A scraping sound came from above us now, and we saw Jimmy making his way down the hillside toward the fence. He lost his footing but managed to rebalance himself, despite the weight of binoculars and camera, bouncing against his chest. He stopped a few feet from the fence gap and raised the camera again.

Bentley asked what we should do. Surprised, I stared at him. The cool, big-man look was gone; he was as scared as I was. I shook my head, unable to answer. I turned toward Solomon, who was already finding his way back down, and followed him, because I didn't want to keep climbing or stand there in the stink. Bentley followed, too. We all slipped going down and slid on our asses in the dirt, and for a few gasping seconds I thought I might fall straight down into the pit, into that deadly water, even though it was way past the base of the hill. I grabbed a jutting rock, scraping my leg as it broke my fall. I reached and felt blood.

At the bottom of the hill, Jimmy was looking through the binoculars again and spotted us. He waved his arms in frantic gestures for us to stay back. We stood there, between the fenced area and the dumping truck, whose driver had gotten out and was looking down into the pit. It was Andy Velman.

Jimmy now turned and hurried toward the trucks still behind the fence. He didn't try to hide himself, and he strode defiantly, without hesitation. Two men were now standing at the fence's opening, and one of them began shouting at Jimmy to get the hell away from there. The other man stood watching awhile then reached into a pouch at his side and pulled out a gun. Jimmy kept walking forward, quickening his pace, and as he got closer the guy with the drawn gun said something to him quietly but firmly and then, more loudly, "Stop right there." But Jimmy kept advancing until two pops echoed off the dark hills and he stumbled, grasping his left arm near the elbow.

"No," I said, my voice loud in my ears, although I hadn't shouted. Jimmy stood awhile, as if awaiting another shot, before he turned and started running.

"Jesus," said the other man. The shooter stood his ground, lowering his gun as a third man approached, running from somewhere on the other side of the trucks. He grabbed the gun out of the shooter's unresisting hand and whacked him across the face.

And now I recognized the third man: Jimmy's father. I felt a sudden squeezing in my chest and head and started bawling. I could not control it. Bentley stared at me with his mouth open. He was trying to catch his breath. I wanted to scream for my own father, who might be able to help us and do something.

"Stop it," Bentley said, and then he shouted it.

The cold terror in his voice cut off my crying, but deep, sobbing spasms heaved my chest, and blood trickled down my leg. I felt as if the whole world had shrunk to that stinking dark mound and we were stuck in it.

I looked over at Andy, who was still gazing into the pit and didn't seem to have heard the commotion over the truck's noise. I looked back. Jimmy was hurrying in our direction with his left arm pressed against his chest. With the other arm he waved us away again. No one was following him; his father stood with his head bowed, the gun in his hand.

"Should we go help?" I said, and I grabbed Solomon's wrist. He turned and shook me off with a strong sideward thrust.

"No," he said. "We should get our butts out of here is what we should do."

He and Bentley started back past the pit, where the truck still sat rumbling. I hesitated, glancing back at Jimmy. He shouted at me to get going, and I ran after Bentley and Solomon. But now Andy had turned and spotted us and Jimmy. He looked stunned, though, and didn't move as we made our way back across the pits and through the woods toward Claytown. I kept looking back and saw Jimmy dash by Andy, who grabbed him. Jimmy pulled away and shouted something, and Andy yelled back but didn't try to stop him again. "Loser!" he screamed after Jimmy.

This time we headed toward the road, where we noticed a car parked to one side, half in the brush. The glow from the one streetlight lit up the area around the car, which looked like Jimmy's new one. We had gotten only a few yards along the road when we heard a rustling sound in the woods behind us. Solomon began walking faster—aiming for home, I figured—but then Bentley said, "It's Jimmy." We all turned and saw Jimmy walking quickly toward the parked car. I started back, and they both stood watching as I hugged the side of the road, in darkness, and made my way to a spot near the car, but outside the circle of light around it. And I was suddenly aware that Jimmy had parked right near the tree he'd smashed into.

Solomon and Bentley caught up, and we stood watching Jimmy. He pulled at the car door but got it only partway open before he yanked his arm away, saying, "Dammit." Wincing, he squeezed himself through the half-open door and slumped into the driver's seat, but he didn't close the door or start the engine. He just sat there with his hands covering his face. None of us said anything, and I wasn't sure if I could move now if I tried.

We stood there a long time. The only sounds were the dark trees whooshing and the chirps of what seemed like a million crickets, until these sounds were joined then overpowered by an approaching car's motor. It was a Lincoln Continental. It parked near Jimmy's car and out stepped Gerthoff Senior. He walked over to the other car and leaned into the open door. He said something to Jimmy, who did not move or reply.

Then Gerthoff said, distinctly, "You're coming home."

Jimmy shook his head.

"You don't know what you're doing. Always messing up. First the Portuguese girl and now that Theona and all this. You need help."

Again Jimmy gave no answer.

"You'd rather live with that man."

Now Jimmy looked up and said, loudly, "Maybe I would."

Gerthoff slammed the car door shut and strode away. He paced awhile with hands on hips before returning to Jimmy's car. He spoke into the window, his profile ghost-pale in the streetlight glare.

"You're wounded," he said.

"Grazed my arm. I'm fine. Get the hell away from me. Leave me alone."

Gerthoff was silent a moment.

"You know," he said, more loudly. "Life isn't as simple as you think. I told you just do your work and mind your business, didn't I? I told you stay away from this side of the dump. Those black people were in the way, and they'll all benefit from leaving. They didn't want or need your help. Can't even help yourself."

Jimmy's head sank to his chest and he sat silent. I had a horrible feeling, watching him there in that still car on the dark quiet road, that he really had been badly wounded, that he would never move again.

Feen stood in her nightdress, her arms folded, as we sat in her kitchen trying to explain what had happened. We'd walked back after Gerthoff drove away and after Jimmy, a few minutes later, started up his car and drove off, too. Feen was holding her temper, relieved that Solomon was all right. She had come back from the church, she told us, to find a note he'd left—it sat there in front of us on the table—saying he was sleeping at my house. (I looked at Solomon, wondering why he would have written that.) She had found this peculiar but hadn't questioned its truth. She'd gone to bed early and couldn't sleep, feeling that something was very wrong, that Solomon wasn't safe. She'd gotten up, paced the kitchen debating whether to call my house, and had just finished some warm milk to help her sleep when our knock came at the back door. And now she wanted answers.

When Solomon finished the telling, including everything about Jimmy and his father, Feen didn't say anything to him. "Your folks must be worried sick," she said to Bentley and me. She picked up the phone and ran her finger across a piece of notepaper next to it. She said she was calling my parents; I knew better than to object. My father answered, and after she told him all that we'd told her, she was quiet, listening. I could hear my father's voice but not distinct words. She nodded a few times and said, a little impatient, "Yes, of course, they're fine now. Why don't you come and get them?"

Solomon was staring at us again in that distant way, almost as if the months we'd known him had vanished and we were suspicious strangers, even though he'd brought us back there to his house again.

Feen noticed the blood on my leg and told me she'd tend to my gash immediately. She ordered Solomon to bed. Neither of us argued. After washing and peroxiding my wound in the bathroom, Feen brought Bentley and me into the living room to wait, and nobody spoke. There was loud snoring from another room. After what seemed like an hour in which Bentley and I avoided looking at Feen but couldn't look at each other for long either, a car drove up and cut its engine. Feen got up and looked out the window. "I think it's your father, Luke," she said.

She opened the door as Dad was walking up the front path. He stopped before he got to the door. He and Feen looked at each other but said nothing as Bentley and I walked out, heads down, and stood near him.

"Dad," I said, as if asking a question, or a lot of questions.

He gave me a look that seemed angry, confused, and worst of all, ashamed.

"Get in the car, both of you," he said, in a weary voice. He thanked Feen.

"Something has to be done," she said, sounding tired, too.

Dad nodded, as Bentley and I walked past him to the car.

We drove home in complete silence, stopping at Bentley's house to drop him off. His father was standing at the screen door when we drove up, and he met Bentley halfway up the walk. He grabbed his son by the arm and gave him a slap on the side of the face—not an injuring slap but a serious one. He pulled him up the stairs and into the house.

Riley came back down to the car and put his head in the window. He spoke across me to my father, telling Dad he'd like to talk more about all this soon. He thanked Dad for calling him. It was all very restrained and calm. When we got home, Dad told me to get to bed. And be quiet, he added, your mother's lying down. I did as he said, walking softly past the closed door of my parents' room.

My father didn't go to work the next day. School hadn't started yet, so I was home, too. There were withering leis around the house and lots of leftovers in the refrigerator. My mother had come into my room the night before, shortly after I'd come home. She hadn't said much, just "I'm glad you're safe." She'd kissed me on the head and left the room, looking like she was still in that state between

euphoria and shock that she'd fallen into after Diane's outburst at the luau.

She didn't say much more in the morning, as she sat with
Dad and me at breakfast. Diane wasn't there, and neither
was Avo. My father was mostly silent, too, and I watched
his face for signs of anger or anything else that would tell
me what he felt about the night before. As we finished our
cereal, he turned to me and let out a long breath.

"Buddy," he said. "What did you think you were doing
out there late at night?"

He hadn't called me "buddy" in a very long time. I
couldn't answer.

"You guys were snooping around, huh? It's not so bad
you going to Claytown. And it's good to have friends. But
following Jimmy Gerthoff into that landfill, that's something else. And he should know better than to involve kids."

"It wasn't his doing," I said. "And we're not kids."

My mother asked what were we then, and my father
said maybe I'd understand better about business when I was
older, and I gave a sharp quick laugh, like my grandfather.

"You can laugh, but money's a powerful thing—for
good and bad," Dad said. "People do crazy things sometimes when they have to make a living."

Like try to kill their own sons, I thought, but I couldn't
say it to my father's face. I felt my eyes burn and I tried
to hold back the wet burning as I thought about how I'd
wanted him there the night before. How scary and lonely it
all was. Nothing he was saying seemed to have anything to
do with what had happened, what I'd experienced.

"I'll explain it later," he said. "We love you, you know
that, you and Diane."

I nodded, but his words, especially that word he rarely
used, *love*, pressed my own words down into my throat.
Love, too, seemed in need of explanation.

Peter Riley came by a few days later, in the evening. He told my father that Bentley was grounded until the start of school, and Dad said something about the curiosity of boys. (He hadn't punished me, at least not so far.) They were talking in the backyard, drinking beers, Riley smoking a cigar, and they weren't trying to be quiet. The strung lanterns illuminated them strangely in the fading light. I stood next to the screened sliding door, concealed, lifting my weights. Dad wondered if we had told the truth or were letting our imaginations run wild, and Riley said he was pretty sure it had occurred the way we'd said and that it was all part of a complicated situation.

"A big mess," Riley said. "Now you'd think there'd be some kind of conscience here. Building houses knowing they were near that toxic shit. Burying it where people already lived."

"Conscience," my father said. "Moral responsibility."

"Yeah, call it what you want. Here we're trying to teach our kids to be decent and there's this crap going on. Hell, those guys probably lecture their kids about right and wrong."

"I'm sure they do," Dad said. "You think they all knew? The Underbridge boys?"

Riley laughed. "You'd know better than me. They must have, wouldn't you say?"

"Yes, some of them, at least," my father said. He let out a long breath and put his hand to his head. "The money was the main thing. They were paid by Gerthoff and Randono and Velman to work at the landfill. Off the books, so they probably didn't care if it was legal. They strayed onto Claytown land. And then they started focusing on Jimmy, especially once he got involved with Claytown. They were mad at a lot of things, for a long time, and they took it out on him."

"Well, yeah, him and the Claytown people," Riley said. "The big boys were good at stirring up gripes and hatred." He took a puff on his cigar, and nasty-smelling smoke wafted in. I suppressed a cough. I remembered how Riley had deflected our questions about the landfill; had he already suspected what was happening?

They sat quietly for a few minutes. Crickets chirped, a distant car whirred by, fading. I wondered again what Jimmy thought he was doing, and how my father could've gotten mixed up in all of it. Shouldn't they know better? Wouldn't I know better? I wasn't sure.

Another cloud of smoke hit my nose and mouth.

The two men went on talking. Dad mentioned the evening Eddie and Andy were parked outside our house. Dad was supposed to go with them to meet with Gerthoff Senior, Randono, and some other guys—mob guys, Dad suspected. But Dad had changed his mind. He'd spent that night in his car, parked by the old Bultmann house, near Claytown. He'd stayed up almost till dawn, rethinking things. He'd never much liked Randono or some of the men he dealt with. They reminded him of guys he saw when he was growing up, guys who'd strut around the neighborhood in flashy clothes, acting like they ruled the streets. He'd been wary of men like that ever since. It was Gerthoff Senior who had gotten Dad involved. He'd met with Gerthoff one night at the Underbridge, and that's when it all started. Dad had been feeling restless, frustrated with his job, the town, lots of things. Gerthoff wanted some financial advice and said he'd pay nicely, that there was a big windfall coming. Gerthoff introduced Dad to some of the men at the Underbridge, and Dad started going there regularly.

"I wouldn't normally fall for schemes like that," Dad said. "But some things the guys were saying made sense.

They never talked about the bigger picture, just how they wanted to protect the town from crime and drugs and delinquency. They claimed Gerthoff's new development would help."

"Oh?" Riley said.

"Well, Gerthoff persuaded them. I know, it was naïve. We were all naïve. And greedy. Gerthoff, too, I think. In fact, I'm pretty sure Gerthoff tried to get out of the whole deal once he realized who was behind it all, but then he couldn't. Not even when they went after Jimmy."

"Yeah, that's the really sickening part," Riley said. "Threatening your own son."

"Well, Gerthoff didn't do that himself," Dad said. "That was Randono and Velman and their mob friends, I think. Maybe Gerthoff went along, thinking they would scare Jimmy so he'd keep his two cents out of things. Maybe he needed scaring. But the Underbridge guys got carried away, I figure. And you could say he brought it on himself, the kid. He could've walked away. Instead he continued helping out. But he was still working with Ward and the people in Claytown."

"There was more to it than that," Riley said. "Jimmy was pretty shook up after the accident and the attack on his house. But he was loyal to his father and the business. There was all that money involved. Maybe he was trying to please his old man, somehow. Maybe he didn't know it was all connected, or didn't want to know."

"But they suspected Jimmy was still spying on them," Dad said. "And that one goon panicked when he saw Jimmy out at the dump site again."

"Yeah, well, that'll all be part of our investigation. What I don't get, though, is why would Jimmy go back there at all, once they got after him? Why did he put himself in danger like that?"

"Good questions," Dad said.

"Got any answers?"

"Me? How would I know?"

"So you don't?"

"Of course not. I was just fed up with the kid. Fed up with a lot of things, like I said. And I thought Jimmy was treating his old man badly. And then he gets our boys involved. Who knows what he was thinking? Jimmy's a crazy kid, like a lot of these kids."

Our boys. Crazy kids. I wanted to protest: we weren't the crazy ones, were we?

Riley said he would be talking to Gerthoff Senior about all this soon, and Dad mumbled something about how he himself shared some guilt, too. I shook my head, as if to un-hear those words. Even if it was true, I didn't want Dad to be saying it, as if confessing to Riley. I grasped the weights tighter as I lifted them faster, causing another muffled cough.

Riley asked, "Do you think those guys planned to do damage at Claytown?"

"I think their intention, at first, was to scare people, not to hurt them," Dad said. He was scratching under his chin the way he sometimes did when working on figures. "But you know—intentions." He took another long breath. He leaned his head forward into his hand now, and Riley asked if he was okay. Dad raised his head and nodded.

"You know that elderly man is out of the hospital," Riley said. "The one they assaulted with the bat."

"How's he doing?"

"Recovering. Slowly. Couldn't identify the guys, though. Jerks were wearing party masks. Didn't see the license plates, either. But it was a green truck, like Gerthoff and Son construction has, so maybe they were using one of theirs."

"Probably. Like they did to chase Jimmy. I didn't know about any of that."

"Well, I'm glad you came to me that night they ganged up on Jimmy. I just wish you'd told me more then. I still can't believe you went along with it as far as you did. You let the kid get to you."

Dad shrugged, like a kid himself for a moment, confronted. "I guess so. But I never wanted to hurt him. I've been mad at him, sure, but I also admire his energy, all those big dreams and ideas. He doesn't know what to do with all he has. It's a waste. There's just something about him makes you want him to learn a lesson."

"Well, maybe he did."

"Maybe *I* did."

Riley chuckled. More puffing and smoke.

"Also," Riley said. "You have some personal history with him."

I waited for Dad to say something about Diane and Jimmy. Riley couldn't have been aware of all that had happened. But Dad only said "Yes," and Riley didn't pursue it.

"So you didn't know about the bigger plans when you were hanging out with those bozos?" he asked.

Dad shook his head. "Oh, no. No."

"And you never actually took money from Gerthoff or Randono?"

"No, no. It never got that far."

It sounded like the truth. Riley stopped asking questions. Putting down my weights, feeling the burn of building muscle, I watched the two men, who were looking away from one another in silence.

Seventeen

An uneasy sort of normalcy dropped over our house after the landfill events. Routines resumed. School reopened. I heard that Jimmy was treated at the hospital and released, but otherwise the shooting wasn't mentioned—not in the paper, not by anyone in my household. Jimmy went back to stay with Ward, for a while. I had begun to understand why Jimmy might have taken refuge there. He didn't want to return to his house, probably wanted out of it altogether but felt like he couldn't leave town. It wasn't so easy to break free, maybe, or to know what freedom was or why you wanted it.

For several days after overhearing my father and Riley, I kept thinking about Jimmy—spreading his arms in the doorway that night they mobbed him, striding toward that drawn gun at the landfill. Ward, in his own way, offered Jimmy a kind of love —I could see that now, in an obscure, fearful, awed way. And maybe a different model of privilege. But was that what Jimmy was looking for? And how long could he stay in Ward's strange old house, like a child? The more I'd seen of that house, the more I felt that its apartness in space and time, which had seemed so magical at first, could be a trap. It stood on the edge of Wardville, facing away, but it was also part of the town, its ambiguous memory, the loneliness within its community. I understood all that, inchoately, not yet in words.

I used Ward's library a few times. I borrowed the second book of *Lord of the Rings* from it. I had finally been allowed into the "game room," but no one else was there, and everything in the room seemed forlorn, obsolete, future junk. Reverend Wilson had cut the links between Ward and the Claytown church, and the children of Claytown no longer livened the place. Rumors continued about the youth program, but they remained rumors, with the mistiness of speculation, never coalescing into fact or proof or even accusation. Still, the reverend probably wanted no part of the landfill scandal that was about to erupt, even if Ward didn't have much to do with it. And maybe Wilson didn't want Ward's help anymore because he resented that rich descendent of overlords—like lots of people did.

A couple of weeks after the landfill confrontation, Ward asked a few of us to come by for a sort of farewell party. Bentley, Solomon, and I didn't much want to see Jimmy, and we were fairly cool toward the party. Solomon seemed especially sore at Jimmy—a wounded anger. He still liked Ward, the way you like a teacher or a benefactor, but he was again pulling back. "Maybe Gran's right about him," he said to me. We did end up going to the party, but we mostly kept our distance from Jimmy. Solomon gave him a hello before going off to play some tennis with Mark. He was much friendlier toward the North Shore and Brooklyn kids than he had been, but he sat with me and Bentley for lunch. Something had changed, though, since Labor Day; it was clear we were no longer a trio as we'd become for a while over the summer. Jimmy and Ward had brought us together, but it seemed the fragile connections were crumbling.

Ward was mostly indoors, holding court almost, visiting with his guests individually or in small groups in the parlor. He sat with me there for half an hour or so, while Jimmy sprawled in a chair on the other side of the room, near a window, reading a book about Frank Lloyd Wright. Ward looked out at the broad lawn, which was losing its green, and asked me questions about myself—what did I want to do, where did I want to go. I hadn't decided on anything except that I knew I wouldn't be a banker. Ward laughed when I told him that. And I said I didn't know where I'd be going after high school but that I would be leaving Wardville and the island. As I said it, looking at this man, like some wizard-prince alone in his isolated realm, a patriarch without progeny, I realized that I truly believed what I'd said. I felt it strongly as a fact, whereas before it had been more like a desire or a dream. Ward sighed and told me he thought that was a good idea, that Wardville was not the world. He continued gazing out at his walled property and didn't say anything else to me.

As I talked to Ward, I'd kept glancing over at Jimmy. Now I sat watching him. Despite his posture, he didn't look relaxed: one leg was moving up and down in that restless way, almost shaking, and he didn't seem to be focusing on his book. He would repeatedly push his glasses up the bridge of his nose and run a hand through his hair. Ward asked him several times to do things—some chore outside, some activity with "the guests"—and each time Jimmy answered that he just wanted to read a few more pages. After the fourth or fifth round of this, Ward told Jimmy that no one was forcing him to stay if he didn't want to. Jimmy stared at Ward with a surprised, hurt look, as if he hadn't really thought of that before, or hadn't expected Ward to speak that way. And Ward stared back, his lips set tight and one hand clasping the other, as if suppressing panic or rage, and it seemed like those hands might be burning to grasp Jimmy's throat. I swallowed hard. But Ward's tension seemed to pass, and he sat back with a sort of perturbed weariness.

Jimmy jumped up, threw the book on the chair, and walked past Ward, who grasped his arm, the one without the wound. They looked at one another until Jimmy pulled away and told Ward in a calm, unemotional voice that he'd do what he was asked. The rest of the time I was there, I didn't see Jimmy and Ward together.

Late that afternoon, as I sat on the swing, moving it gently with my foot, Jimmy walked up and asked if he could join me. I shrugged and said sure. He sat across from me and pushed the swing a little higher, smiling, as if this were an old joke between us. Even with a large bandage on his arm, he looked healthier than the last time I'd seen him there. Except for that shakiness in his body and his voice. I couldn't bring myself to mention his father and the shooting.

"When you starting high school?" he asked.

I hesitated—didn't he know when? Finally I said, "Next year."

He told me to be careful, not for the first time. More than ever, it seemed like odd advice from him, and I wasn't sure how to take it.

"I'm back in college," he continued, "but I don't want to stay there."

"What do you want to do?" I asked.

He said he was leaving New York, transferring to a college out West. He'd like to be a sort of carpenter-architect, somebody who designs things but also gets to help build them. He wanted to be close to what he was designing—not the usual kind of architect, and not a contractor or a builder, either. The West was more open to things like that, he figured. He wouldn't do things just for money. He'd work for people. He wanted to know that what he was doing had some larger purpose. I looked at him, not knowing what to say, not quite understanding or believing. Then he abruptly said, "I want to make it right," ambiguous words full of regret and failure, and that got me; he watched me with those distantly gazing yet seen-it-all eyes, as if looking through and past me, and I felt a resurging awe and anger toward him. But this feeling faded. I kept seeing him on that waste mound, moving boldly or crazily toward those men with guns.

I had no answer for him. I could tell this was a sort of apology, for a lot of things that only he could truly know about, but I was the one hearing it, and I didn't want that weight. If this had to do with Diane, then shouldn't he be explaining to her, making it up to her somehow? I knew he had hurt her, or maybe they'd hurt each other. It seemed that Diane both clung to some dream about him and also rejected those feelings, as she probably mourned a child that never was while not wanting it at all. But I wasn't sure about any of it. No one had mentioned a baby again, and the possibility had receded back into the haze of half-real things dimly understood. Much later, I would piece together a story, from hints dropped, from talk overheard, from my retrospective imagining: that Jimmy broke with Diane when she told him she was pregnant, that he let his father deal with it all, that Gerthoff Senior had pressured for an abortion and made arrangements with some doctor friend, that my ambivalent parents tried to convince Diane, who felt resentful and coerced, even though she saw the sense of it. And that one day, in a druggy maelstrom of emotions, she went into labor and miscarried. Which would explain the secrecy about that anxious late-night trip to the hospital, the fuzzy details about her stay there. I never asked Diane directly about it, and she never told me.

And who else would have told me? Was Jimmy trying to tell me that late summer afternoon? All I knew there on that swing with him was that he felt guilty, sad, angry about a lot of things, as if he'd taken on all the troubles around him (his own and everybody else's) and wanted to be free of them. It was oppressive, bewildering. I didn't want his concern or his weird repentance.

Although I wasn't responding much, he went on talking. But not about Diane. We were trying to help, he kept saying (the "we" unclear). There were powers on both sides, he said, but nobody was really listening to the people caught in the middle, the Claytown people especially. They were the ones who'd lose out. He'd asked Pete Riley's advice and would help with Riley's investigation, even if it hurt his old man. He paused, then went on as if answering questions the silence had asked; he'd waited a long time, he explained, because he and Ward wanted to be certain of the truth. He'd kept working at the landfill because he was trying to stop what was happening.

After another pause, he said, like an afterthought, "You know Ward's family had put a lot of money into the Bultmann factory. And the clay quarries. That's what kept the Ward family fortune going after the oyster industry went bust. That and real estate."

These plain-fact statements were like further clues to a mystery Jimmy was trying to solve. They explained a lot. They explained nothing.

Listening to Jimmy, I dimly understood that his interest in me, in all of us, had some deeper, more obscure goal. I knew I couldn't believe everything he was saying, and this awareness seemed like part of his effect on me. Of course, he'd affected lots of people, who saw larger questions—about themselves, about our place and time—in his confused and ambivalent actions. Questions they didn't necessarily want raised or answered.

For a long while afterward, I would try to put the things Jimmy told me together with what I'd heard from my father and Riley, and from others, along with all the things I'd seen. I knew that some people in Claytown wanted to sell their property and were trying to get the rest of the town to agree. Jimmy's father was pressuring people to sell, too, the way he'd done at Spanish Settlement. Ward was fighting against selling and so was fighting part of the town while trying to save it. Jimmy was sort of working both sides, helping Randono and Velman even while trying to undermine them.

I wanted to work this all out. Maybe Jimmy did, too. But the pieces still wouldn't fit. I'd probably never find out for sure why Jimmy was driving that truck on Labor Day. Spying? Attempting to help his father? Trying to get himself hurt? And I'd never know Ward's true motives either. Nor, I had to admit to myself, would I know my father's actual role or reasons: whether he wanted to get away from us or provide for us or had acted from some mixed-up combination of urges. But being sure about things felt less important now, and less real. Jimmy was moving further into uncertainty and so would I. Into the world, of course. I kept thinking of the city with its shining towers, ever newer and higher, that island of possibilities that Jimmy loved and loathed. And the West he talked about more and more. To me they still seemed full of the future.

Now, finished talking, Jimmy stared off into space (as Ward had earlier) and didn't seem to notice as I left through the garden gate.

He didn't move back home. Before transferring out West, Jimmy found himself a rented room near the Hill College for the fall term and rarely came to town. I would sometimes see him drive by, alone, on his way to visit his mother. There were rumors that she had taken to her bedroom, from which neighbors heard shouts and screaming. She was afraid, the speculation ran, that she'd be abandoned by her son and her possibly jail-bound husband. I heard Jimmy wasn't speaking to his father, who would soon be indicted along with Randono, Velman, and their associates. I also heard Theona had broken up with Jimmy.

On one of these visits to town, Jimmy stopped his car and called out to me as I walked past.

"Hey, Luke, need a ride?"

I considered it, looking at the new car, shiny in the sun. "No," I said.

Our eyes met briefly but he looked away, faced forward. "Well, then, see ya round."

"Like a donut," I said, and Jimmy laughed at my father's ancient joke.

And, yes, I saw him around, but we never spoke again before he left. (Later on, he boomeranged back to care for his mother, but by then I was already gone myself.)

I had been attending religious instruction class that September, but by the second or third week I'd made a decision: I wasn't going to continue and I wouldn't receive Confirmation. I told my parents. My father was ready to agree, but my mother said they'd have to talk it over. She'd rediscovered Catholicism and had been talking to Sister Michael Mary regularly, as I'd sensed. The next day they told me I could drop the classes if I wanted to, but I'd have to tell Sister M myself, and tell her why.

I talked to Sister in her office at Stella Maris School. Her habit looked different on her somehow, like a costume. I told her my decision, and tried to explain that being confirmed felt like saying I knew the truth when I didn't. She gave me a slight smile. I had expected something more dramatic.

"You've been having a difficult time," she said. "Your whole family has. The whole community, in fact. It isn't easy to know the right thing to do."

"No," I said.

She talked about my journal, most of which I'd shown her. It revealed thought, perceptiveness, growth, she told me. I said I was only trying to figure things out, and she said that was pretty much the same thing. She explained again what the Church meant by Confirmation. Maybe the sacrament should be called Complication, she added.

"It really begins our adult quest," she said. "There's a word to look up. *Quest.* We're given grace but not answers, not a life without problems. Maybe we're all finding our own paths to the Church. Or away from it." She laughed in her abrupt, self-conscious way and told me not to repeat that.

She seemed to be saying, without saying it, that I could define Confirmation for myself, that the defining was some sort of equivalent. We talked a little more about family and school, never mentioning Jimmy or Ward or Claytown, although they seemed like the undercurrent in all we said.

As I was leaving, she said "You'll be fine," and her face had more relief in it than disapproval.

On the way out, I paused at my classroom. The empty desks seemed small and confining but also secure. I looked up at the crucifix above the newly washed and shiny black-board. How must it have felt? The body pulled down by earth, the flesh torn against those rigid piercing spikes. The pain of slowly dying, unable to move or resist. In one way or another, it was happening to people every day. But I remembered what we'd been told in that classroom: God had taken on this suffering to bring us closer to Him, and so He could be closer to us. Everything that seemed painful and obscure and terrifying was part of a vast, sometimes harsh, and incomprehensible love. The Son had bridged our separation from the Father, and we could be free. But we couldn't fly off; we weren't angels. There would always be suffering, sorrow, evil somewhere, inside us and around us, and maybe the way to God was through it, not beyond it or away from it.

Maybe. I closed the door and hurried down the hall, grateful for my moving legs as I strode out into the crisp sunshine, unambiguously real.

My birthday near the end of September passed pretty much like any other birthday. The day itself didn't change anything, but I was more aware of how things were changing. Doris and I went to a movie together in the afternoon, and it felt strange. She was a little somber; she talked about the High Holy Days, about atonement and scattering sins on the water. We both somehow knew that we wouldn't have simple, fun times together much longer. I didn't want her as a girlfriend (and I wasn't her idea of a boyfriend), we didn't want to touch or kiss (although I thought about it), and it no longer felt right to be pals. It all made me revved-up, jumpy, and sad underneath, like my feelings for Bentley, Solomon, Jimmy. I wanted them as friends but with some deep, gut-twisting, urgent attraction that it seemed no one would understand. If only we could all live someplace where we wouldn't have to follow the expected patterns, the normal ways. I felt confusion like a constant, electric need to move without knowing where to go. I sometimes wondered if I might have actually been taken away by aliens, turned into some humanoid Ziggy Stardust kid, during those spaceship-angel dreams.

Later on, Doris, Bentley, and I went out for pizza; Solomon said he couldn't join us. Back home, my mother baked a cake (therapy, she said) and everyone sang "Happy Birthday." Diane grasped my shoulders and segued into the Beatles' "Birthday," and we all laughed.

Diane and Avo were spending more and more time together in September, usually out in the garden. I watched them from my window or the patio: Diane would sit on the ground, Avo in a lawn chair, and Diane would talk while he listened. She spoke much less to the rest of us. Her outburst at the luau had never been mentioned, at least not around me. She was seeing her doctor less often but was still on medication. She started focusing her discontents in more practical ways, vowing to crack the books so she could get away to college. Maybe Berkeley, she said, to Mom's dismay. She even mentioned careers: environmentalism, social work, civil rights law.

Avo was still keeping track, more quietly, of his particular obsessions. He always picked up the newspaper first, from the front steps or from the newsboy himself, and one evening he walked up to the living room reading aloud from the *Vantage*. His accent spiced the familiar journalese: "An investigation has begun into criminal activity at the Kills landfill, possibly involving private garbage haulers, construction companies, and elements of organized crime. Payments were allegedly made by industries and businesses citywide to criminal groups who arranged for illegal dumping in remote sections of the sprawling facility. At the same time, according to sources close to the investigation, contaminated city land, once intended for a park, was sold to private developers near the landfill, in an apparent collusion among waste haulers, builders, and city officials."

Avo read us the entire article, as if speaking someone else's words had enabled coherent sentences again. My mother, my father, and I sat watching *Eyewitness News*, which hadn't said anything about the scandal. When he'd finished, Avo closed the paper and tossed it down on the coffee table. He shook his head. "Some of the truth," he said, "not the whole. Won't allow that."

I looked at my father. He continued to gaze at the TV as if he hadn't heard a word of what Avo had said.

I wondered then how I could write about Claytown for the school paper or anywhere except my own journal; it had become part of a larger story, now being revealed. I was only beginning to learn it.

There were no more incidents at Claytown that fall. The harassment had stopped, at least in its violent forms. The resentments didn't go away, of course, nor did the conflicts, but they got quieter—more internalized and discreet, I guess, in the usual Wardville way. But the pressures on Claytown continued, and they mainly had to do with money. The land there was too valuable to be left alone, and fewer people seemed to share Dalton's defiance. Ward's efforts to have the whole town declared "historical" didn't get very far; the city bureaucracy didn't care, and the residents didn't either. More and more of them decided they could live just as well elsewhere—probably better, with the cash they could get for their property.

My father explained all this to me one cool September evening after another back-to-normal, non-tropical dinner of pot roast, as he sat sipping his coffee. I had mentioned Claytown after seeing a report in the *Vantage* about the declining congregation at the church there. Reverend Wilson was quoted in the article, talking about an inevitable exodus and how he'd advised people for a long time to do what was best for their survival. In fact, Solomon had told us that his grandmother had had a big fight with the reverend after he'd counseled her to sell her house.

Dad agreed with the reverend and mentioned again the large amounts of money people were getting. His urge to explain seemed defensive but also like experienced wisdom, offered with rough-edged love and concern. It felt like he too was trying to work out answers but had been trying a lot longer than me. He never told me about what he'd done the way he'd described it to Peter Riley, and I never told him what I'd overheard.

•

I saw less of Solomon after my birthday. We were both busy with school, but it was more than that: things had changed in Claytown. George and Feen kept their house, but they were more and more isolated. George had gotten sicker, and Feen and Solomon spent a lot of time caring for him. On my one or two visits there in the fall, things felt different, as though there was less time for everything. Solomon didn't feel like talking and had lots of chores. Neither of us wanted to venture into the woods, and we couldn't get far into them anyway—a big chain link fence topped with barbwire had been put up near the pits. Trucks and machinery sat inside the fence doing nothing, like sick zoo animals. We did go up to the fence one day, and I asked Solomon if he thought there really were bodies buried down there. I mentioned the old graveyard. He gave me a strange, blank look and said, "Well, it wouldn't surprise me, since nobody was allowed to live or die in peace." His voice was calm and quiet, which only made his words eerier, sadder, more unanswerable. They were like the words of a much older person, with experience someone our age shouldn't have.

When the school term ended, Solomon left Claytown for good and went to live with his mother. She wanted Solomon with her permanently, and he was ready to give it a try. I said goodbye to him one brisk morning in his front yard. We stood not really looking at one another, trying to be cool about the whole thing. He said he'd be glad to see his mother but didn't mention her husband, and he didn't sound glad at all. I felt heat behind my eyes, creeping back toward my ears. He'd been matter-of-fact about leaving his grandparents, but now I could see how much it hurt. The burning in my head wanted release in questions, about how he felt toward his mother, and who would look after his grandparents, and a bigger question I figured I'd never ask if I didn't ask now: What happened to your father? But it came out a different question.

"You like your stepfather?"

He shook his head. "I don't call him that. Only met him once. He's okay but he's not my father nohow. My father's in California."

"Oh," I said.

"Someday I'll go see my father. Maybe I'll live there."

He said this as if challenging me to say it wouldn't happen, or asking me to tell him it would. But I couldn't do either.

He put out a hand and we shook. It brought back our earlier touching, the fear and thrill of it; maybe because of that, and because I was alone so much, like him, it felt like a farewell to a friend I'd known much longer.

We let go and looked away from each other. He said he wasn't sure when he'd be back to visit.

Neither of us mentioned Jimmy. I knew he'd let Solomon down somehow. Had Solomon wanted Jimmy to stop the threats to Claytown? Or, beyond that, bring Solomon out of his isolation, even somehow unify Claytown and Wardville? If so, Solomon seemed to have let go of any such hopes or expectations. Maybe he saw that these things were happening anyway, although not how he'd wanted them to.

Earlier Feen had told me not to be a stranger. She'd also said it was for the best that Solomon was leaving, that Claytown was no place for the young. Her voice was confident, but she kept looking at Solomon, as if he might suddenly vanish.

My mother had been very quiet in the weeks after the luau. She seemed to have stopped lecturing Diane and focused on the transition to fall: storing summer clothes in plastic mothballed bags, cleaning the storm windows, taking me shopping for school supplies. After my decision about Confirmation, she continued meeting with Sister M and joined an adult Catholic education class at Stella Maris. One day I saw the open box of photographs again in her room, while she was doing laundry downstairs. I ran to get the photo of my grandfather and placed it in the box, toward the bottom of the stack. She had never said anything about missing it.

Maybe it was partly this change in Mom, but it seemed that things were calmer between my parents. Dad was working very hard at the bank. He would come home and fall asleep on the sofa. There were no arguments, at least none that I witnessed. In mid-September, at my mother's suggestion, they began discussing a trip to Hawaii. I'd thought Mom had gotten that out of her system, but I guess she'd quietly decided to turn her fantasies into reality. Maybe they were finally acting on their long-contained restlessness. Brochures with palm trees and a turquoise ocean appeared in our mail, and there were phone calls to travel agents. Dad seemed as enthusiastic as Mom once he got into the trip planning.

Also, around that time, Dad announced that he was looking for a new job. He did look, for a while, but decided not to leave the bank, especially after he got a promotion to vice president ("there are only about a thousand of those in the company," he joked). The day after Thanksgiving, my mother began composing her Christmas letter. She was looking forward, she wrote, to the happiest of holidays, one to savor and cherish. She described some of the events of that eventful year. She emphasized the brighter side of what she chose to tell, and most of it was, in its own way, true.

About the Author

PHOTO BY GLENN LUNDEN

FRANK MEOLA has published work in a variety of forms and places, including *New England Review* and the *New York Times*. His *Times* travel essay on Rachel Carson in Maine was published in the book *Footsteps*. He has written frequently on Emerson and Thoreau. His newest essay, in *Michigan Quarterly Review*, centers on the ambiguities of Hispanic identity in America, based partly on his own experience. Several of Meola's stories have been finalists or won first place in fiction competitions. He has an MFA from Columbia University, and teaches writing and humanities at NYU. Frank lives in Brooklyn, NY with his husband and their two cats.